Bloodthirsty Dinosaurs!

IT WAS OF ENORMOUS SIZE AND POWER, LIKE AN ERECT elephant, but its movements, in spite of its bulk, were exceedingly alert. For a moment, as I saw its shape, I hoped that it was an iguanodon, which I knew to be harmless, but, ignorant as I was, I soon saw that this was a very different creature. This beast had a broad, squat, toad-like face like that which had alarmed us in our camp. His ferocious cry and the horrible energy of his pursuit both assured me that this was surely one of the great flesh-eating dinosaurs, the most terrible beasts which have ever walked this earth. As the huge brute loped along it dropped forward upon its fore-paws and brought its nose to the ground every twenty yards or so. *It was smelling out my trail.*

THE LOST WORLD

SIR ARTHUR CONAN DOYLE

A TOM DOHERTY ASSOCIATES BOOK
NEW YORK

THE LOST WORLD

A Tor Book
Published by Tom Doherty Associates, Inc.
175 Fifth Avenue
New York, NY 10010

Tor® is a registered trademark of Tom Doherty Associates, Inc.

ISBN: 0-812-56483-9

First Tor edition: November 1993

Printed in the United States of America

0 9 8 7 6 5 4 3 2

CONTENTS

I have wrought my simple plan
If I give one hour of joy
To the boy who's half a man,
Or the man who's half a boy.

There Are Heroisms
All Round Us

MR. HUNGERTON, HER FATHER, REALLY WAS THE MOST TACT-less person upon earth—a fluffy, feathery, untidy cockatoo of a man, perfectly good-natured, but absolutely centered upon his own silly self. If anything could have driven me from Gladys, it would have been the thought of such a father-in-law. I am convinced that he really believed in his heart that I came round to the Chestnuts three days a week for the pleasure of his company, and very especially to hear his views upon bimetallism—a subject upon which he was by way of being an authority.

For an hour or more that evening I listened to his monotonous chirrup about bad money driving out good, the token value of silver, the depreciation of the rupee, and the true standards of exchange.

"Suppose," he cried, with feeble violence, "that all the debts in the world were called up simultaneously and immediate payment insisted upon. What, under our present conditions, would happen then?"

I gave the self-evident answer that I should be a ruined

man, upon which he jumped from his chair, reproved me my habitual levity, which made if impossible for him to discuss any reasonable subject in my presence, and bounced off out of the room to dress for a Masonic meeting.

At last I was alone with Gladys, and the moment of fate had come! All that evening I had felt like the soldier who awaits the signal which will send him on a forlorn hope, hope of victory and fear of repulse alternating in his mind.

She sat with that proud, delicate profile of hers outlined against the red curtain. How beautiful she was! And yet how aloof! We had been friends, quite good friends; but never could I get beyond the same comradeship which I might have established with one of my fellow-reporters upon the *Gazette*—perfectly frank, perfectly kindly, and perfectly unsexual. My instincts are all against a woman being too frank and at her ease with me. It is no compliment to a man. Where the real sex feelings begins, timidity and distrust are its companions, heritage from old wicked days when love and violence went often hand in hand. The bent head, the averted eye, the faltering voice, the wincing figure—these, and not the unshrinking gaze and frank reply, are the true signals of passion. Even in my short life I had learned as much as that—or had inherited it in that race-memory which we call instinct.

Gladys was full of every womanly quality. Some judged her to be cold and hard, but such a thought was treason. That delicately-bronzed skin, almost Oriental in its coloring, that raven hair, the large liquid eyes, the full but exquisite lips—all the stigmata of passion were there. But I was sadly conscious that up to now I had never found the secret of drawing it forth. However, come what might, I should have done with suspense and bring matters to a head to-night. She could but refuse me, and better be a repulsed lover than an accepted brother.

So far my thoughts had carried me, and I was about to break the long and uneasy silence when two critical dark eyes looked round at me, and the proud head was shaken in smiling reproof.

"I have a presentiment that you are going to propose, Ned. I do wish you wouldn't for things are so much nicer as they are."

I drew my chair a little nearer.

"Now, how did you know that I was going to propose?" I asked, in genuine wonder.

"Don't women always know? Do you suppose any woman in the world was ever taken unawares? But, oh, Ned, our friendship has been so good and so pleasant! What a pity to spoil it! Don't you feel how splendid it is that a young man and a young woman should be able to talk face to face as we have talked?"

"I don't know, Gladys. You see, I can talk face to face with—with the station-master." I can't imagine how that official came into the matter, but in he trotted and set us both laughing. "That does not satisfy me in the least. I want my arms round you and your head on my breast, and, oh, Gladys, I want—"

She had sprung from her chair as she saw signs that I proposed to demonstrate some of my wants.

"You've spoiled everything, Ned," she said. "It's all so beautiful and natural until this kind of thing comes in. It is such a pity. Why can't you control yourself?"

"I didn't invent it," I pleaded. "It's nature. It's love!"

"Well, perhaps if both love it may be different. I have never felt it."

"But, you must —you, with your beauty, with your soul! Oh, Gladys, you were made for love! You must love!"

"One must wait till it comes."

"But why can't you love me, Gladys? Is it my appearance, or what?"

She did unbend a little. She put forward a hand—such a gracious, stooping attitude it was—and she pressed back my head. Then she looked into my upturned face with a very wistful smile.

"No, it isn't that," she said at last. "You're not a conceited boy by nature, and so I can safely tell you that it is not that. It's deeper."

"My character?"

She nodded severely.

"What can I do to mend it? Do sit down and talk it over. No, really I won't, if you'll only sit down!"

She looked at me with a wondering distrust which was much more to my mind than her whole-hearted confidence. How primitive and bestial it looks when you put it down in black and white! And perhaps after all it is only a feeling peculiar to myself. Anyhow, she sat down.

"Now tell me what's amiss with me."

"I'm in love with somebody else," said she.

It was my turn to jump out of my chair.

"It's nobody in particular," she explained, laughing at the expression on my face, "only an ideal. I've never met the kind of man I mean."

"Tell me about him. What does he look like?"

"Oh, he might look very much like you."

"How dear of you to say that! Well, what is it that he does that I don't do? Just say the word—teetotal, vegetarian, aeronaut, Theosophist, Superman—I'll have a try at it, Gladys, if you will only give me an idea what would please you."

She laughed at the elasticity of my character. "Well, in the first place, I don't think my ideal would speak like that," she said. "He wold be a harder, sterner man, not so ready to adapt himself to a silly girl's whim. But above all he must be a man who could do, who could act, who would look death in the face and have no fear of him—a man of great deeds and strange experiences. It is never a man that I should love, but always the glories he had won, for they would be reflected upon me. Think of Richard Burton! When I read his wife's life of him I could so understand her love. And Lady Stanley! Did you ever read the wonderful last chapter of that book about her husband? These are the sort of men that a woman could worship with all her soul and yet be the greater, not the less, on account of her love, honored by all the world as the inspirer of noble deeds."

She looked so beautiful in her enthusiasm that I nearly brought down the whole level of the interview. I gripped myself hard, and went on with the argument.

"We can't all be Stanleys and Burtons," said I. "Besides, we don't get the chance—at least, I never had the chance. If I did I should try to take it."

"But chances are all around you. It is the mark of the kind of man I mean that he makes his own chances. You can't hold him back. I've never met him, and yet I seem to know him so well. There are heroisms all round us waiting to be done. It's for men to do them, and for women to reserve their love as a reward for such men. Look at that young Frenchman who went up last week in a balloon. It was blowing a gale of wind, but because he was announced to go he insisted on starting. The wind blew him one thousand five hundred miles in twenty-four hours, and he fell in the middle of Russia. That was the kind of man I mean. Think of the woman he loved, and how other women must have envied her! That's what I should like—to be envied for my man."

"I'd have done it to please you."

"But you shouldn't do it merely to please me. You should do it because you can't help it, because it's natural to you—because the man in you is crying out for heroic expression. Now, when you described the Wigan coal explosion last month, could you not have gone down and helped those people, in spite of the choke-damp?"

"I did."

"You never said so."

"There was nothing worth bucking about."

"I didn't know." She looked at me with rather more interest. "That was brave of you."

"I had to. If you want to write good copy you must be where the things are."

"What a prosaic motive! It seems to take all the romance out of it. But still, whatever your motive, I am glad that you went down that mine." She gave me her hand, but with such sweetness and dignity that I could only stoop and kiss it. "I dare say I am merely a foolish woman with a young girl's fancies. And yet it is so real with me, so entirely part of my very self, that I cannot help acting upon it. If I marry, I do want to marry a famous man."

"Why should you not?" I cried. "It is women like you who brace men up. Give me a chance and see if I will take it! Besides, as you say, men ought to *make* their own chances, and not wait until they are given. Look at Clive— just a clerk, and he conquered India. By George! I'll do something in the world yet!"

She laughed at my sudden Irish effervescence.

"Why not?" she said. "You have everything a man could have—youth, health, strength, education, energy. I was sorry you spoke. And now I am glad—so glad—if it wakens these thoughts in you."

"And if I do——?"

Her hand rested like warm velvet upon my lips.

"Not another word, sir. You should have been at the office for even in dutying half an hour ago, only I hadn't the heart to remind you. Some day, perhaps, when you have won your place in the world, we shall talk it over again."

And so it was that I found myself that foggy November evening pursuing the Camberwell tram with my heart glowing within me, and with the eager determination that not another day should elapse before I should find some deed which was worthy of my lady. But who in all this wide world could ever have imagined the incredible shape which that deed was to take, or the strange steps by which I was led to the doing of it?

And, after all, this opening chapter will seem to the reader to have nothing to do with my narrative; and yet there would have been no narrative without it, for it is only when a man goes out into the world with the thought that there are heroisms all round him, and with the desire all alive in his heart to follow any which may come within sight of him, that he breaks away as I did from the life he knows, and ventures forth into the wonderful mystic twilight land where lie the great adventures and the great rewards. Behold me, then, at the office of the *Daily Gazette*, on the staff of which I was a most insignificant unit, with the settled determination that very night, if possible, to find the quest which should be worthy of my Gladys! Was it hardness, was it selfishness, that she should ask me to risk my life for her own glorification? Such thoughts may come to middle age, but never to ardent three-and-twenty in the fever of his first love.

2

Try Your Luck with Professor Challenger

I ALWAYS LIKED McARDLE, THE CRABBED OLD, ROUND backed, redheaded news editor, and I rather hoped that he liked me. Of course, Beaumont was the real boss, but he lived in the rarified atmosphere of some Olympian height from which he could distinguish nothing smaller than an international crisis or a split in the Cabinet. Sometimes we saw him passing in lonely majesty to his inner sanctum with his eyes staring vaguely and his mind hovering over the Balkans or the Persian Gulf. He was above and beyond us. But McArdle was his first lieutenant, and it was he that we knew. The old man nodded as I entered the room, and he pushed his spectacles far up on his bald forehead.

"Well, Mr. Malone, from all I hear, you seem to be doing very well," said he, in his kindly Scotch accent.

I thanked him.

"The colliery explosion was excellent. So was the Southwark fire. You have the true descreeptive touch. What did you want to see me about?"

"To ask a favor."

He looked alarmed and his eyes shunned mine.

"Tut! tut! What is it?"

"Do you think, sir, that you could possibly send me on some mission for the paper? I would do my best to put it through and get you some good copy."

"What sort of a meesion had you in your mind, Mr. Malone?"

"Well, sir, anything that had adventure and danger in it. I would really do my very best. The more difficult it was the better it would suit me."

"You seem very anxious to lose your life."

"To justify my life, sir."

"Dear me, Mr. Malone, this is very—very exalted. I'm afraid the day for this sort of thing is rather past. The expense of the 'special meesion' business hardly justifies the result, and, of course, in any case it would only be an experienced man with a name that would command public confidence who would get such an order. The big blank spaces in the map are all being filled in, and there's no room for romance anywhere. Wait a bit, though!" he added, with a sudden smile upon his face. "Talking of the blank spaces of the map gives me an idea. What about exposing a fraud—a modern Munchausen—and making him rideeculous? You could show him up as the liar that he is! Eh, man, it would be fine. How does it appeal to you?"

"Anything—anywhere—I care nothing."

McArdle was plunged in thought for some minutes.

"I wonder whether you could get on friendly—or at least on talking terms with the fellow," he said, at last. "You seem to have a sort of genius for establishing relations with people—seempathy, I suppose, or animal magnetism, or youthful vitality, or something. I am conscious of it myself."

"You are very good, sir."

"So why should you not try your luck with Professor Challenger, of Enmore Park?"

I dare say I looked a little startled.

"Challenger!" I cried. "Professor Challenger, the famous zoologist! Wasn't he the man who broke the skull of Blundell, of the *Telegraph*?"

The news editor smiled grimly.

"Do you mind? Didn't you say it was adventures you were after?"

"It is all in the way of business, sir," I answered.

"Exactly. I don't suppose he can always be so violent as that. I'm thinking that Blundell got him at the wrong moment, maybe, or in the wrong fashion. You may have better luck, or more tact in handling him. There's something in your line there, I am sure, and the *Gazette* should work it."

"I really know nothing about him," said I. "I only remember his name in connection with the police-court proceedings, for striking Blundell."

"I have a few notes for your guidance, Mr. Malone. I've had my eye on the Professor for some little time." He took a paper from a drawer. "Here is a summary of his record. I give it you briefly:—

" 'Challenger, George Edward. *Born*: Largs, N.B., 1863. *Educ.*: Largs Academy; Edinburgh University. British Museum Assistant, 1892. Assistant-Keeper of Comparative Anthropology Department, 1893. Resigned after acrimonious Correspondence same year. Winner of Crayston Medal for Zoological Research. Foreign Member of'—well, quite a lot of things, about two inches of small type—'Société Belge, American Academy of Sciences, La Plata, etc., etc. Ex-President Palaeontological Society. Section H, British Association'—so on, so on!—'*Publications*: "Some Observations Upon a Series of Kalmuck Skulls"; "Outlines of

Vertebrate Evolution"; and numerous papers, including "The Underlying Fallacy of Weissmannism," which caused heated discussion at the Zoological Congress of Vienna. *Recreations*: Walking, Alpine climbing. *Address*: Enmore Park, Kensington, W.'

"There, take it with you. I've nothing more for you tonight."

I pocketed the slip of paper.

"One moment, sir," I said, as I realized that it was a pink bald head, and not a red face, which was fronting me. "I am not very clear yet why I am to interview this gentleman. What has he done?"

The face flashed back again.

"Went to South America on a solitary expedeetion two years ago. Came back last year. Had undoubtedly been to South America, but refused to say exactly where. Began to tell his adventures in a vague way, but something started to pick holes, and he just shut up like an oyster. Something wonderful happened—or the man's champion liar, which is the more probable supposeetion. Had some damaged photographs, said to be fakes. Got so touchy that he assaults anyone who asks questions, and heaves reporters doun the stairs. In my opinion he's just a homicidal megalomaniac with a turn for silence. That's you man, Mr. Malone. Now, off you run, and see what you can make of him. You're big enough to look after youself. Anyway, you are all safe. Employers' Liability Act, you know."

A grinning red face turned once more into a pink oval, fringed with gingery fluff: the interview was at an end.

I walked across to the Savage Club, but instead of turning into it I leaned upon the railings of Adelphi Terrace and gazed thoughtfully for a long time at the brown, oily river. I can always think more sanely and clearly in the open air. I took out the list of Professor Challenger's exploits, and I read it over under the electric lamp. Then I had what I can only regard as an inspiration. As a Pressman, I felt sure from what I had been told that I could never hope to get into touch with this cantankerous Professor. But these recriminations, twice mentioned in his skeleton biography, could only mean that he was a fanatic in science. Was there not an exposed margin there upon which he might be accessible? I would try.

I entered the club. It was just after eleven, and the big room was fairly full, though the rush had not yet set in. I noticed a tall, thin, angular man seated in an armchair by the fire. He turned as I drew my chair up to him. It was the man of all others whom I should have chosen—Tarp Henry of the staff of *Nature*, a thin, dry, leathery creature, who was full, to those who knew him, of kindly humanity. I plunged instantly into my subject.

"What do you know of Professor Challenger?"

"Challenger?" He gathered his brows in scientific disapproval. "Challenger was the man who came with some cock-and-bull story from South America."

"What story?"

"Oh, it was rank nonsense about some queer animals he had discovered. I believe he has retracted since. Anyhow, he has suppressed it all. He gave an interview to Reuter's, and there was such a howl that he saw it wouldn't do. It was a discreditable business. There were one or two folk who were inclined to take him seriously, but he soon chocked them off."

"How?"

"Well, by his insufferable rudeness and impossible behavior. There was poor old Wadley, of the Zoological Institute. Wadley sent a message: 'The President of the Zoological Institute presents his compliments to Professor Challenger, and would take it as a personal favor if he would do them the honor to come to their next meeting.' The answer was unprintable."

"You don't say?"

"Well, a bowdlerized version of it would run: 'Professor Challenger presents his compliments to the President of the Zoological Institute, and wold take it as a personal favor if he would go to the devil.'"

"Good Lord!"

"Yes, I expect that's what old Wadley said. I remember his wail at the meeting, which began: 'In fifty years' experience of scientific intercourse——' It quite broke the old man up."

"Anything more about Challenger?"

"Well, I'm a bacteriologist, you know. I live in a nine-hundred-diameter microscope. I can hardly claim to take serious notice of anything that I can see with my naked eye. I'm a frontiersman from the extreme edge of the Knowable, and I feel quite out of place when I leave my study and come into touch with all you great, rough, hulking creatures. I'm too detached to talk scandal, and yet at scientific conversaziones I *have* heard something of Challenger, for he is one of those men whom nobody can ignore. He's as clever as they make 'em—a full-charged battery of force and vitality, but a quarrelsome, ill-conditioned faddist, and unscrupulous at that. He had gone the length of faking some photographs over the South American business."

"You say he is a faddist. What is his particular fad?"

"He has a thousand, but the latest is something about Weissmann and Evolution. He had a fearful row about it in Vienna, I believe."

"Can't you tell me the point?"

"Not at the moment, but a translation of the proceedings

exists. We have it filed at the office. Would you care to come?"

"It's just what I want. I have to interview the fellow, and I need some lead up to him. It's really awfully good of you to give me a lift. I'll go with you now, if it is not too late."

Half an hour later I was seated in the newspaper office with a huge tome in front of me, which had been opened at the article "Weissmann *versus* Darwin," with the subheading, "Spirited Protest at Vienna. Lively Proceedings." My scientific education having been somewhat neglected I was unable to follow the whole argument, but it was evident that the English Professor had handled his subject in a very aggressive fashion, and had thoroughly annoyed his Continental colleagues. "Protests," "Uproar," and "General appeal to the Chairman" were three of the first brackets which caught my eye. Most of the matter might have been written in Chinese for any definite meaning that it conveyed to my brain.

"I wish you could translate it into English for me," I said, pathetically, to my helpmate.

"Well, it is a translation."

"Then I'd better try my luck with the original."

"It is certainly rather deep for a layman."

"If I could only get a single good, meaty sentence which seemed to convey some sort of definite human idea, it would serve my turn. Ah, yes, this one will do. I seem in a vague way almost to understand it. I'll copy it out. This shall be my link with the terrible Professor."

"Nothing else I can do?"

"Well, yes; I propose to write to him. If I could frame the letter here and use your address, it would give atmosphere."

"We'll have the fellow round here making a row and breaking the furniture."

"No, no; you'll see the letter—nothing contentious, I assure you."

"Well, that's my chair and desk. You'll find paper there. I'd like to censor it before it goes."

It took some doing, but I flatter myself that it wasn't such a bad job when it was finished. I read it aloud to the critical bacteriologist with some pride in my handiwork.

"*DEAR PROFESSOR CHALLENGER,*" it said. "*As a humble student of Nature, I have always taken the most profound interest in your speculations as to the differences between Darwin and Weissmann. I have recently had occasion to refresh my memory by re-reading——*"

"You infernal liar!" murmured Tarp Henry.

——"*by re-reading your masterly address at Vienna. That lucid and admirable statement seems to be the last word in the matter. There is one sentence in it, however—namely: 'I protest strongly against the insufferable and entirely dogmatic assertion that each separate id is a microcosm possessed of an historical architecture elaborated slowly through the series of generations.' Have you no desire, in view of later research, to modify this statement? Do you not think that it is over-accentuated? With your permission, I would ask the favor of an interview, as I feel strongly upon the subject, and have certain suggestions which I could only elaborate in a personal conversation. With your consent, I trust to have the honor of calling at eleven o'clock the day after tomorrow (Wednesday) morning.*

"I remain, Sir, with assurance of profound respect, yours very truly,

EDWARD D. MALONE."

"How's that?" I asked, triumphantly.

"Well, if your conscience can stand it—"

"It has never failed me yet."

"But what do you mean to do?"

"To get there. Once I am in his room I may see some opening. I may even go to the length of open confession. If he is a sportsman he will be tickled."

"Tickled, indeed! He's much more likely to do the tickling. Chain mail, or an American football suit—that's what you'll want. Well, good-bye. I'll have the answer for you here on Wednesday morning—if he ever deigns to answer you. He is a violent, dangerous, cantankerous character, hated by everyone who comes across him, and the butt of the students, so far as they dare take a liberty with him. Perhaps it would be best for you if you never heard from the fellow at all."

3

He Is a Perfectly Impossible Person

MY FRIEND'S FEAR OF HOPE WAS NOT DESTINED TO BE REALized. When I called on Wednesday there was a letter with the West Kensington postmark upon it, and my name scrawled across the envelope in a handwriting which looked like a barbed-wire railing. The contents were as follows:—

"Enmore Park, W.
"Sir,—I have duly received your note, in which you claim to endorse my views, although I am not aware that they are dependent upon endorsement either from you or anyone else. You have ventured to use the word 'speculation' with regard to my statement upon the subject of Darwinism, and I would call your attention to the fact that such a word in such a connection is offensive to a degree. The context convinces me, however, that you have sinned rather through ignorance and tactlessness than through malice, so I am content to pass the matter by. You

quote an isolated sentence from my lecture, and appear to have some difficulty in understanding it. I should have thought that only a sub-human intelligence could have failed to grasp the point, but if it really needs amplification I shall consent to see you at the hour named, though visits and visitors of every sort are exceedingly distasteful to me. As to your suggestion that I may modify my opinion, I would have you know that it is not my habit to do so after a deliberate expression of my mature views. You will kindly show the envelope of this letter to my man, Austin, when you call, as he has to take every precaution to shield me from the intrusive rascals who call themselves 'journalists.'

"Yours faithfully,
George Edward Challenger."

This was the letter that I read aloud to Tarp Henry, who had come down early to hear the result of my venture. His only remark was, "There's some new stuff, cuticura or something, which is better than arnica." Some people have such extraordinary notions of humor.

It was nearly half-past ten before I had received my message, but a taxicab took me round in good time for my appointment. It was an imposing porticoed house at which we stopped, and the heavily-curtained windows gave every indication of wealth upon the part of this formidable Professor. The door was opened by an odd, swarthy, dried-up person of uncertain age, with a dark pilot jacket and brown leather gaiters. I found afterwards that he was the chauffeur, who filled the gaps left by a succession of fugitive butlers. He looked me up and down with a searching light blue eye.

"Expected?" he asked.

"An appointment."

"Got your letter?"

I produced the envelope.

"Right!" He seemed to be a person of few words. Following him down the passage I was suddenly interrupted by a small woman, who stepped out from what proved to be the dining-room door. She was a bright, vivacious, dark-eyed lady, more French than English in her type.

"One moment," she said. "You can wait, Austin. Step in here, sir. May I ask if you have met my husband before?"

"No, madam, I have not had the honor."

"Then I apologize to you in advance. I must tell you that he is a perfectly impossible person—absolutely impossible. If you are forewarned you will be the more ready to make allowances."

"It is most considerate of you, madam."

"Get quickly out of the room if he seems inclined to be violent. Don't wait to argue with him. Several people have been injured through doing that. Afterwards there is a public scandal, and it reflects upon me and all of us. I suppose it wasn't about South America you wanted to see him?"

I could not lie to a lady.

"Dear me! That is his most dangerous subject. You won't believe a word he says—I'm sure I don't wonder. But don't tell him so, for it makes him very violent. Pretend to believe him, and you may get through all right. Remember he believes it himself. Of that you may be assured. A more honest man never lived. Don't wait any longer or he may suspect. If you find him dangerous—really dangerous—ring the bell and hold him off until I come. Even at his worse I can usually control him."

With these encouraging words the lady handed me over to the taciturn Austin, who had waited like a bronze statue of discretion during our short interview, and I was conducted to the end of the passage. There was a tap at a door, a bull's bellow from within, and I was face to face with the Professor.

He sat in a rotating chair behind a broad table, which was covered with books, maps, and diagrams. As I entered, his seat spun round to face me. His appearance made me gasp. I was prepared for something strange, but not for so overpowering a personality as this. It was his size which took one's breath away—his size and his imposing presence. His head was enormous, the largest I have ever seen upon a human being. I am sure that his top-hat, had I ventured to don it, would have slipped over me entirely and rested on my shoulders. He had the face and beard which I associate with an Assyrian bull; the former florid, the latter so black as almost to have a suspicion of blue, spade-shaped and rippling down over his chest. The hair was peculiar, plastered down in front in a long, curving wisp over his massive forehead. The eyes were blue-grey under great black tufts, very clear, very critical, and very masterful. A huge spread of shoulders and a chest like a barrel were the other parts of him which appeared above the table, save for two enormous hands covered with long black hair. This and a bellowing, roaring, rumbling voice made up my first impression of the notorious Professor Challenger.

"Well?" said he, with a most insolent stare. "What now?"

I must keep up my deception for at least a little time longer, otherwise here was evidently an end of the interview.

"You were good enough to give me an appointment, sir," said I, humbly, producing his envelope.

He took my letter from his desk and laid it out before him.

"Oh, you are the young person who cannot understand plain English, are you? My general conclusions you are good enough to approve, as I understand?"

"Entirely, sir—entirely!" I was very emphatic.

"Dear me! That strengthens my position very much, does it not? Your age and appearance make your support doubly valuable. Well, at least you are better than that herd of swine in Vienna, whose gregarious grunt is, however, not more offensive than the isolated effort of the British hog." He glared at me as the present representative of the beast.

"They seem to have behaved abominably," said I.

"I assure you that I can fight my own battles, and that I have no possible need of your sympathy. Put me alone, sir, and with my back to the wall. G. E. C. is happiest then. Well, sir, let us do what we can to curtail this visit, which can hardly be agreeable to you, and is inexpressibly irksome to me. You had, as I have been led to believe, some comments to make upon the proposition which I advanced in my thesis."

There was a brutal directness about his methods which made evasion difficult. I must still make play and wait for a better opening. It had seemed simple enough at a distance. Oh, my Irish wits, could they not help me now, when I needed help so sorely? He transfixed me with two sharp, steely eyes. "Come, come!" he rumbled.

"I am, of course, a mere student," said I, with a fatuous smile, "hardly more, I might say, than an earnest inquirer. At the same time, it seemed to me that you were a little severe upon Weissmann in this matter. Has not the general evidence since that date tended to—well, to strengthen his position?"

"What evidence?" He spoke with a menacing calm.

"Well, of course, I am aware that there is not any what

you might call *definite* evidence. I alluded merely to the trend of modern thought and the general scientific point of view, if I might so express it."

He leaned forward with great earnestness.

"I suppose you are aware," said he, checking off his points upon his fingers, "that the cranial index is a constant factor?"

"Naturally," said I.

"And that telegony is still *sub judice*?"

"Undoubtedly."

"And that the germ plasm is different from the parthenogenetic egg?"

"Why, surely!" I cried, and gloried in my own audacity.

"But what does that prove?" he asked, in a gentle, persuasive voice.

"Ah, what indeed?" I murmured. "What does it prove?"

"Shall I tell you?" he cooed.

"Pray do."

"It proves," he roared, with a sudden blast of fury, "that you are the rankest impostor in London—a vile, crawling journalist, who has no more science than he has decency in his composition!"

He had sprung to his feet with a mad rage in his eyes. Even at that moment of tension I found time for amazement at the discovery that he was quite a short man, his head not higher than my shoulder—a stunted Hercules whose tremendous vitality had all run to depth, breadth, and brain.

"Gibberish!" he cried, leaning forward, with his fingers on the table and his face projecting. "That's what I have been talking to you, sir—scientific gibberish! Did you think you could match cunning with me—you with your walnut of a brain? You think you are omnipotent, you infernal scribblers, don't you? That your praise can make a

man and your blame can break him? We must all bow to
you, and try to get a favorable word, must we? This man
shall have a leg up, and this man shall have a dressing
down! Creeping vermin, I know you! You've got out of
your station. Time was when your ears were clipped.
You've lost your sense of proportion. Swollen gas-bags!
I'll keep you in your proper place. Yes, sir, you haven't
got over G. E. C. There's one man who is still your master. He warned you off, but if you _will_ come, by the Lord
you do it at your own risk. Forfeit, my good Mr. Malone,
I claim forfeit! You have played a rather dangerous game,
and it strikes me that you have lost it."

"Look here, sir," said I, backing to the door and opening
it; "you can be as abusive as you like. But there is a limit.
You shall not assault me."

"Shall I not?" He was slowly advancing in a peculiarly
menacing way, but he stopped now and put his big hands
into the side pockets of a rather boyish short jacket which
he wore. "I have thrown several of you out of the house.
You will be the fourth or fifth. Three pound fifteen each—
that is how it averaged. Expensive, but very necessary.
Now, sir, why should you not follow your brethren? I
rather think you must." He resumed his unpleasant and
stealthy advance, pointing his toes as he walked, like a
dancing master.

I could have bolted for the hall door, but it would have
been too ignominious. Besides, a little glow of righteous
anger was springing up within me. I had been hopelessly
in the wrong before, but this man's menaces were putting
me in the right.

'I'll trouble you to keep your hands off, sir. I'll not
stand it.'

"Dear me!" His black mustache lifted and a white fang
twinkled in a sneer. "You won't stand it, eh?"

"Don't be such a fool, Professor!" I cried. "What can you hope for? I'm fifteen stone, as hard as nails, and play center three-quarter every Saturday for the London Irish. I'm not the man——"

It was at that moment that he rushed me. It was lucky that I had opened the door, or we should have gone through it. We did a Catherine-wheel together down the passage. Somehow we gathered up a chair upon our way, and bounded on with it towards the street. My mouth was full of his beard, our arms were locked, our bodies intertwined, and that infernal chair radiated its legs all round us. The watchful Austin had thrown open the hall door. We went with a back somersault down the front steps. I had seen the two Macs attempt something of the kind at the halls, but it appears to take some practice to do it without hurting oneself. The chair went to matchwood at the bottom, and we rolled apart into the gutter. He sprang to his feet, waving his fists and wheezing like an asthmatic.

"Had enough?" he panted.

"You infernal bully!" I cried, as I gathered myself together.

Then and there we should have tried the thing out, for he was effervescing with fight, but fortunately I was rescued from an odious situation. A policeman was beside us, his notebook in his hand.

"What's all this? You ought to be ashamed," said the policeman. It was the most rational remark which I had heard in Enmore Park. "Well," he insisted, turning to me, "what is it, then?"

"This man attacked me," said I.

"Did you attack him?" asked the policeman.

The Professor breathed hard and said nothing.

"It's not the first time, either," said the policeman, severely shaking his head. "You were in trouble last month for the same thing. You've blackened this young man's eye. Do you give him in charge, sir?"

I relented.

"No," said I, "I do not."

"What's that?" said the policeman.

"I was to blame myself. I intruded upon him. He gave me fair warning."

The policeman snapped up his notebook.

"Don't let us have any more such goings-on," said he. "Now, then! Move on, there, move on!" This to a butcher's boy, a maid, and one or two loafers who had collected. He clumped heavily down the street, driving this little flock before him. The Professor looked at me, and there was something humorous at the back of his eyes.

"Come in!" said he. "I've not done with you yet."

The speech had a sinister sound, but I followed him none the less into the house. The man-servant, Austin, like a wooden image, closed the door behind us.

4

It's Just the Very Biggest Thing in the World

HARDLY WAS IT SHUT THAN MRS. CHALLENGER DARTED OUT from the dining-room. The small woman was in a furious temper. She barred her husband's way like an enraged chicken in front of a bulldog. It was evident that she had seen my exit, but had not observed my return.

"You brute, George!" she screamed. "You've hurt that nice young man."

He jerked backwards with his thumb.

"Here he is, safe and sound behind me."

She was confused, but not unduly so.

"I am sorry, I didn't see you."

"I assure you, madam, that it is all right."

"He has marked your poor face! Oh, George, what a brute you are! Nothing but scandals from one end of the week to the other. Everyone hating and making fun of you. You've finished my patience. This ends it."

"Dirty linen," he rumbled.

"It's not a secret," she cried. "Do you suppose that the whole street—the whole of London, for that matter——

Get away, Austin, we don't want you here. Do you suppose they don't all talk about you? Where is your dignity? You, a man who should have been Regius Professor at a great University with a thousand students all revering you. Where is your dignity, George?"

"How about yours, my dear?"

"You try me too much. A ruffian—a common brawling ruffian—that's what you have become."

"Be good, Jessie."

"A roaring, raging bully!"

"That's done it! Stool of penance!" said he.

To my amazement he stooped, picked her up, and placed her sitting upon a high pedestal of black marble in the angle of the hall. It was at least seven feet high, and so thin that she could hardly balance upon it. A more absurd object than she presented cocked up there with her face convulsed with anger, her feet dangling, and her body rigid for fear of an upset, I could not imagine.

"Let me down!" she wailed.

"Say 'please.' "

"You brute, George! Let me down this instant!"

"Come into the study, Mr. Malone."

"Really, sir——!" said I, looking at the lady.

"Here's Mr. Malone pleading for you, Jessie. Say 'please,' and down you come."

"Oh, you brute! Please! please!"

He took her down as if she had been a canary.

"You must behave yourself, dear. Mr. Malone is a Pressman. He will have it all in his rag tomorrow, and sell an extra dozen among our neighbors. 'Strange story of high life'—you felt fairly high on that pedestal, did you not? Then a subtitle, 'Glimpse of a singular ménage.' He's a foul feeder, is Mr. Malone, a carrion eater, like all of his kind—*porcus ex grege diaboli*—a swine from the devil's herd. That's it, Malone—what?"

"You are really intolerable!" said I, hotly.

He bellowed with laughter.

"We shall have a coalition presently," he boomed, looking from his wife to me and puffing out his enormous chest. Then, suddenly altering his tone, "Excuse this frivolous family badinage, Mr. Malone. I called you back for some more serious purpose than to mix you up with our little domestic pleasantries. Run away, little woman, and don't fret." He placed a huge hand upon each of her shoulders. "All that you say is perfectly true. I should be a better man if I did what you advise, but I shouldn't be quite George Edward Challenger. There are plenty of better men, my dear, but only one G. E. C. So make the best of him." He suddenly gave her a resounding kiss, which embarrassed me even more than his violence had done. "Now, Mr. Malone," he continued, with a great accession of dignity, "this way if *you* please."

We re-entered the room which we had left so tumultuously ten minutes before. The Professor closed the door carefully behind us, motioned me into in armchair, and pushed a cigar box under my nose.

"Real San Juan Colorado," he said. "Excitable people like you are the better for narcotics. Heavens! Don't bite it! Cut—and cut with reverence! Now lean back, and listen attentively to whatever I may care to say to you. If any remark should occur to you, you can reserve it for some more opportune time.

"First of all, as to your return to my house after your most justifiable expulsion"—he protruded his beard, and stared at me as one who challenges and invites contradiction—"after, as I say, your well-merited expulsion. The reason lay in your answer to that most officious policeman, in which I seemed to discern some glimmering of good feeling upon your part—more, at any rate, than I am accustomed to associate with your profession. In admitting that the fault of the incident lay with you, you gave some evidence of a certain mental detachment and breadth of view which attracted my favorable notice. The sub-species of the human race to which you unfortunately belong has always been below my mental horizon. Your words brought you suddenly above it. You swam up into my serious notice. For this reason I asked you to return with me, as I was minded to make your further acquaintance. You will kindly deposit your ash in the small Japanese tray on the bamboo table which stands at your left elbow."

All this he boomed forth like a professor addressing his class. He had swung round his revolving chair so as to face me, and he sat all puffed out like an enormous bullfrog, his head laid back, and his eyes half-covered by supercilious lids. Now he suddenly turned himself sideways, and all I could see of him was tangled hair with a red, protruding ear. He was scratching about among the litter of papers upon his desk. He faced me presently with what looked like a very tattered sketchbook in his hand.

"I am going to talk to you about South America," said he. "No comments if you please. First of all, I wish you to understand that nothing I tell you now is to be repeated in any public way unless you have my express permission. That permission will, in all human probability, never be given. Is that clear?"

"It is very hard," said I. "Surely a judicious account——"

He replaced the notebook upon the table.

"That ends it," said he. "I wish you a very good morning."

"No, no!" I cried. "I submit to any conditions. So far as I can see, I have no choice."

"None in the world," said he.

"Well, then, I promise."

"Word of honor?"

"Word of honor."

He looked at me with doubt in his insolent eyes.

"After all, what do I know about your honor?" said he.

"Upon my word, sir," I cried, angrily, "you take very great liberties! I have never been so insulted in my life."

He seemed more interested than annoyed at my outbreak.

"Round-headed," he muttered. "Brachycephalic, gray-eyed, black-haired, with suggestion of the negroid. Celtic, I presume?"

"I am an Irishman, sir."

"Irish Irish?"

"Yes, sir."

"That, of course, explains it. Let me see; you have given me your promise that my confidence will be respected? That confidence, I may say, will be far from complete. But I am prepared to give you a few indications which will be of interest. In the first place, you are probably aware that two years ago I made a journey to South America—one which will be classical in the scientific history of the world? The object of my journey was to verify some conclusions of Wallace and of Bates, which could only be done by observing their reported facts under the same conditions in which they had themselves noted them. If my expedition had no other results it would still have been noteworthy, but a curious incident occurred to me while there which opened up an entirely fresh line of inquiry.

"You are aware—or probably, in this half-educated age, you are not aware—that the country round some parts of the

Amazon is still only partially explored, and that a great number of tributaries, some of them entirely uncharted, run into the main river. It was my business to visit this little-known back-country and to examine its fauna, which furnished me with the materials for several chapters for that great and monumental work upon zoology which will be my life's justification. I was returning, my work accomplished, when I had occasion to spend a night at a small Indian village at a point where a certain tributary—the name and position of which I withhold—opens into the main river. The natives were Cucama Indians, an amiable but degraded race, with mental powers hardly superior to the average Londoner. I had effected some cures among them upon my way up the river, and had impressed them considerably with my personality, so that I was not surprised to find myself eagerly awaited upon my return. I gathered from their signs that someone had urgent need of my medical services, and I followed the chief to one of his huts. When I entered I found that the sufferer to whose aid I had been summoned had that instant expired. He was, to my surprise, no Indian, but a white man; indeed, I may say a very white man, for he was flaxen-haired and had some characteristics of an albino. He was clad in rags, was very emaciated, and bore every trace of prolonged hardship. So far as I could understand the account of the natives, he was a complete stranger to them, and had come upon their village through the woods alone and in the last stage of exhaustion.

"The man's knapsack lay beside the couch, and I examined the contents. His name was written upon a tab within it—Maple White, Lake Avenue, Detroit, Michigan. It is a name to which I am prepared always to lift my hat. It is not too much to say that it will rank level with my own when the final credit of this business comes to be apportioned.

"From the contents of the knapsack it was evident that this man had been an artist and poet in search of effects. There were scraps of verse. I do not profess to be a judge of such things, but they appeared to me to be singularly wanting in merit. There were also some rather commonplace pictures of river scenery, a paint box, a box of colored chalks, some brushes, that curved bone which lies upon my inkstand, a volume of Baxter's 'Moths and Butterflies,' a cheap revolver, and a few cartridges. Of personal equipment he either had none or he had lost it in his journey. Such were the total effects of this strange American Bohemian.

"I was turning away from him when I observed that something projected from the front of his ragged jacket. It was this sketchbook, which was as dilapidated then as you see it now. Indeed, I can assure you that a first folio of Shakespeare could not be treated with greater reverence than this relic has been since it came into my possession. I hand it to you now, and I ask you to take it page by page and to examine the contents."

He helped himself to a cigar and leaned back with a fiercely critical pair of eyes, taking note of the effect which this document would produce.

I had opened the volume with some expectation of a revelation, though of what nature I could not imagine. The first page was disappointing, however, as it contained nothing but the picture of a very fat man in a pea jacket, with the legend, "Jimmy Colver on the Mail-boat," written beneath it. There followed several pages which were filled with small sketches of Indians and their ways. Then came a picture of a cheerful and corpulent ecclesiastic in a shovel hat, sitting opposite a very thin European, and the inscription: "Lunch with Fra Cristofero at Rosario." Studies of women and babies accounted for several more pages, and then there was an unbroken series of animal drawings with such explanations as "Manatee upon Sandbank," "Turtles and their Eggs," "Black Ajouti under a Miriti Palm"—the latter disclosing some sort of pig-like animal; and finally came a double page of studies of long-snouted and very unpleasant saurians. I could make nothing of it, and said so to the Professor.

"Surely these are only crocodiles?"

"Alligators! Alligators! There is hardly such a thing as a true crocodile in South America. The distinction between them——"

"I meant that I could see nothing unusual—nothing to justify what you have said."

He smiled serenely.

"Try the next page," said he.

I was still unable to sympathize. It was a full-page sketch of a landscape roughly tinted in color—the kind of painting which an open-air artist takes as a guide to a future more elaborate effort. There was a pale-green foreground of feathery vegetation, which sloped upwards and ended in a line of cliffs dark red in color, and curiously ribbed like some basaltic formations which I have seen. They extended in an unbroken wall right across the background. At one point was an isolated pyramidal rock, crowned by a great tree, which appeared to be separated by a cleft from the main crag. Behind it all, a blue tropical sky. A thin green line of vegetation fringed the summit of the ruddy cliff. On the next page was another watercolor wash of the same place, but much nearer, so that one could clearly see the details.

"Well?" he asked.

"It is no doubt a curious formation," said I, "but I am not geologist enough to say that it is wonderful."

"Wonderful!" he repeated. "It is unique. It is incredible.

No one on earth has ever dreamed of such a possibility. Now the next."

I turned it over, and gave an exclamation of surprise. There was a full-page picture of the most extraordinary creature that I had ever seen. It was the wild dream of an opium smoker, a vision of delirium. The head was like that of a fowl, the body that of a bloated lizard, the trailing tail was furnished with upward-turned spikes, and the curved back was edged with a high serrated fringe, which looked like a dozen cocks' wattles placed behind each other. In front of this creature was an absurd mannikin, or dwarf in the human form, who stood staring at it.

"Well, what do you think of that?" cried the Professor, rubbing his hands with an air of triumph.

"It is monstrous—grotesque."

"But what made him draw such an animal?"

"Trade gin, I should think."

"Oh, that's the best explanation you can give, is it?"

"Well, sir, what is yours?"

"The obvious one that the creature exists. That it is actually sketched from the life."

I should have laughed only that I had a vision of our doing another Catherine-wheel down the passage.

"No doubt," said I, "no doubt," as one humors an imbecile. "I confess, however," I added, "that this tiny human figure puzzles me. If it were an Indian we could set it down as evidence of some pigmy race in America, but it appears to be a European in a sun-hat."

The Professor snorted like an angry buffalo. "You really touch the limit," said he. "You enlarge my view of the possible. Cerebral paresis! Mental inertia! Wonderful!"

He was too absurd to make me angry. Indeed, it was a waste of energy, for if you were going to be angry with this man you would be angry all the time. I contented myself with smiling wearily. "It struck me that the man was small," said I.

"Look here!" he cried, leaning forward and dabbing a great hairy sausage of a finger on to the picture. "You see that plant behind the animal; I suppose you thought it was a dandelion or a brussels sprout—what? Well, it is a vegetable ivory palm, and they run to about fifty or sixty feet. Don't you see that the man is put in for a purpose? He couldn't really have stood in front of that brute and lived to draw it. He sketched himself in to give a scale of heights. He was, we will say, over five feet high. The tree is ten times bigger, which is what one would expect."

"Good heavens!" I cried. "Then you think the beast was—— Why, Charing Cross Station would hardly make a kennel for such a brute!"

"Apart from exaggeration, he is certainly a well-grown specimen," said the Professor, complacently.

"But," I cried, "surely the whole experience of the human race is not to be set aside on account of a single sketch"—I had turned over the leaves and ascertained that there was nothing more in the book—"a single sketch by a wandering American artist who may have done it under hashish, or in the delirium of fever, or simply in order to gratify a freakish imagination. You can't, as a man of science, defend such a position as that."

For answer the Professor took a book down from a shelf.

"This is an excellent monograph by my gifted friend, Ray Lankester!" said he. "There is an illustration here which would interest you. Ah, yes, here it is! The inscription beneath it runs: 'Probably appearance in life of the Jurassic Dinosaur Stegosaurus. The hind leg alone is twice as tall as a full-grown man.' Well, what do you make of that?"

He handed me the open book. I started as I looked at the

picture. In this reconstructed animal of a dead world there was certainly a very great resemblance to the sketch of the unknown artist.

"That is certainly remarkable," said I.

"But you won't admit that it is final?"

"Surely it might be a coincidence, or this American may have seen a picture of the kind and carried it in his memory. It would be likely to recur to a man in a delirium."

"Very good," said the Professor, indulgently, "we leave it at that. I will now ask you to look at this bone." He handed over the bone which he had already described as part of the dead man's possessions. It was about six inches long, and thicker than my thumb, with some indications of dried cartilage at one end of it.

"To what known creature does that bone belong?" asked the Professor.

I examined it with care, and tried to recall some half-forgotten knowledge.

It might be a very thick human collarbone," I said.

My companion waved his hand in contemptuous deprecation.

"The human collarbone is curved. This is straight. There is a groove upon its surface showing that a great tendon played across it, which could not be the case with a clavicle.'

"Then I must confess that I don't know what it is."

"You need not be ashamed to expose your ignorance, for I don't suppose the whole South Kensington staff could give a name to it." He took a little bone the size of a bean out of a pill-box. "So far as I am a judge this human bone is the analogue of the one which you hold in your hand. That will give you some idea of the size of the creature. You will observe from the cartilage that this is no fossil specimen, but recent. What do you say to that?"

"Surely in an elephant——"

He winced as if in pain.

"Don't! Don't talk of elephants in South America. Even in these days of Board Schools—"

"Well," I interrupted, "any large South American animal—a tapir, for example."

"You may take it, young man, that I am versed in the elements of my business. This is not a conceivable bone either of a tapir or of any other creature known to zoology. It belongs to a very large, a very strong, and, by all analogy, a very fierce animal which exists upon the face of the earth, but has not yet come under the notice of science. You are unconvinced?"

"I am at least deeply interested."

"Then your case is not hopeless. I feel that there is reason lurking in you somewhere, so we will patiently grope round for it. We will now leave the dead American and proceed with my narrative. You can imagine that I could hardly come away from the Amazon without probing deeper into the matter. There were indications as to the direction from which the dead traveler had come. Indian legends would alone have been my guide, for I found that rumours of a strange land were common among all the riverine tribes. You have heard, no doubt, of Curupuri?"

"Never."

"Curupuri is the spirit of the woods, something terrible, something malevolent, something to be avoided. None can describe its shape or nature, but it is a word of terror along the Amazon. Now all tribes agree as to the direction in which Curupuri lives. It was the same direction from which the American had come. Something terrible lay that way. It was my business to find out what it was."

"What did you do?" My flippancy was all gone. This massive man compelled one's attention and respect.

"I overcame the extreme reluctance of the natives—a reluctance which extends even to talk upon the subject—and by judicious persuasion and gifts, aided, I will admit, by some threats of coercion, I got two of them to act as guides. After many adventures which I need not describe, and after traveling a distance which I will not mention, in a direction which I withhold, we came at last to a tract of country which has never been described, nor, indeed, visited save by my unfortunate predecessor. Would you kindly look at this?"

He handed me a photograph—half-plate size.

"The unsatisfactory appearance of it is due to the fact," said he, "that on descending the river the boat was upset and the case which contained the undeveloped films was broken, with disastrous results. Nearly all of them were totally ruined—an irreparable loss. This is one of the few which partially escaped. This explanation of deficiencies or abnormalities you will kindly accept. There was talk of faking. I am not in a mood to argue such a point."

The photograph was certainly very off-colored. An unkind critic might easily have misinterpreted that dim surface. It was a dull gray landscape, and as I gradually deciphered the details of it I realized that it represented a long and enormously high line of cliffs exactly like an immense cataract seen in the distance, with a sloping, tree-clad plain in the foreground.

"I believe it is the same place as the painted picture," said I.

"It *is* the same place," the Professor answered. "I found traces of the fellow's camp. Now look at this."

It was a nearer view of the same scene, though the photograph was extremely defective. I could distinctly see the isolated, tree-crowned pinnacle of rock which was detached from the crag.

"I have no doubt of it at all," said I.

"Well, that is something gained," said he. "We progress, do we not? Now, will you please look at the top of that rocky pinnacle? Do you observe something there?"

"An enormous tree."

"But on the tree?"

"A large bird," said I.

He handed me a lens.

"Yes," I said, peering through it, "a large bird stands on the tree. It appears to have a considerable beak. I should say it was a pelican."

"I cannot congratulate you upon your eyesight," said the Professor. "It is not a a pelican, nor, indeed, is it a bird. It may interest you to know that I succeeded in shooting that particular specimen. It was the only absolute proof of my experiences which I was able to bring away with me."

"You have it, then?" Here at last was tangible corroboration.

"I had it. It was unfortunately lost with so much else in the same boat accident which ruined my photographs. I clutched at it as it disappeared in the swirl of the rapids, and part of its wing was left in my hand. I was insensible when washed ashore, but the miserable remnant of my superb specimen was still intact; I now lay it before you."

From a drawer he produced what seemed to me to be the upper portion of the wing of a large bat. It was at least two feet in length, a curved bone, with a membranous veil beneath it.

"A monstrous bat!" I suggested.

"Nothing of the sort," said the Professor, severely. "Living, as I do, in an educated and scientific atmosphere, I could not have conceived that the first principles of zoology were so little known. Is it possible that you do not know the elementary fact in comparative anatomy, that the wing of a bird is really the forearm, while the wing of a bat consists of three elongated fingers with membranes between? Now, in this case, the bone is certainly not the forearm, and you can see for yourself that this is a single membrane hanging upon a single bone, and therefore that it cannot belong to a bat. But if it is neither bird nor bat, what is it?"

My small stock of knowledge was exhausted.

"I really do not know," said I.

He opened the standard work to which he had actually referred me.

"Here," said he, pointing to the picture of an extraordinary flying monster, "is an excellent reproduction of the dimorphodon, or pterodactyl, a flying reptile of the Jurassic period. On the next page is a diagram of the mechanism of its wing. Kindly compare it with the specimen in your hand."

A wave of amazement passed over me as I looked. I was convinced. There could be no getting away from it. The cumulative proof was overwhelming. The sketch, the photographs, the narrative, and now the actual specimen—the evidence was complete. I said so—I said so warmly, for I felt that the Professor was an ill-used man. He leaned back in his chair with drooping eyelids and a tolerant smile, basking in this sudden gleam of sunshine.

"It's just the very biggest thing that I ever heard of!" said I, though it was my journalistic rather than my scientific enthusiasm that was roused. "It is colossal. You are a Columbus of science who has discovered a lost world. I'm really awfully sorry if I seemed to doubt you. It was all so unthinkable. But I understand evidence when I see it, and this should be good enough for anyone."

The Professor purred with satisfaction.

"And then, sir, what did you do next?"

"It was the wet season, Mr. Malone, and my stores were

exhausted. I explored some portion of this huge cliff, but I was unable to find any way to scale it. The pyramidal rock upon which I saw and shot the pterodactyl was more accessible. Being something of a cragsman, I did manage to get half way to the top of that. From that height I had a better idea of the plateau upon the top of the crags. It appeared to be very large; neither to east nor to west could I see any end to the vista of green-capped cliffs. Below, it is a swampy, jungly region, full of snakes, insects, and fever. It is a natural protection to this singular country."

"Did you see any other trace of life?"

"No, sir, I did not; but during the week that we lay encamped at the base of the cliff we heard some very strange noises from above."

"But the creature that the American drew? How do you account for that?"

"We can only suppose that he must have made his way to the summit and seen it there. We know, therefore, that there *is* a way up. We know equally that it must be a very difficult one, otherwise the creatures would have come down and overrun the surrounding country. Surely that is clear?"

"But how do they come to be there?"

"I do not think that the problem is a very obscure one," said the Professor; "there can only be one explanation. South America is, as you may have heard, a granite continent. At this single point in the interior there has been, in some far distant age, a great, sudden volcanic upheaval. These cliffs, I may remark, are basaltic, and therefore plutonic. An area, as large as Sussex, has been lifted up *en bloc* with all its living contents, and cut off by perpendicular precipices of a hardness which defies erosion from all the rest of the continent. What is the result? Why, the ordinary laws of nature are suspended. The various checks which influence the struggle for existence in the world at large are all neutralized or altered. Creatures survive which would otherwise disappear. You will observe that both the pterodactyl and the stegosaurus are Jurassic, and therefore of a great age in the order of life. They have been artificially conserved by those strange accidental conditions."

"But surely your evidence is conclusive. You have only to lay it before the proper authorities."

"So, in my simplicity, I had imagined," said the Professor, bitterly. "I can only tell you that it was not so, that I was met at eery turn by incredulity, born partly of stupidity and partly of jealousy. It is not my nature, sir, to cringe to any man, or to seek to prove a fact if my word has been doubted. After the first I have not condescended to show such corroborative proofs as I possess. The subject became hateful to me—I would not speak of it. When men like yourself, who represent the foolish curiosity of the public, came to disturb my privacy I was unable to meet them with dignified reserve. By nature I am, I admit, somewhat fiery, and under provocation I am inclined to be violent. I fear you may have remarked it."

I nursed my eye and was silent.

"My wife has frequently remonstrated with me upon the subject, and yet I fancy that any man of honour would feel the same. Tonight, however, I propose to give an extreme example of the control of the will over the emotions. I invite you to be present at the exhibition." He handed me a card from his desk. "You will perceive that Mr. Percival Waldron, a naturalist of some popular repute, is announced to lecture at eight-thirty at the Zoological Institute's Hall upon 'The Record of the Ages.' I have been specially invited to be present upon the platform, and to move a vote of thanks to the lecturer. While doing so, I shall make it my business, with infinite tact and delicacy, to throw out a few remarks which may arouse the interest of the audience and cause some of them to desire to go more deeply into the matter. Nothing contentious, you understand, but only an indication that there are greater deeps beyond. I shall hold myself strongly in leash, and see whether by this self-restraint I attain a more favorable result."

"And I may come?" I asked eagerly.

"Why, surely," he answered, cordially. He had an enormously massive genial manner, which was almost as overpowering as his violence. His smile of benevolence was a wonderful thing, when his cheeks would suddenly bunch into two red apples, between his half-closed eyes and his great black beard. "By all means, come. It will be a comfort to me to know that I have one ally in the hall, however inefficient and ignorant of the subject he may be. I fancy there will be a large audience, for Waldron, though an absolute charlatan, has a considerable popular following. Now, Mr. Malone, I have given you rather more of my time than I had intended. The individual must not monopolize what is meant for the world. I shall be pleased to see you at the lecture tonight. In the meantime, you will understand that no public use is to be made of any of the material that I have given you."

"But Mr. McArdle—my news editor, you know—will want to know what I have done."

"Tell him what you like. You can say, among other things, that if he sends anyone else to intrude upon me I shall call upon him with a riding whip. But I leave it to you that nothing of all this appears in print. Very good. Then the Zoological Institute's Hall at eight-thirty tonight." I had a last impression of red cheeks, blue rippling beard, and intolerant eyes, as he waved me out of the room.

5

Question!

WHAT WITH THE PHYSICAL SHOCKS INCIDENTAL TO MY FIRST interview with Professor Challenger and the mental ones which accompanied the second, I was a somewhat demoralized journalist by the time I found myself in Enmore Park once more. In my aching head the one thought was throbbing that there really *was* truth in this man's story, that it was of tremendous consequence, and that it would work up into inconceivable copy for the *Gazette* when I could obtain permission to use it. A taxicab was waiting at the end of the road, so I sprang into it and drove down to the office. McArdle was at his post as usual.

"Well," he cried, expectantly, "what may it run to? I'm thinking, young man, you have been in the wars. Don't tell me that he assaulted you."

"We had a little difference at first."

"What a man it is! What did you do?"

"Well, he became more reasonable and we had a chat. But I got nothing out of him—nothing for publication."

"I'm not so sure about that. You got a black eye out of

him, and that's for publication. We can't have this reign of
terror, Mr. Malone. We must bring the man to his bearings.
I'll have a leaderette on him tomorrow that will raise a
blister. Just give me the material and I will engage to
brand the fellow for ever. Professor Munchausen—how's
that for an inset headline? Sir John Mandeville redivivus—
Cagliostro—all the impostors and bullies in history. I'll
show him up for the fraud he is."

"I wouldn't do that, sir."

"Why not?"

"Because he is not a fraud at all."

"What!" roared McArdle. "You don't meant to say you
really believe this stuff of his about mammoths and mas-
todons and great sea sairpents?"

"Well, I don't know about that. I don't think he makes
any claims of that kind. But I do believe that he has got
something new."

"Then for Heaven's sake, man, write it up!"

"I'm longing to, but all I know he gave me in confidence and on condition that I didn't." I condensed into a
few sentences the Professor's narrative. "That's how it
stands."

McArdle looked deeply incredulous.

"Well, Mr. Malone," he said at last, "about this scientific meeting tonight; there can be no privacy about that,
anyhow. I don't suppose any paper will want to report it,
for Waldron has been reported already a dozen times, and
no one is aware that Challenger will speak. We may get a
scoop, if we are lucky. You'll be there in any case, so
you'll just give us a pretty full report. I'll keep space up
to midnight."

"My day was a busy one, and I had an early dinner at
the Savage Club with Tarp Henry, to whom I gave some
account of my adventures. He listened with a sceptical

smile on his gaunt face, and roared with laughter on hearing that the Professor had convinced me.

"My dear chap, things don't happen like that in real life. People don't stumble upon enormous discoveries and then lose their evidence. Leave that to the novelists. The fellow is as full of tricks as the monkey house at the Zoo. It's all absolute bosh."

"But the American poet?"

"He never existed."

"I saw his sketchbook."

"Challenger's sketchbook."

"You think he drew that animal?"

"Of course he did. Who else?"

"Well, then, the photographs?"

"There was nothing in the photographs. By your own admission you only saw a bird."

"A pterodactyl."

"That's what *he* says. He put the pterodactyl into your head."

"Well, then, the bones?"

"First one out of an Irish stew. Second one vamped up for the occasion. If you are clever and you know your business you can fake a bone as easily as you can a photograph."

I began to feel uneasy. Perhaps, after all, I had been premature in my acquiescence. Then I had a sudden happy thought.

"Will you come to the meeting?" I asked.

Tarp Henry looked thoughtful.

"He is not a popular person, the genial Challenger," said he. "A lot of people have accounts to settle with him. I should say he is about the best-hated man in London. If the medical students turn out there will be no end of a rag. I don't want to get into a bear-garden."

"You might at least do him the justice to hear him state his own case."

"Well, perhaps it's only fair. All right. I'm your man for the evening.".

When we arrived at the hall we found a much greater concourse than I had expected. A line of electric broughams discharged their little cargoes of white-bearded professors, while the dark stream of humbler pedestrians, who crowded through the arched doorway, showed that the audience would be popular as well as scientific. Indeed, it became evident to us as soon as we had taken our seats that a youthful and even boyish spirit was abroad in the gallery and the back portions of the hall. Looking behind me, I could see rows of faces of the familiar medical student type. Apparently the great hospitals had each sent down their contingent. The behavior of the audience at present was good-humored, but mischievous. Scraps of popular songs were chorused with an enthusiasm which was a strange prelude to a scientific lecture, and there was already a tendency to personal chaff which promised a jovial evening to others, however embarrassing it might be to the recipients of these dubious honors.

Thus, when old Doctor Meldrum, with his well-known curly-brimmed opera hat, appeared upon the platform, there was such a universal query of "Where *did* you get that tile?" that he hurriedly removed it, and concealed it furtively under his chair. When gouty Professor Wadley limped down to his seat there were general affectionate inquiries from all parts of the hall as to the exact state of his poor toe, which caused him obvious embarrassment. The greatest demonstration of all, however, was at the entrance of my new acquaintance, Professor Challenger, when he passed down to take his place at the extreme end of the front row of the platform. Such a yell of welcome broke forth when his black beard first protruded round the corner that I began to suspect Tarp Henry was right in his surmise, and that this assemblage was there not merely for the sake of the lecture, but because it had got rumored abroad that the famous Professor would take part in the proceedings.

There was some sympathetic laughter on his entrance among the front benches of well-dressed spectators, as though the demonstration of the students in this instance was not unwelcome to them. That greeting was, indeed, a frightful outburst of sound, the uproar of the carnivora cage when the step of the bucket-bearing keeper is heard in the distance. There was an offensive tone in it, perhaps, and yet in the main it struck me as mere riotous outcry, the noisy reception of one who amused and interested them, rather than of one they disliked or despised. Challenger smiled with weary and tolerant contempt, as a kindly man would meet the yapping of a litter of puppies. He sat slowly down, blew out his chest, passed his hand caressingly down his beard, and looked with drooping eyes at the crowded hall before him. The uproar of his advent had not yet died away when Professor Ronald Murray, the Chairman, and Mr. Waldron, the lecturer, threaded their way to the front, and the proceedings began.

Professor Murray will, I am sure, excuse me if I say that he has the common fault of most Englishmen of being inaudible. Why on earth people who have something to say which is worth hearing should not take the slight trouble to learn how to make it heard is one of the strange mysteries of modern life. Their methods are as reasonable as to try to pour some precious stuff from the spring to the reservoir through a non-conducting pipe, which could by the least effort be opened. Professor Murray made several profound remarks to his white tie and to the water-carafe upon the table, with a humorous, twinkling aside to the silver candlestick upon his right. Then he sat down, and Mr. Waldron, the famous lecturer, rose amid a general murmur of applause. He was a stern, gaunt man, with a harsh voice and an aggressive manner, but he had the merit of knowing how to assimilate the ideas of other men, and to pass them on in a way which was intelligible and even interesting to the lay public, with a happy knack of being funny about the most unlikely objects, so that the precession of the Equinox or the formation of a vertebrate became a highly humorous process as treated by him.

It was a bird's-eye view of creation, as interpreted by science, which, in language always clear and sometimes picturesque, he unfolded before us. He told us of the globe, a huge mass of flaming gas, flaring through the heavens. Then he pictured the solidification, the cooling, the wrinkling which formed the mountains, the steam which turned to water, the slow preparation of the stage upon which was to be played the inexplicable drama of life. On the origin of life itself he was discreetly vague. That the germs of it could hardly have survived the original roasting was, he declared, fairly certain. Therefore it had come later. Had it built itself out of the cooling, inorganic elements of the globe? Very likely. Had the germs of it arrived from outside upon a meteor? It was hardly conceivable. On the whole, the wisest man was the least dogmatic upon the point. We could not—or at least we had not succeeded up to date in making organic life in our laboratories out of inorganic materials. The gulf between the dead and the living was something which our chemistry could not as yet bridge. But there was a higher and subtler chemistry of Nature, which, working with great forces over long epochs, might well produce results which were impossible for us. There the matter must be left.

This brought the lecturer to the great ladder of animal life, beginning low down in molluscs and feeble sea creatures, then up rung by rung through reptiles and fishes, till at last we came to a kangaroo-rat, a creature which brought forth its young alive, the direct ancestor of all mammals, and presumably, therefore, of everyone in the audience. ("No, no," from a sceptical student in the back row.) If the young gentleman in the red tie who cried "No, no," and who presumably claimed to have been hatched out of an egg, would wait upon him after the lecture, he would be glad to see such a curiosity. (Laughter.) It was strange to think that the climax of all the age-long processes of Nature had been the creation of that gentleman in the red tie. But had the process stopped? Was this gentleman to be taken as the final type—the be-all and end-all of development? He hoped that he would not hurt the feelings of the gentleman in the red tie if he maintained that, whatever virtues that gentleman might possess in private life, still the vast processes of the universe were not fully justified if they were to end entirely in his production. Evolution was not a spent force, but one still working, and even greater achievements were in store.

Having thus, amid a general titter, played very prettily with his interrupter, the lecturer went back to his picture of the past, the drying of the seas, the emergence of the sand-bank, the sluggish, viscous life which lay upon their margins, the overcrowded lagoons, the tendency of the sea creatures to take refuge upon the mud-flats, the abundance of food awaiting them, their consequent enormous growth. "Hence, ladies and gentlemen," he added, "that frightful brood of saurians which still afright our eyes when seen in the Wealden or in the Solenhofen slates, but which were fortunately extinct long before the first appearance of mankind upon this planet."

"Question!" boomed a voice from the platform.

Mr. Waldron was a strict disciplinarian with a gift of acid humour, as exemplified upon the gentleman with the red tie, which made it perilous to interrupt him. But this interjection appeared to him so absurd that he was at a loss how to deal with it. So looks the Shakespearean who is confronted by a rancid Baconian, or the astronomer who is assailed by a flat-earth fanatic. He paused for a moment, and then, raising his voice, repeated slowly the words: "Which were extinct before the coming of man."

"Question!" boomed the voice once more.

Waldron looked with amazement along the line of professors upon the platform until his eyes fell upon the figure of Challenger, who leaned back in his chair with closed eyes and an amused expression, as if he were smiling in his sleep. "I see!" said Waldron, with a shrug. "It is my friend Professor Challenger," and amid laughter he renewed his lecture as if this was a final explanation and no more need to be said.

But the incident was far from being closed. Whatever path the lecturer took amid the wilds of the past seemed invariably to lead him to some assertion as to extinct or prehistoric life which instantly brought the same bull's bellow from the Professor. The audience began to anticipate it and to roar with delight when it came. The packed benches of students joined in, and every time Challenger's beard opened, before any sound could come forth, there was a yell of "Question!" from a hundred voices, and an answering counter cry of "Order!" and "Shame!" from as many more. Waldron, though a hardened lecturer and a strong man, became rattled. He hesitated, stammered, repeated himself, got snarled in a long sentence, and finally turned furiously upon the cause of his troubles.

"This is really intolerable!" he cried, glaring across the

platform. "I must ask you, Professor Challenger, to cease these ignorant and unmannerly interruptions."

There was a hush over the hall, the students rigid with delight at seeing the high gods on Olympus quarrelling among themselves. Challenger levered his bulky figure slowly out of his chair.

"I must in turn ask you, Mr. Waldron," he said, "to cease to make assertions which are not in strict accordance with scientific fact."

The words unloosed a tempest. "Shame! Shame!" "Give him a hearing!" "Put him out!" "Shove him off the platform!" "Fair play!" emerged from a general roar of amusement or execration. The chairman was on his feet flapping both his hands and bleating excitedly. "Professor Challenger—personal—views—later," were the solid peaks above his clouds of inaudible mutter. The interrupter bowed, smiled, stroked his beard, and relapsed into his chair. Waldron, very flushed and warlike, continued his observations. Now and then, as he made an assertion, he shot a venomous glance at his opponent, who seemed to be slumbering deeply, with the same broad, happy smile upon his face.

At last the lecture came to an end—I am inclined to think that it was a premature one, as the peroration was hurried and disconnected. The thread of the argument had been rudely broken, and the audience was restless and expectant. Waldron sat down, and, after a chirrup from the chairman, Professor Challenger rose and advanced to the edge of the platform. In the interests of my paper I took down his speech verbatim.

"Ladies and Gentlemen," he began, amid a sustained interruption from the back. "I beg pardon—Ladies, Gentlemen, and Children—I must apologize, I had inadvertently omitted a considerable section of this audience" (tumult, during which the Professor stood with one hand raised and his enormous head nodding sympathetically, as if he were bestowing a pontifical blessing upon the crowd), "I have been selected to move a vote of thanks to Mr. Waldron for the very picturesque and imaginative address to which we have just listened. There are points in it with which I disagree, and it has been my duty to indicate them as they arose, but, none the less, Mr. Waldron has accomplished his object well, that object being to give a simple and interesting account of what he conceives to have been the history of our planet. Popular lecturers are the easiest to listen to, but Mr. Waldron" (here he beamed and blinked at the lecturer) "will excuse me when I say that they are necessarily both superficial and misleading, since they have to be graded to the comprehension of an ignorant audience." (Ironical cheering.) "Popular lecturers are in their nature parasitic." (Angry gesture of protest from Mr. Waldron.) "They exploit for fame or cash the work which has been done by the indigent and unknown brethren. One smallest new fact obtained in the laboratory, one brick built into the temple of science, far outweighs any second-hand exposition which passes an idle hour, but can leave no useful result behind it. I put forward this obvious reflection, not out of any desire to disparage Mr. Waldron in particular, but that you may not lose your sense of proportion and mistake the acolyte for the high priest." (At this point Mr. Waldron whispered to the chairman, who half rose and said something severely to his water-carafe.) "But enough of this!" (Loud and prolonged cheers.) "Let me pass to some subject of wider interest. What is the particular point upon which I, as an original investigator, have challenged our lecturer's accuracy? It is upon the permanence of certain types of animal life upon the earth. I do not speak upon this subject as an amateur, nor, I may add, as a popular lecturer, but I speak as one whose scientific conscience compels him to adhere closely to facts, when I say that Mr. Waldron is very wrong in supposing that because he has never himself seen a so-called prehistoric animal, therefore these creatures no longer exist. They are indeed, as he has said, our ancestors, but they are, if I may use the expression, our contemporary ancestors, who can still be found with all their hideous and formidable characteristics if one has but the energy and hardihood to seek their haunts. Creatures which were supposed to be Jurassic, monsters who would hunt down and devour our largest and fiercest mammals, still exist." (Cries of "Bosh!" "Prove it!" "How do *you* know?" "Question!") "How do I know? you ask me. I know because I have visited their secret haunts. I know because I have seen some of them." (Applause, uproar, and a voice, "Liar!") "Am I a liar?" (General hearty and noisy assent.) "Did I hear someone say that I was a liar? Will the person who called me a liar kindly stand up that I may know him?" (A voice, "Here he is, sir!" and an inoffensive little person in spectacles, struggling violently, was held up among a group of students.) "Did you venture to call me a liar?" ("No, sir, no!" shouted the accused, and disappeared like a Jack-in-the-box.) "If any person in this hall dares to doubt my veracity, I shall be glad to have a few words with him after the lecture." ("Liar!") "Who said that?" (Again the inoffensive one, plunging desperately, was elevated high in the air.) "If I come down among you—" (General chorus of "Come, love, come!" which interrupted the proceedings for some moments, while the chairman, standing up and waving his arms, seemed to be conducting the music. The Professor, with his face flushed, his nostrils dilated, and his beard bristling, was now in a proper Berserk mood.) "Every great discoverer has been met with the same incredulity—the sure brand of a generation of fools. When great facts are laid before you, you have not the intuition, the imagination which would help you to understand them. You can only throw mud at the men who have risked their lives to open new fields to science. You persecute the prophets! Galileo, Darwin, and I—" (Prolonged cheering and complete interruption.)

All this is from my hurried notes taken at the time, which give little notion of the absolute chaos to which the assembly had by this time been reduced. So terrific was the uproar that several ladies had already beaten a hurried retreat. Grave and reverend seniors seemed to have caught the prevailing spirit as badly as the students, and I saw white-bearded men rising and shaking their fists at the obdurate Professor. The whole great audience seethed and simmered like a boiling pot. The Professor took a step forward and raised both his hands. There was something so big and arresting and virile in the man that the clatter and shouting died gradually away before his commanding gesture and his masterful eyes. He seemed to have a definite message. They hushed to hear it.

"I will not detain you," he said. "It is not worth it. Truth is truth, and the noise of a number of foolish young men—and, I fear I must add, of their equally foolish seniors—cannot affect the matter. I claim that I have opened a new field of science. You dispute it." (Cheers.) "Then I put you to the test. Will you accredit one or more of your own number to go out as your representatives and test my statement in your name?"

Mr. Summerlee, the veteran Professor of Comparative Anatomy, rose among the audience, a tall, thin, bitter man, with the withered aspect of a theologian. He wished, he said, to ask Professor Challenger whether the results to which he had alluded in his remarks had been obtained during a journey to the headwaters of the Amazon made by him two years before.

Professor Challenger answered that they had.

Mr. Summerlee desired to know how it was that Professor Challenger claimed to have made discoveries in those regions which had been overlooked by Wallace, Bates, and other previous explorers of established scientific repute.

Professor Challenger answered that Mr. Summerlee appeared to be confusing the Amazon with the Thames; that it was in reality a somewhat larger river; that Mr. Summerlee might be interested to know that with the Orinoco, which communicated with it, some fifty thousand miles of country were opened up, and that in so vast a space it was not impossible for one person to find what another had missed.

Mr. Summerlee declared, with an acid smile, that he fully appreciated the difference between the Thames and the Amazon, which lay in the fact that any assertion about the former could be tested, while about the latter it could not. He would be obliged if Professor Challenger would give the latitude and the longitude of the country in which prehistoric animals were to be found.

Professor Challenger replied that he reserved such information for good reasons of his own, but would be prepared to give it with proper precautions to a committee chosen from the audience. Would Mr. Summerlee serve on such a committee and test his story in person?

Mr. Summerlee: "Yes, I will." (Great cheering.)

Professor Challenger: "Then I guarantee that I will place in your hands such material as will enable you to find your way. It is only right, however, since Mr. Summerlee goes to check my statement that I should have one or more with him who may check his. I will not disguise from you that there are difficulties and dangers. Mr.

Summerlee will need a younger colleague. May I ask for volunteers?"

It is thus that the great crisis of a man's life springs out at him. Could I have imagined when I entered that hall that I was about to pledge myself to a wilder adventure than had ever come to me in my dreams? But Gladys—was it not the very opportunity of which she spoke? Gladys would have told me to go. I had sprung to my feet. I was speaking, and yet I had prepared no words. Tarp Henry, my companion, was plucking at my skirts and I heard him whispering, "Sit down, Malone! Don't make a public ass of yourself." At the same time I was aware that a tall, thin man, with dark gingery hair, a few seats in front of me, was also upon his feet. He glared back at me with hard angry eyes, but I refused to give way.

"I will go, Mr. Chairman," I kept repeating over and over again.

"Name! Name!" cried the audience.

"My name is Edward Dunn Malone. I am the reporter of the *Daily Gazette*. I claim to be an absolutely unprejudiced witness."

"What is *your* name, sir?" the chairman asked of my tall rival.

"I am Lord John Roxton. I have already been up the Amazon, I know all the ground, and have special qualifications for this investigation."

"Lord John Roxton's reputation as a sportsman and a traveler is, of course, world-famous," said the chairman, "at the same time it would certainly be as well to have a member of the Press upon such an expedition."

"Then I move," said Professor Challenger, "that both these gentlemen be elected, as representatives of this meeting, to accompany Professor Summerlee upon his journey to investigate and to report upon the truth of my statements."

And so, amid shouting and cheering, our fate was decided, and I found myself borne away in the human current which swirled towards the door, with my mind half stunned by the vast new project which had risen so suddenly before it. As I emerged from the hall I was conscious for a moment of a rush of laughing students down the pavement, and of an arm wielding a heavy umbrella, which rose and fell in the midst of them. Then, amid a mixture of groans and cheers, Professor Challenger's electric brougham slid from the kerb, and I found myself walking under the silvery lights of Regent Street, full of thoughts of Gladys and of wonder as to my future.

Suddenly there was a touch at my elbow. I turned, and found myself looking into the humorous, masterful eyes of the tall, thin man who had volunteered to be my companion on this strange quest.

"Mr. Malone, I understand," said he. "We are to be companions—what? My rooms are just over the road, in the Albany. Perhaps you would have the kindness to spare me half an hour, for there are one or two things that I badly want to say to you."

6

I Was the Flail of the Lord

LORD JOHN ROXTON AND I TURNED DOWN VIGO STREET together and through the dingy portals of the famous aristo-
cratic rookery. At the end of a long drab passage my new
acquaintance pushed open a door and turned on an electric
switch. A number of lamps shining through tinted shades
bathed the whole great room before us in a ruddy radiance.
Standing in the doorway and glancing round me, I had a
general impression of extraordinary comfort and elegance
combined with an atmosphere of masculine virility. Everywhere there were mingled the luxury of the wealthy man
of taste and the careless untidiness of the bachelor. Rich
furs and strange iridescent mats from some Oriental bazaar
were scattered upon the floor. Pictures and prints which
even my unpracticed eyes could recognize as being of
great price and rarity hung thick upon the walls. Sketches
of boxers, of ballet girls, and of racehorses alternated with
a sensuous Fragonard, a martial Girardet, and a dreamy
Turner. But amid these varied ornaments there were scattered the trophies which brought back strongly to my re-

collection the fact that Lord John Roxton was one of the great all-round sportsmen and athletes of his day. A dark-blue oar crossed with a cherry-pink one above his mantelpiece spoke of the old Oxonian and Leander man, while the foils and boxing gloves above and below them were the tools of a man who had won supremacy with each. Like a dado round the room was the jutting line of splendid heavy game-heads, the best of their sort from every quarter of the world, with the rare white rhinoceros of the Lado Enclave drooping its supercilious lip above them all.

In the center of the rich red carpet was a black and gold Louis Quinze table, a lovely antique, now sacrilegiously desecrated with marks of glasses and the scars of cigar-stumps. On it stood a silver tray of smokables and a burnished spirit-stand, from which an adjacent siphon my silent host proceeded to charge two high glasses. Having indicated an armchair to me and placed my refreshment near it, he handed me a long, smooth Havana. Then, seating himself, opposite to me, he looked at me long and fixedly with his strange, twinkling, reckless eyes—eyes of a cold light blue, the color of a glacier lake.

Through the thin haze of my chair smoke I noted the details of a face which was already familiar to me from many photographs—the strongly-curved nose, the hollow, worn cheeks, the dark, ruddy hair, thin at the top, the crisp, virile mustaches, the small, aggressive tuft upon his projecting chin. Something there was of Napoleon III, something of Don Quixote, and yet again something which was the essence of the English country gentleman, the keen, alert, open-air lover of dogs and of horses. His skin was of a rich flower-pot red from sun and wind. His eyebrows were tufted and overhanging, which gave those naturally cold eyes an almost ferocious aspect, an impression which was increased by his strong and furrowed brow. In figure he was spare, but very strongly built—indeed, he had often proved that there were few men in England capable of such sustained exertions. His height was a little over six feet, but he seemed shorter on account of a peculiar rounding of the shoulders. Such was the famous Lord Roxton as he sat opposite to me, biting hard upon his cigar and watching me steadily in a long and embarrassing silence.

"Well," said he, at last, "we've gone and done it, young fellah-my-lad." (This curious phrase he pronounced as if it were all one word—"young fellah-my-lad.") "Yes, we've taken a jump, you an' me. I suppose, now, when you went into that room there was no such notion in your head—what?"

"No thought of it."

"The same here. No thought of it. And here we are, up to our necks in the tureen. Why, I've only been back three weeks from Uganda, and taken a place in Scotland, and signed the lease and all. Pretty goin's on—what? How does it hit you?"

"Well, it is all in the main line of my business. I am a journalist on the *Gazette*."

"Of course—you said so when you took it on. By the way, I've got a small job for you, if you'll help me."

"With pleasure."

"Don't mind takin' a risk, do you?"

"What is the risk?"

"Well, it's Ballinger—he's the risk. You've heard of him?"

"No."

"Why, young fellah, where *have* you lived? Sir John Ballinger is the best gentleman jock in the north country. I could hold him on the flat at my best, but over jumps he's my master. Well, it's an open secret that when he's out of trainin' he drinks hard—strikin' an average, he calls it. He got delirium on Toosday, and has been ragin' like a devil ever since. His room is above this. The doctors say that it is all up with the old dear unless some food is got into him, but as he lies in bed with a revolver on his coverlet, and swears he will put six of the best through anyone that comes near him, there's been a bit of a strike among the serving-men. He's a hard nail, is Jack, and a dead shot, too, but you can't leave a Grand National winner to die like that—what?"

"What do you mean to do, then?" I asked.

"Well, my idea was that you and I could rush him. He may be dozin', and at the worst he can only wing one of us, and the other should have him. If we can get his bolster-cover round his arms and then 'phone up a stomach-pump, we'll give the old dear the supper of his life."

It was rather a desperate business to come suddenly into one day's work. I don't think that I am a particularly brave man. I have an Irish imagination which makes the unknown and the untried more terrible than they are. On the other hand, I was brought up with a horror of cowardice and with a terror of such a stigma. I dare say that I could throw myself over a precipice, like the Hun in the history books, if my courage to do it were questioned, and yet it would surely be pride and fear, rather than courage, which would be my inspiration. Therefore, although every nerve in my body shrank from the whiskey-maddened figure which I pictured in the room above, I still answered, in as careless a voice as I could command, that I was ready to go. Some further remark of Lord Roxton's about the danger only made me irritable.

"Talking won't make it any better," said I. "Come on." I rose from my chair and he from his. Then, with a little confidential chuckle of laughter, he patted me two or three times on the chest, finally pushing me back into my chair.

"All right, sonny my lad—you'll do," said he.

I looked up in surprise.

"I saw after Jack Ballinger myself this mornin'. He blew a hole in the skirt of my kimono, bless his shaky old hand, but we got a jacket on him, and he's to be all right in a week. I say, young fellah, I hope you don't mind—what? You see, between you an' me close-tiled, I look on this South American business as a mighty serious thing, and if I have a pal with me I want a man I can bank on. So I sized you down, and I'm bound to say that you came well out of it. You see, it's all up to you and me, for this old Summerlee man will want dry-nursin' from the first. By the way, are you by any chance the Malone who is expected to get his Rugby cap for Ireland?"

"A reserve, perhaps."

"I thought I remembered your face. Why, I was there when you got that try against Richmond—as fine a swervin' run as I saw the whole season. I never miss a Rugby match if I can help it, for it is the manliest game we have left. Well, I didn't ask you in here just to talk sport. We've got to fix our business. Here are the sailin's, on the first page of *The Times*. There's a Booth boat for Para next Wednesday week, and if the Professor and you can work it, I think we should take it—what? Very good, I'll fix it with him. What about your outfit?"

"My paper will see to that."

"Can you shoot?"

"About average Territorial standard."

"Good Lord! as bad as that? It's the last thing you young fellahs think of learnin'. You're all bees without stings, so far as lookin' after the hive goes. You'll look silly, some o' these days, when someone comes along an' sneaks the honey. But you'll need to hold your gun straight in South America, for, unless our friend the Professor is a madman or a liar, we may see some queer things before we get back. What gun have you?"

He crossed to an oaken cupboard, and as he threw it open I caught a glimpse of glistening rows of parallel barrels, like the pipes of an organ.

"I'll see what I can spare you out of my own battery," said he.

One by one he took out a succession of beautiful rifles, opening and shutting them with a snap and a clang, and then patting them as he put them back into the rack as tenderly as a mother would fondle her children.

"This is a Bland's .577 axite express," said he. "I got that big fellow with it." He glanced up at the white rhinoceros. "Ten more yards, and he'd have added me to *his* collection.

'On that conical bullet his one chance hangs,

''Tis the weak one's advantage fair.'

"Hope you know your Gordon, for he's the poet of the horse and the gun and the man that handles both. Now, here's a useful tool—.470, telescopic sight, double ejector, point-blank up to three-fifty. That's the rifle I used against the Peruvian slave drivers three years ago. I was the flail of the Lord up in those parts, I may tell you, though you won't find it in any Blue-book. There are times, young fellah, when every one of us must make a stand for human right and justice, or you never feel clean again. That's why I made a little war on my own. Declared it myself, waged it myself, ended it myself. Each of those nicks is for a slave murderer—a good row of them—what? That big one is for Pedro Lopez, the king of them all, that I killed in a backwater of the Putomayo River. Now, here's something that would do for you." He took out a beautiful brown-

and-silver rifle. "Well rubbered at the stock, sharply sighted, five cartridges to the clip. You can trust your life to that." He handed it to me and closed the door of his oak cabinet. "By the way," he continued, coming back to his chair, "what do you know of this Professor Challenger?"

"I never saw him till to-day."

"Well, neither did I. It's funny we should both sail under sealed orders from a man we don't know. He seemed an uppish old bird. His brothers of science don't seem too fond of him, either. How came you to take an interest in the affair?"

I told him shortly my experiences of the morning, and he listened intently. Then he drew out a map of South America and laid it on the table.

"I believe every single word he said to you was the truth," said he, earnestly, "and, mind you, I have something to go on when I speak like that. South America is a place I love, and I think, if you take it right through the Darien to Fuego, it's the grandest, richest, most wonderful bit of earth upon this planet. People don't know it yet, and don't realize what it may become. I've been up an' down it from end to end, and had two dry seasons in those very parts, as I told you when I spoke of the war I made on the slave-dealers. Well, when I was up there I heard some yarns of the kind—traditions of Indians and the like, but with somethin' behind them, no doubt. The more you knew of that country, young fellah, the more you would understand that anythin' was possible—*anythin.*' There are just some narrow waterlanes along which folk travel, and outside that it is all darkness. Now, down here in the Matto Grosso"—he swept his cigar over a part of the map—"or up in this corner where three countries meet, nothin' would surprise me. As that chap said tonight, there are fifty thousand miles of waterway runnin' through a forest that is very near the size of Europe. You and I could be as far away from each other as Scotland is from Constantinople, and yet each of us be in the same great Brazilian forest. Man has just made a track here and a scrape there in the maze. Why, the river rises and falls the best part of forty feet, and half the country is a morass that you can't pass over. Why shouldn't somethin' new and wonderful lie in such a country? And why shouldn't we be the men to find it out? Besides," he added, his queer, gaunt face shining with delight, "there's a sportin' risk in every mile of it. I'm like an old golf ball—I've had all the white paint knocked off me long ago. Life can whack me about now and it can't leave a mark. But a sportin' risk, young fellah, that's the salt of existence. Then it's worth livin' again. We're all gettin' a deal too soft and dull and comfy. Give me the great waste lands and the wide spaces, with a gun in my fist and somethin' to look for that's worth findin'. I've tried war and steeplechasin' and airplanes, but this huntin' of beasts that look like a lobster-supper dream is a brand-new sensation." He chuckled with glee at the prospect.

Perhaps I have dwelt too long upon this new acquaintance, but he is to be my comrade for many a day, and so I have tried to set him down as I first saw him, with his quaint personality and his queer little tricks of speech and of thought. It was only the need of getting in the account of my meeting which drew me at last from his company. I left him seated amid his pink radiance, oiling the lock of his favorite rifle, while he still chuckled to himself at the thought of the adventures which awaited us. It was very clear to me that if dangers lay before us I could not in all England have found a cooler head or a braver spirit with which to share them.

That night, wearied as I was after the wonderful happenings of the day, I sat with McArdle, the news editor, explaining to him the whole situation, which he thought important enough to bring next morning before the notice of Sir George Beaumont, the chief. It was agreed that I should write home full accounts of my adventures in the shape of successive letters to McArdle, and that these should either be edited for the *Gazette* as they arrived, or held back to be published later, according to the wishes of Professor Challenger, since we could not yet know what conditions he might attach to those directions which should guide us to the unknown land. In response to a telephone inquiry, we received nothing more definite than a fulmination against the Press, ending up with the remark that if we would notify our boat he would hand us any directions which he might think it proper to give us at the moment of starting. A second question from us failed to elicit any answer at all, save a plaintive bleat from his wife to the effect that her husband was in a very violent temper already, and that she hoped we would do nothing to make it worse. A third attempt, later in the day, provoked a terrific crash, and a subsequent message from the Central Exchange that Professor Challenger's receiver had been shattered. After that we abandoned all attempt at communication.

And now, my patient readers, I can address you directly no longer. From now onwards (if, indeed, any continuation of this narrative should ever reach you) it can only be through the paper which I represent. In the hands of the editor I leave this account of the events which have led up to one of the most remarkable expeditions of all time, so that if I never return to England there shall be some record as to how the affair came about. I am writing these last lines in the saloon of the Booth liner *Francisca*, and they will go back by the pilot to the keeping of Mr. McArdle.

Let me draw one last picture before I close the notebook—a picture which is the last memory of the old country which I bear away with me. It is a wet, foggy morning in the late spring; a thin, cold rain is falling. Three shining mackintoshed figures are walking down the quay, making for the gangplank of the great liner from which the blue-peter is flying. In front of them a porter pushes a trolley piled high with trunks, wraps, and gun cases. Professor Summerlee, a long, melancholy figure, walks with dragging steps and drooping head, as one who is already profoundly sorry for himself. Lord John Roxton steps briskly, and his thin, eager face beams forth between his hunting cap and his muffler. As for myself, I am glad to have got the bustling days of preparation and the pangs of leave-taking behind me, and I have no doubt that I show it in my bearing. Suddenly, just as we reach the vessel, there is a shout behind us. It is Professor Challenger, who had promised to see us off. He runs after us, a puffing, red-faced, irascible figure.

"No, thank you," says he; "I should much prefer not to go aboard. I have only a few words to say to you, and they can very well be said where we are. I beg you not to imagine that I am in any way indebted to you for making this journey. I would have you to understand that it is a matter of perfect indifference to me, and I refuse to entertain the most remote sense of personal obligation. Truth is truth, and nothing which you can report can affect it in any way, though it may excite the emotions and allay the curiosity of a number of very ineffectual people. My directions for your instruction and guidance are in this sealed envelope. You will open it when you reach a town upon the Amazon which is called Manaos, but not until the date and hour which is marked upon the outside. Have I made myself clear? I leave the strict observance of my conditions en-

tirely to your honor. No, Mr. Malone, I will place no re-
striction upon your correspondence, since the ventilation
of the facts is the object of your journey; but I demand
that you shall give no particulars as to your exact destination, and that nothing be actually published until your return. Good-bye, sir. You have done something to mitigate
my feelings for the loathsome profession to which you unhappily belong. Good-bye, Lord John. Science is, as I understand, a sealed book to you; but you may congratulate
yourself upon the hunting-field which awaits you. You
will, no doubt, have the opportunity of describing in the
Field how you brought down the rocketing dimorphodon.
And good-bye to you also, Professor Summerlee. If you
are still capable of self-improvement, of which I am
frankly unconvinced, you will surely return to London a
wiser man."

So he turned upon his heel, and a minute later from the
deck I could see his short, squat figure bobbing about in
the distance as he made his way back to his train. Well, we
are well down Channel now. There's the last bell for letters, and it's good-bye to the pilot. We'll be "down, hull-
down, on the old trail" from now on. God bless all we
leave behind us, and send us safely back.

7

Tomorrow We Disappear into the Unknown

I WILL NOT BORE THOSE WHOM THIS NARRATIVE MAY REACH BY
an account of our luxurious voyage upon the Booth liner,
nor will I tell of our week's stay at Para (save that I should
wish to acknowledge the great kindness of the Pereira da
Pinta Company in helping us to get together our equipment). I will also allude very briefly to our river journey
up a wide, slow-moving, clay-tinted stream, in a streamer
which was little smaller than that which had carried us
across the Atlantic. Eventually we found ourselves through
the narrows of Obidos and reached the town of Manaos.
Here we were rescued from the limited attractions of the
local inn by Mr. Shortman, the representative of the British
and Brazilian Trading Company. In his hospitable fazenda
we spent our time until the day when we were empowered
to open the letter of instructions given to us by Professor
Challenger. Before I reach the surprising events of that
date I would desire to give a clearer sketch of my comrades in this enterprise, and of the associates whom we
had already gathered together in South America. I speak

freely, and I leave the use of my material to your own discretion, Mr. McArdle, since it is through your hands that this report must pass before it reaches the world.

The scientific attainments of Professor Summerlee are too well known for me to trouble to recapitulate them. He is better equipped for a rough expedition of this sort than one would imagine at first sight. His tall, gaunt, stringy figure is insensible to fatigue, and his dry, half-sarcastic, and often wholly unsympathetic manner is uninfluenced by any change in his surroundings. Though in his sixty-sixth year, I have never heard him express any dissatisfaction at the occasional hardships which we have had to encounter. I had regarded his presence as a encumbrance to the expedition, but, as a matter of fact, I am now well convinced that his power of endurance is as great as my own. In temper he is naturally acid and sceptical. From the beginning he has never concealed his belief that Professor Challenger is an absolute fraud, that we are all embarked on an absurd wild-goose chase and that we are likely to reap nothing but disappointment and danger in South America, and corresponding ridicule in England. Such are the views which, with much passionate distortion of his thin features and wagging of his thin, goat-like beard, he poured into our ears all the way from Southampton to Manaos. Since landing from the boat he has obtained some consolation from the beauty and variety of the insect and bird life around him, for he is absolutely wholehearted in his devotion to science. He spends his days flitting through the woods with his shotgun and his butterfly-net, and his evenings in mounting the many specimens he has acquired. Among his minor peculiarities are that he is careless as to his attire, unclean in his person, exceedingly absentminded in his habits, and addicted to smoking a short briar pipe, which is seldom out of his mouth. He has been upon several scientific expeditions in his youth (he was with Robertson in Papua), and the life of the camp and the canoe is nothing fresh to him.

Lord John Roxton has some points in common with Professor Summerlee and others in which they are the very antithesis to each other. He is twenty years younger, but has something of the same spare, scraggy physique. As to his appearance, I have, as I recollect, described it in that portion of my narrative which I have left behind me in London. He is exceedingly neat and prim in his ways, dresses always with great care in white drill suits and high brown mosquito-boots, and shaves at least once a day. Like most men of action, he is laconic in speech, and sinks readily into his own thoughts, but he is always quick to answer a question or join in a conversation, talking in a queer, half-humorous fashion. His knowledge of the world, and very especially of South America, is surprising, and he has a wholehearted belief in the possibilities of our journey which is not to be dashed by the sneers of Professor Summerlee. He has a gentle voice and a quiet manner, but behind his twinkling blue eyes there lurks a capacity for furious wrath and implacable resolution, the more dangerous because they are held in leash. He spoke little of his own exploits in Brazil and Peru, but it was a revelation to me to find the excitement which was caused by his presence among the riverine natives, who looked upon him as their champion and protector. The exploits of the Red Chief, as they called him, had become legends among them, but the real facts, as far as I could learn them, were amazing enough.

These were that Lord John had found himself some years before in that no-man's-land which is formed by the half-defined frontiers between Peru, Brazil, and Colombia. In this great district the wild rubber tree flourishes, and has become, as in the Congo, a curse to the natives which can only be compared to their forced labor under the Spaniards upon the old silver mines of Darien. A handful of villainous half-breeds dominated the country, armed such Indians as would support them, and turned the rest into slaves, terrorizing them with the most inhuman tortures in order to force them to gather the india-rubber, which was then floated down the river to Para. Lord John Roxton expostulated on behalf of the wretched victims, and received nothing but threats and insults for his pains. He then formally declared war against Pedro Lopez, the leader of the slave drivers, enrolled a band of runaway slaves in his service, armed them, and conducted a campaign, which ended by his killing with his own hands the notorious half-breed and breaking down the system which he represented.

No wonder that the ginger-headed man with the silky voice and the free and easy manners was now looked upon with deep interest upon the banks of the great South American river, though the feelings he inspired were naturally mixed, since the gratitude of the natives was equalled by the resentment of those who desired to exploit them. One useful result of his former experiences was that he could talk fluently in the Lingoa Geral, which is the peculiar talk, one-third Portuguese and two-thirds Indian, which is current all over Brazil.

I have said before the Lord John Roxton was a South Americomaniac. He could not speak of that great country without ardor, and this ardor was infectious, for, ignorant as I was, he fixed my attention and stimulated my curiosity. How I wish I could reproduce the glamour of his discourses, the peculiar mixture of accurate knowledge and of racy imagination which gave them their fascination, until even the Professor's cynical and sceptical smile would gradually vanish from his thin face as he listened. He would tell the history of the mighty river so rapidly explored (for some of the first conquerors of Peru actually crossed the entire continent upon its waters), and yet so unknown in regard to all that lay behind its ever-changing banks.

"What is there?" he would cry, pointing to the north. "Wood and marsh and unpenetrated jungle. Who knows what it may shelter? And there to the south? A wilderness of swampy forests, where no white man has ever been. The unknown is up against us on every side. Outside the narrow lines of the rivers what does anyone know? Who will say what is possible in such a country? Why should old man Challenger not be right?" At which direct defiance the stubborn sneer would reappear upon Professor Summerlee's face, and he would sit, shaking his sardonic head in unsympathetic silence, behind the cloud of his briar-root pipe.

So much, for the moment, for my two white companions, whose characters and limitations will be further exposed, as surely as my own, as this narrative proceeds. But already we have enrolled certain retainers who may play no small part in what is to come. The first is a gigantic negro named Zambo, who is a Hercules. Him we enlisted at Para, on the recommendation of the steamship company, on whose vessels he had learned to speak a halting English.

It was at Para also that we engaged Gomez and Manuel, two half-breeds from up the river, just come down with a cargo of redwood. They were swarthy fellows, bearded and fierce, as active and wiry as panthers. Both of them had spent their lives in those upper waters of the Amazon which we were about to explore, and it was this recommendation which had caused Lord John to engage them. One of them, Gomez, had the further advantage that he could speak excellent English. These men were willing to act as our personal servants, to cook, to row, or to make themselves useful in any way at a payment of fifteen dollars a month. Besides these, we had engaged three Mojo Indians from Bolivia, who are the most skillful at fishing and boat work of all the river tribes. The chief of these we called Mojo, after his tribe, and the others are known as José and Fernando. Three white men, then, two half-breeds, one negro, and three Indians made up the personnel of the little expedition which lay waiting for its instructions at Manaos, before starting upon its singular quest.

At last after a weary week, the day had come and the hour. I ask you to picture the shaded sitting-room of the Fazenda Santa Ignacia, two miles inland from the town of Manaos. Outside lay the yellow, brassy glare of the sunshine, with the shadows of the palm trees as black and definite as the trees themselves. The air was calm, full of the eternal hum of insects, a tropical chorus of many octaves, from the deep drone of the bee to the high, keen pipe of the mosquito. Beyond the veranda was a small cleared garden, bounded with cactus hedges and adorned with clumps of flowering shrubs, round which the great blue butterflies and the tiny hummingbirds fluttered and darted in crescents of sparkling light. Within we were seated round the cane table, on which lay a sealed envelope. Inscribed upon it, in the jagged handwriting of Professor Challenger, were the words:

"Instructions to Lord John Roxton and party. To be opened at Manaos upon July 15th, at 12 o'clock precisely."

Lord John had placed his watch upon the table beside him.

"We have seven more minutes," said he. "The old dear is very precise."

Professor Summerlee gave an acid smile as he picked up the envelope in his gaunt hand.

"What can it possibly matter whether we open it now or in seven minutes?" said he. "It is all part and parcel of the same system of quackery and nonsense for which I regret to say that the writer is notorious."

"Oh, come, we must play the game accordin' to rules," said Lord John. "It's old man Challenger's show and we are here by his good will, so it would be rotten bad form if we didn't follow his instructions to the letter."

"A pretty business it is!" cried the Professor, bitterly. "It struck me as preposterous in London, but I'm bound to say that it seems even more so upon closer acquaintance. I don't know what is inside this envelope, but, unless it is something pretty definite, I shall be much tempted to take the next down-river boat and catch the *Bolivia* at Para. After all, I have some more responsible work in the world than to run about disproving the assertions of a lunatic. Now, Roxton, surely it is time."

"Time it is," said Lord John. "You can blow the whistle." He took up the envelope and cut it with his penknife. From it he drew a folded sheet of paper. This he carefully opened out and flattened on the table. It was a blank sheet. He turned it over. Again it was blank. We looked at each other in a bewildered silence, which was broken by a discordant burst of derisive laughter from Professor Summerlee.

"It is an open admission," he cried. "What more do you want? The fellow is a self-confessed humbug. We have only to return home and report him as the brazen impostor that he is."

"Invisible ink!" I suggested.

"I don't think!" said Lord Roxton, holding the paper to the light. "No, young fellah-my-lad, there is no use deceiving yourself. I'll go bail for it that nothing has ever been written upon this paper."

"May I come in?" boomed a voice from the veranda.

The shadow of a squat figure had stolen across the patch of sunlight. That voice! That monstrous breadth of shoulder! We sprang to our feet with a gasp of astonishment as Challenger, in a round, boyish straw-hat with a colored ribbon—Challenger, with his hands in his jacket-pockets and his canvas shoes daintily pointing as he walked—appeared in the open space before us. He threw back his head, and there he stood in the golden glow with all his old Assyrian luxuriance of beard, all his native insolence of drooping eyelids and intolerant eyes.

"I fear," said he, taking out his watch, "that I am a few minutes too late. When I gave you this envelope I must confess that I had never intended that you should open it, for it had been my fixed intention to be with you before the hour. The unfortunate delay can be apportioned between a blundering pilot and an intrusive sandbank. I fear that it has given my colleague, Professor Summerlee, occasion to blaspheme."

"I am bound to say, sir," said Lord John, with some sternness of voice, "that your turning up is a considerable relief to us, for our mission seemed to have come to a premature end. Even now I can't for the life of me understand why you should have worked it in so extraordinary a manner."

Instead of answering, Professor Challenger entered, shook hands with myself and Lord John, bowed with ponderous insolence, to Professor Summerlee, and sank back into a basket-chair, which creaked and swayed beneath his weight.

"Is all ready for your journey?" he asked.

"We can start tomorrow."

"Then so you shall. You need no chart of directions now, since you will have the inestimable advantage of my own guidance. From the first I had determined that I would myself preside over your investigation. The most elaborate charts would, as you will readily admit, be a poor substitute for my own intelligence and advice. As to the small ruse which I played upon you in the matter of the envelope, it is clear that, had I told you all my intentions, I should have been forced to resist unwelcome pressure to travel out with you."

"Not from me, sir!" exclaimed Professor Summerlee, heartily. "So long as there was another ship upon the Atlantic."

Challenger waved him away with his great hairy hand.

"Your common sense will, I am sure, sustain my objection and realize that it was better that I should direct my own movements and appear only at the exact moment when my presence was needed. That moment has now arrived. You are in safe hands. You will not now fail to reach your destination. From henceforth I take command of this expedition, and I must ask you to complete your preparations tonight, so that we may be able to make an early start in the morning. My time is of value, and the same thing may be said, no doubt, in a lesser degree of your own. I propose, therefore, that we push on as rapidly as possible, until I have demonstrated what you have come to see."

Lord John Roxton had chartered a large steam-launch, the *Esmeralda*, which was to carry us up the river. So far as climate goes, it was immaterial what time we chose for our expedition, as the temperature ranges from seventy-five to ninety degrees both summer and winter, with no appreciable difference in heat. In moisture, however, it is otherwise; from December to May is the period of the rains, and during this time the river slowly rises until it attains a height of nearly forty feet above its low-water mark. It floods the banks, extends in great lagoons over a monstrous waste of country, and forms a huge district, called locally the Gapo, which is for the most part too marshy for foot-travel and too shallow for boating. About June the waters begin to fall, and are at their lowest at October or November. Thus our expedition was at the time of the dry season, when the great river and its tributaries were more or less in a normal condition.

The current of the river is a slight one, the drop being not greater than eight inches in a mile. No stream could be more convenient for navigation, since the prevailing wind is south-east, and sailing boats may make a continuous progress to the Peruvian frontier, dropping down again with the current. In our own case the excellent engines of the *Esmeralda* could disregard the sluggish flow of the stream, and we made as rapid progress as if we were navigating a stagnant lake. For three days we steamed northwestwards up a stream which even here, a thousand miles from its mouth, was still so enormous that from its centre the two banks were mere shadows upon the distant skyline. On the fourth day after leaving Manaos we turned into a tributary which at its mouth was little smaller than the main stream. It narrowed rapidly, however, and after two more days' steaming we reached an Indian village, where the Professor insisted that we should land, and that the *Esmeralda* should be sent back to Manaos. We should soon come upon rapids, he explained, which would make its further use impossible. He added privately that we were now approaching the door of the unknown country, and that the fewer whom we took into our confidence the better it would be. To this end also he made each of us give our word of honor that we would publish or say nothing which would give any exact clue as to the whereabouts of our travels, while the servants were all solemnly sworn to the same effect. It is for this reason that I am compelled to be vague in my narrative, and I would warn my readers that in any map or diagram which I may give the relation of places to each other may be correct, but the points of the compass are carefully confused, so that in no way can it be taken as an actual guide to the country. Professor Challenger's reasons for secrecy may be valid or not, but we had no choice but to adopt them, for he was prepared to abandon the whole expedition rather than modify the conditions upon which he would guide us.

It was August 2nd when we snapped our last link with the outer world by bidding farewell to the *Esmeralda*. Since then four days have passed, during which we have engaged two large canoes from the Indians, made of so light a material (skins over a bamboo framework) that we should be able to carry them round any obstacle. These we have loaded with all our effects, and have engaged two additional Indians to help us in the navigation. I understand that they are the very two—Ataca and Ipetu by name—who accompanied Professor Challenger upon his previous journey. They appeared to be terrified at the prospect of repeating it, but the chief has patriarchal powers in these countries, and if the bargain is good in his eyes the clansman has little choice in the matter.

So tomorrow we disappear into the unknown. This account I am transmitting down the river by canoe, and it may be our last word to those who are interested in our fate. I have, according to our arrangement, addressed it to you, my dear Mr. McArdle, and I leave it to your discretion to delete, alter, or do what you like with it. From the assurance of Professor Challenger's manner—and in spite of the continued scepticism of Professor Summerlee—I have no doubt that our leader will make good his statement, and that we are really on the eve of some most remarkable experiences.

8

The Outlying Pickets
of the New World

OUR FRIENDS AT HOME MAY WELL REJOICE WITH US, FOR WE are at our goal, and up to a point, at least, we have shown that the statement of Professor Challenger can be verified. We have not, it is true, ascended the plateau, but it lies before us, and even Professor Summerlee is in a more chastened mood. Not that he will for an instant admit that his rival could be right, but he is less persistent in his incessant objections, and has sunk for the most part into an observant silence. I must hark back, however, and continue my narrative from where I dropped it. We are sending home one of our local Indians who is injured, and I am committing this letter to his charge, with considerable doubts in my mind as to whether it will ever come to hand.

When I wrote last we were about to leave the Indian village where we had been deposited by the *Esmeralda*. I have to begin my report by bad news, for the first serious personal trouble (I pass over the incessant bickerings between the Professors) occurred this evening, and might have had a tragic ending. I have spoken of our English-speaking half-breed, Gomez—a fine worker and a willing fellow, but afflicted, I fancy, with the vice of curiosity, which is common enough among such men. On the last evening he seems to have hid himself near the hut in which we were discussing our plans, and, being observed by our huge negro Zambo, who is faithful and has the hatred which all his race bear to the half-breeds, he was dragged out and carried into our presence. Gomez whipped out his knife, however, and but for the huge strength of his captor, which enabled him to disarm him with one hand, he would certainly have stabbed him. The matter has ended in reprimands, the opponents have been compelled to shake hands, and there is every hope that all will be well. As to the feuds of the two learned men, they are continuous and bitter. It must be admitted that Challenger is provocative in the last degree, but Summerlee has an acid tongue, which makes matters worse. Last night Challenger said that he never cared to walk on the Thames Embankment and look up the river, as it was always sad to see one's own eventual goal. He is convinced, of course, that he is destined for Westminster Abbey. Summerlee retorted, however, with a sour smile, by saying that he understood that Millbank Prison had been pulled down. Challenger's conceit is too colossal to allow him to be really annoyed. He only smiled in his beard and repeated "Really! Really!" in the pitying tone one would use to a child. Indeed, they are children both—the one wizened and cantankerous, the other formidable and overbearing, yet each with a brain which has put him in the front rank of his scientific age. Brain, character, soul—only as one sees more of life does one understand how distinct is each.

The very next day we did actually make our start upon

this remarkable expedition. We found that all our possessions fitted very easily into the two canoes, and we divided our personnel, six in each, taking the obvious precaution in the interests of peace of putting one Professor into each canoe. Personally, I was with Challenger, who was in a beatific humor, moving about as one in a silent ecstasy and beaming benevolence from every feature. I have had some experience of him in other moods, however, and shall be the less surprised when the thunderstorms suddenly come up amidst the sunshine. If it is impossible to be at your ease, it is equally impossible to be dull in his company, for one is always in a state of half-tremulous doubt as to what sudden turn his formidable temper may take.

For two days we made our way up a good-sized river, some hundreds of yards broad, and dark in color, but transparent, so that one could usually see the bottom. The affluents of the Amazon are, half of them, of this nature, while the other half are whitish and opaque, the difference depending upon the class of country through which they have flowed. The dark indicate vegetable decay, while the others point to clayey soil. Twice we came across rapids, and in each case made a portage of half a mile or so to avoid them. The woods on either side were primeval, which are more easily penetrated than woods of the second growth, and we had no great difficulty in carrying our canoes through them. How shall I ever forget the solemn mystery of it? The height of the trees and the thickness of the boles exceeding anything which I in my town-bred life could have imagined, shooting upwards in magnificent columns until, at an enormous distance above our heads, we could dimly discern the spot where they threw out their side-branches into Gothic upward curves which coalesced to form one great matted roof of verdure, through which only an occasional golden ray of sunshine shot downwards to trace a thin dazzling line of light amidst the majestic obscurity. As we walked noiselessly amid the thick, soft carpet of decaying vegetation the hush fell upon our souls which comes upon us in the twilight of the Abbey, and even Professor Challenger's full-chested notes sank into a whisper. Alone, I should have been ignorant of the names of these giant growths, but our men of science pointed out the cedars, the great silk cotton trees, and the redwood trees, with all that profusion of various plants which has made this continent the chief supplier to the human race of those gifts of nature which depend upon the vegetable world, while it is the most backward in those products which come from animal life. Vivid orchids and wonderful colored lichens smouldered upon the swarthy tree-trunks, and where a wandering shaft of light fell full upon the golden allamanda, the scarlet star-clusters of the tacsonia, or the rich deep blue of ipomaea the effect was as a dream of fairyland. In these great wastes of forest, life, which abhors darkness, struggles ever upwards to the light. Every plant, even the smaller ones, curls and writhes to the green surface, twining itself round its stronger and taller brethren in the effort. Climbing plants are monstrous and luxuriant, but others which have never been known to climb elsewhere learn the art as an escape from that somber shadow, so that the common nettle, the jasmine, and even the jacitara palm tree can be seen circling the stems of the cedars and striving to reach their crowns. Of animal life there was no movement amid the majestic vaulted aisles which stretched from us as we walked, but a constant movement far above our heads told of that multitudinous world of snake and monkey, bird and sloth, which lived in the sunshine, and looked down in wonder at our tiny, dark stumbling figures in the obscure depths immeasurably below them. At dawn and at sunset the howler monkeys screamed together and the parakeets broke into shrill chatter, but during the hot hours of the day, only the full drone of insects like the beat of a distant surf, filled the ear, while nothing moved amid the solemn vistas of stupendous trunks, fading away into the darkness which held us in. Once some bandy-legged, lurching creature, an anteater or a bear, scuttled clumsily amid the shadows. It was the only sign of earth life which I saw in this great Amazonian forest.

And yet there were indications that even human life itself was not far from us in those mysterious recesses. On the third day out we were aware of a singular deep throbbing in the air, rhythmic and solemn, coming and going fitfully throughout the morning. The two boats were paddling within a few yards of each other when we first heard it, and our Indians remained motionless, as if they had been turned to bronze, listening intently with expressions of terror upon their faces.

"What is it, then?" I asked.

"Drums," said Lord John, carelessly; "war drums. I have heard them before."

"Yes, sir, war drums," said Gomez, the half-breed. "Wild Indians, bravos, not mansos; they watch us every mile of the way; kill us if they can."

"How can they watch us?" I asked, gazing into the dark, motionless void.

The half-breed shrugged his broad shoulders.

"The Indians know. They have their own way. They watch us. They talk the drum talk to each other. Kill us if they can."

By the afternoon of that day—my pocket diary shows me that it was Tuesday, August 18th— at least six or seven drums were throbbing from various points. Sometimes they beat quickly, sometimes slowly, sometimes in obvious question and answer, one far to the east breaking out in a high staccato rattle, and being followed after a pause by a deep roll from the north. There was something indescribably nerve-shaking and menacing in that constant mutter, which seemed to shape itself into the very syllables of the half-breed, endlessly repeated, "We will kill you if we can. We will kill you if we can." No one ever moved in the silent woods. All the peace and soothing of quiet Nature lay in that dark curtain of vegetation, but away from behind there came ever the one message from our fellow-man. "We will kill you if we can," said the men in the east. "We will kill you if we can," said the men in the north.

All day the drums rumbled and whispered, while their menace reflected itself in the faces of our colored companions. Even the hardy, swaggering half-breed seemed cowed. I learned, however, that day once for all that both Summerlee and Challenger possessed that highest type of bravery, the bravery of the scientific mind. Theirs was the spirit which upheld Darwin among the gauchos of the Argentine or Wallace among the headhunters of Malaya. It is decreed by a merciful Nature that the human brain cannot think of two things simultaneously, so that if it be steeped in curiosity as to science it has no room for merely personal considerations. All day amid that incessant and mysterious menace our two Professors watched every bird upon the wing, and every shrub upon the bank, with many a sharp wordy contention, when the snarl of Summerlee came quick upon the deep growl of Challenger, but with no more sense of danger and no more reference to drum-beating Indians than if they were seated together in the smoking-room of the Royal Society's Club in St. James's Street. Once only did they condescend to discuss them.

"Miranha or Amajuaca cannibals," said Challenger, jerking his thumb toward the reverberating wood.

"No doubt, sir," Summerlee answered. "Like all such tribes, I shall expect to find them of polysynthetic speech and of Mongolian type."

"Polysynthetic certainly," said Challenger, indulgently. "I am not aware that any other type of language exists in this continent, and I have notes of more than a hundred. The Mongolian theory I regard with deep suspicion."

"I should have thought that even a limited knowledge of comparative anatomy would have helped to verify it," said Summerlee, bitterly.

Challenger thrust out his aggressive chin until he was all beard and hat-rim. "No doubt, sir, a limited knowledge would have that effect. When one's knowledge is exhaustive, one comes to other conclusions." They glared at each other in mutual defiance, while all round rose the distant whisper, "We will kill you—we will kill you if we can."

That night we moored our canoes with heavy stones for anchors in the center of the stream, and made every preparation for a possible attack. Nothing came, however, and with the dawn we pushed upon our way, the drum-beating dying out behind us. About three o'clock in the afternoon we came to a very steep rapid, more than a mile long—the very one in which Professor Challenger has suffered disaster upon his first journey. I confess that the sight of it consoled me, for it was really the first direct corroboration, slight as it was, of the truth of his story. The Indians carried first our canoes and then our stores through the brushwood, which is very thick at this point, while we four whites, our rifles on our shoulders, walked between them and any danger coming from the woods. Before evening we had successfully passed the rapids, and made our way some ten miles above them, where we anchored for the night. At this point I reckoned that we had come not less than a hundred miles up the tributary from the main stream.

It was in the early forenoon of the next day that we made the great departure. Since dawn Professor Challenger had been acutely uneasy, continually scanning each bank of the river. Suddenly he gave an exclamation of satisfaction and pointed to a single tree, which projected at a peculiar angle over the side of the stream.

"What do you make of that?" he asked.

"It is surely an Assai palm," said Summerlee.

"Exactly. It was an Assai palm which I took for my landmark. The secret opening is half a mile onwards upon the other side of the river. There is no break in the trees. That is the wonder and the mystery of it. There where you see light-green rushes instead of dark-green undergrowth, there between the great cotton woods, that is my private gate into the unknown. Push through, and you will understand."

It was indeed a wonderful place. Having reached the spot marked by a line of light-green rushes, we poled our two canoes through them for some hundreds of yards, and eventually emerged into a placid and shallow stream, running clear and transparent over a sandy bottom. It may have been twenty yards across, and was banked in on each side by most luxuriant vegetation. No one who had not observed that for a short distance reeds had taken the place of shrubs could possibly have guessed the existence of such a stream or dreamed of the fairyland beyond.

For a fairyland it was—the most wonderful that the imagination of man could conceive. The thick vegetation met overhead, interlacing into a natural pergola, and through this tunnel of verdure in a golden twilight flowed the green, pellucid river, beautiful in itself, but marvelous from the strange tints thrown by the vivid light from above filtered and tempered in its fall. Clear as crystal, motionless as a sheet of glass, green as the edge of an iceberg, it stretched in front of us under its leafy archway, every stroke of our paddles sending a thousand ripples across its shining surface. It was a fitting avenue to a land of wonders. All sign of the Indians had passed away, but animal life was more frequent, and the tameness of the creatures showed that they knew nothing of the hunter. Fuzzy little black-velvet monkeys, with snow-white teeth and gleaming mocking eyes, chattered at us as we passed. With a dull, heavy splash an occasional cayman plunged in from the bank. Once a dark, clumsy tapir stared at us from a gap in the bushes, and then lumbered away through the forest; once, too, the yellow, sinuous form of a great puma whisked amid the brushwood, and its green, baleful eyes glared hatred at us over its tawny shoulder. Bird life was abundant, especially the wading birds, stork, heron, and ibis gathering in little groups, blue, scarlet, and white, upon every log which jutted from the bank, while beneath us the crystal water was alive with fish of every shape and color.

For three days we made our way up this tunnel of hazy green sunshine. On the longer stretches one could hardly tell as one looked ahead where the distant green water ended and the distant green archway began. The deep peace of this strange waterway was unbroken by any sign of man.

"No Indian here. Too much afraid. Curupuri," said Gomez.

"Curupuri is the spirit of the woods," Lord John explained. "It's the name for any kind of devil. The poor beggars think that there is something fearsome in this direction, and therefore they avoid it."

On the third day it became evident that our journey in the canoes could not last much longer, for the stream was rapidly growing more shallow. Twice in as many hours we stuck upon the bottom. Finally we pulled the boats up among the brushwood and spent the night on the bank of the river. In the morning Lord John and I made our way for a couple of miles through the forest, keeping parallel with the stream; but as it grew ever shallower we returned and reported, what Professor Challenger had already suspected, that we had reached the highest point to which the canoes could be brought. We drew them up, therefore, and concealed them among the bushes, blazing a tree with our axes, so that we should find them again. Then we distributed the various burdens among us—guns, ammunition, food, a tent, blankets, and the rest—and, shouldering our packages, we set forth upon the more laborious stage of our journey.

An unfortunate quarrel between our pepperpots marked the outset of our new stage. Challenger had from the moment of joining us issued directions to the whole party, much to the evident discontent of Summerlee. Now, upon his assigning some duty to his fellow-Professor (it was only the carrying of an aneroid barometer), the matter suddenly came to a head.

"May I ask, sir," said Summerlee, with vicious calm, "in what capacity you take it upon yourself to issue these orders?"

Challenger glared and bristled.

"I do it, Professor Summerlee, as leader of this expedition."

"I am compelled to tell you, sir, that I do not recognize you in that capacity."

"Indeed!" Challenger bowed with unwieldy sarcasm. "Perhaps you would define my exact position."

"Yes, sir. You are a man whose veracity is upon trial, and this committee is here to try it. You walk sir, with your judges."

"Dear me!" said Challenger, seating himself on the side of one of the canoes. "In that case you will, of course, go on your way, and I will follow at my leisure. If I am not the leader you cannot expect me to lead."

Thank heaven that there were two sane men—Lord John Roxton and myself—to prevent the petulance and folly of our learned Professors from sending us back empty-handed to London. Such arguing and pleading and explaining before we could get them mollified! Then at last Summerlee, with his sneer and his pipe, would move forwards, and Challenger would come rolling and grumbling after. By some good fortune we discovered about this time that both our savants had the very poorest opinion of Dr. Illingworth of Edinburgh. Thenceforward that was our one safety, and every strained situation was relieved by our introducing the name of the Scottish zoologist, when both our Professors would form a temporary alliance and friendship in their detestation and abuse of this common rival.

Advancing in single file along the bank of the stream, we soon found that it narrowed down to a mere brook, and finally that it lost itself in a great green morass of sponge-like mosses, into which we sank up to our knees. The place was horribly haunted by clouds of mosquitoes and every form of flying pest, so we were glad to find solid ground again and to make a circuit among the trees, which enabled us to outflank this pestilent morass, which droned like an organ in the distance, so loud was it with insect life.

On the second day after leaving our canoes we found that the whole character of the country changed. Our road was persistently upwards, and as we ascended the woods became thinner and lost their tropical luxuriance. The huge trees of the alluvial Amazonian plain gave place to the Phœnix and coco palms, growing in scattered clumps, with thick brushwood between. In the damper hollows the Mauritia palms threw out their graceful drooping fronds. We travelled entirely by compass, and once or twice there were differences of opinion between Challenger and the two Indians, when, to quote the Professor's indignant words, the whole party agreed to "trust the fallacious instincts of undeveloped savages rather than the highest product of modern European culture." That we were justified in doing so was shown upon the third day, when Challenger admitted that he recognized several landmarks of his former journey, and in one spot we actually came upon four fire-blackened stones, which must have marked a camping place.

The road still ascended, and we crossed a rock-studded slope which took two days to traverse. The vegetation had again changed, and only the vegetable ivory tree remained, with a great profusion of wonderful orchids, among which I learned to recognize the rare *Nuttonia Vexillaria* and the glorious pink and scarlet blossoms of Cattleya and odontoglossum. Occasional brooks with pebbly bottoms and fern-draped banks gurgled down the shallow gorges in the hill, and offered good camping-grounds every evening on the banks of some rock-studded pool, where swarms of little blue-backed fish, about the size and shape of English trout, gave us a delicious supper.

On the ninth day after leaving the canoes, having done, as I reckon, about a hundred and twenty miles, we began to emerge from the trees, which had grown smaller until they were mere shrubs. Their place was taken by an immense wilderness of bamboo, which grew so thickly that

we could only penetrate it by cutting a pathway with the
machetes and bill-hooks of the Indians. It took us a long
day, traveling from seven in the morning till eight at night,
with only two breaks of one hour each, to get through this
obstacle. Anything more monotonous and wearying could
not be imagined, for, even at the most open places, I could
not see more than ten or twelve yards, while usually my
vision was limited to the back of Lord John's cotton jacket
in front of me, and to the yellow wall within a foot of me
on either side. From above came one thin knife-edge of
sunshine, and fifteen feet over our heads one saw the tops
of the reeds swaying against the deep blue sky. I do not
know what kind of creatures inhabit such a thicket, but
several times we heard the plunging of large, heavy animals quite close to us. From their sounds Lord John
judged them to be some form of wild cattle. Just as night
fell we cleared the belt of bamboos, and at once formed
our camp, exhausted by the interminable day.

Early next morning we were again afoot, and found that
the character of the country had changed once again. Behind us was the wall of bamboo, as definite as if it marked
the course of a river. In front was an open plain, sloping
slightly upwards and dotted with clumps of tree-ferns, the
whole curving before us until it ended in a long, whale-
backed ridge. This we reached about midday, only to find
a shallow valley beyond, rising once again into a gentle incline which led to a low, rounded skyline. It was here,
while we crossed the first of these hills, that an incident
occurred which may or may not have been important.

Professor Challenger, who, with the two local Indians,
was in the van of the party, stopped suddenly and pointed
excitedly to the right. As he did so we saw, at the distance
of a mile or so, something which appeared to be a huge
grey bird flap slowly up from the ground and skim

smoothly off, flying very low and straight, until it was lost among the tree-ferns.

"Did you see it?" cried Challenger, in exultation. "Summerlee, did you see it?"

His colleague was staring at the spot where the creature had disappeared.

"What do you claim it was?" he asked.

"To the best of my belief, a pterodactyl."

Summerlee burst into derisive laughter. "A ptero-fiddle-stick!" said he. "It was a stork, if ever I saw one."

Challenger was too furious to speak. He simply swung his pack upon his back and continued upon his march. Lord John came abreast of me, however, and his face was more grave than was his wont. He had his Zeiss glasses in his hand.

"I focused it before it got over the trees," said he. "I won't undertake to say what it was, but I'll risk my reputation as a sportsman that it wasn't any bird that ever I clapped eyes on in my life."

So there the matter stands. Are we really just at the edge of the unknown, encountering the outlying pickets of this lost world of which our leader speaks? I give you the incident as it occurred and you will know as much as I do. It stands alone, for we saw nothing more which could be called remarkable.

And now, my readers, if ever I have any, I have brought you up the broad river, and through the screen of rushes, and down the green tunnel, and up the long scope of palm trees, and through the bamboo brake, and across the plain of tree-ferns. At last our destination lay in full sight of us. When we had crossed the second ridge we saw before us an irregular, palm-studded plain, and then the line of high red cliffs which I have seen in the picture. There it lies,

ROUGH CHART OF JOURNEY
(NEITHER ORIENTATED NOR TO SCALE)

MAPLE-WHITE LAND

BASALT CLIFF

△ CAMP

STRANGE GREY
THING SEEN HERE ✗

PLAIN OF
TREE FERNS

GIANT CANE-BRAKE

ROCKY SLOPE

SEMI-TROPICAL VEGETATION

MANY SNAKES & TARANTULAS

UNEXPLORED

LOW HILLS
SPONGY MORASS

CANOES
HIDDEN

CONCEALED RIVER

UNEXPLORED HILLS
(ON FAR HORIZON)

WOODS

DRUMBEATING INDIANS

RAPIDS
(WHERE CHALLENGER LOST
SPECIMENS ~ FIRST
JOURNEY)

(WHERE MAPLE WHITE died)
INDIAN VILLAGE
COOGO

GAPO OR MARSH

AMAZON

WOODS

even as I write, and there can be no question that it is the same. At the nearest point it is about seven miles from our present camp, and it curves away, stretching as far as I can see. Challenger struts about like a prize peacock, and Summerlee is silent, but still sceptical. Another day should bring some of our doubts to an end. Meanwhile, as José, whose arm was pierced by a broken bamboo, insists upon returning, I send this letter back in his charge, and only hope that it may eventually come to hand. I will write again as the occasion serves. I have enclosed with this a rough chart of our journey, which may have the effect of making the account rather easier to understand.

9

Who Could Have Foreseen It?

A DREADFUL THING HAS HAPPENED TO US. WHO COULD HAVE foreseen it? I cannot foresee any end to our troubles. It may be that we are condemned to spend our whole lives in this strange, inaccessible place. I am still so confused that I can hardly think clearly of the facts of the present or of the chances of the future. To my astounded senses the one seems most terrible and the other as black as night.

No men have ever found themselves in a worse position; nor is there any use in disclosing to you our exact geographical situation and asking our friends for a relief party. Even if they could send one, our fate will in all human probability be decided long before it could arrive in South America.

We are, in truth, as far from any human aid as if we were on the moon. If we are to win through, it is only our own qualities which can save us. I have as companions three remarkable men, men of great brain-power and of unshaken courage. There lies our one and only hope. It is only when I look upon the untroubled faces of my comrades that I see some glimmer through the darkness. Outwardly I trust that I appear as unconcerned as they. Inwardly I am filled with apprehension.

Let me give you, with as much detail as I can, the sequence of events which have led us to this catastrophe.

When I finished my last letter I stated that we were within seven miles from an enormous line of ruddy cliffs which encircled, beyond all doubt, the plateau of which Professor Challenger spoke. Their height, as we approached them, seemed to me in some places to be greater than he had stated—running up in parts to at least a thousand feet—and they were curiously striated, in a manner which is, I believe, characteristic of basaltic upheavals. Something of the sort is to be seen in Salisbury Crags at Edinburgh. The summit showed every sign of a luxuriant vegetation, with bushes near the edge, and farther back many high trees. There was no indication of any life that we could see.

That night we pitched our camp immediately under the cliff—a most wild and desolate spot. The crags above us were not merely perpendicular, but curved outwards at the top, so that ascent was out of the question. Close to us was the high, thin pinnacle of rock which I believe I mentioned earlier in this narrative. It is like a broad red church spire, the top of it being level with the plateau, but a great chasm gaping between. On the summit of it there grew on high tree. Both pinnacle and cliff were comparatively low—some five or six hundred feet, I should think.

"It was on that," said Professor Challenger, pointing to this tree, "that the pterodactyl was perched. I climbed halfway up the rock before I shot him. I am inclined to think that a good mountaineer like myself could ascend the rock to the top, though he would, of course, be no nearer to the plateau when he had done so."

As Challenger spoke of his pterodactyl I glanced at Professor Summerlee, and for the first time I seemed to see some signs of a dawning credulity and repentance. There was no sneer upon his thin lips, but, on the contrary, a grey, drawn look of excitement and amazement. Challenger saw it, too, and revelled in the first taste of victory.

"Of course," said he, with his clumsy and ponderous sarcasm, "Professor Summerlee will understand that when I speak of a pterodactyl I mean a stork—only it is the kind of stork which has no feathers, a leathery skin, membranous wings, and teeth in its jaws." He grinned and blinked and bowed until his colleague turned and walked away.

In the morning, after a frugal breakfast of coffee and manioc—we had to be economical of our stores—we held a council of war as to the best method of ascending to the plateau above us.

Challenger presided with a solemnity as if he were the Lord Chief Justice on the Bench. Picture him seated upon a rock, his absurd boyish straw hat tilted on the back of his head, his supercilious eyes dominating us from under his drooping lids, his great black beard wagging as he slowly defined our present situation and our future movements.

Beneath him you might have seen the three of us—myself, sunburnt, young, and vigorous after our open-air tramp; Summerlee, solemn, but still critical, behind his eternal pipe; Lord John, as keen as a razor-edge, with his supple, alert figure leaning upon his rifle, and his eagle eyes fixed eagerly upon the speaker. Behind us were grouped the two swarthy half-breeds and the little knot of Indians, while in front and above us towered those huge, ruddy ribs of rocks which kept us from our goal.

"I need not say," said our leader, "that on the occasion of my last visit I exhausted every means of climbing the cliff, and where I failed I do not think that anyone else is likely to succeed, for I am something of a mountaineer. I had none of the appliances of a rock-climber with me, but I have taken the precaution to bring them now. With their aid I am positive I could climb that detached pinnacle to the summit; but so long as the main cliff overhangs, it is vain to attempt ascending that. I was hurried upon my last visit by the approach of the rainy season and by the exhaustion of my supplies. These considerations limited my time, and I can only claim that I have surveyed about six miles of the cliff to the east of us, finding no possible way up. What, then, shall we now do?"

"There seems to be only one reasonable course," said Professor Summerlee. "If you have explored the east, we should travel along the base of the cliff to the west, and seek for a practicable point for our ascent."

"That's it," said Lord John. "The odds are that this plateau is of no great size, and we shall travel round it until we either find an easy way up it, or come back to the point from which we started."

"I have already explained to our young friend here," said Challenger (he has a way of alluding to me as if I were a school child ten years old), "that it is quite impossible that there should be an easy way up anywhere, for the simple reason that if there were the summit would not be isolated, and those conditions would not obtain which have effected so singular an interference with the general laws of survival. Yet I admit that there may very well be places where an expert human climber may reach the summit, and yet a cumbrous and heavy animal be unable to descend. It is certain that there *is* a point where an ascent is possible."

"How do you know that, sir?" asked Summerlee, sharply.

"Because my predecessor, the American Maple White, actually made such an ascent. How otherwise could he have seen the monster which he sketched in his notebook?"

"There you reason somewhat ahead of the proved facts," said the stubborn Summerlee. "I admit your plateau, because I have seen it; but I have not as yet satisfied myself that it contains any form of life whatever."

"What you admit, sir, or what you do not admit, is really of inconceivably small importance. I am glad to perceive that the plateau itself has actually obtruded itself upon your intelligence." He glanced up at it, and then, to our amazement, he sprang from his rock, and, seizing Summerlee by the neck, he tilted his face into the air. "Now, sir!" he shouted, hoarse with excitement. "Do I help you to realize that the plateau contains some animal life?"

I have said that a thick fringe of green overhung the edge of the cliff. Out of this there had emerged a black, glistening object. As it came slowly forth and overhung the chasm, we saw that it was a very large snake with a peculiar flat spade-like head. It wavered and quivered above us for a minute, the morning sun gleaming upon its sleek, sinuous coils. Then it slowly drew inwards and disappeared.

Summerlee had been so interested that he had stood unresisting while Challenger tilted his head into the air. Now he shook his colleague off and came back to his dignity.

"I should be glad, Professor Challenger," said he, "if you could see your way to make any remarks which may occur to you without seizing me by the chin. Even the appearance of a very ordinary rock python does not appear to justify such a liberty."

"But there is life upon the plateau all the same," his colleague replied in triumph. "And now, having demonstrated this important conclusion so that it is clear to anyone, however prejudiced or obtuse, I am of opinion that we cannot do better than break up our camp and travel westward until we find some means of ascent."

The ground at the foot of the cliff was rocky and broken, so that the going was slow and difficult. Suddenly we came, however, upon something which cheered our hearts. It was the site of an old encampment, with several empty Chicago meat tins, a bottle labelled "Brandy," a broken tin-opener, and a quantity of other travellers' debris. A crumpled, disintegrated newspaper revealed itself as the *Chicago Democrat*, though the date had been obliterated.

"Not mine," said Challenger. "It must be Maple White's."

Lord John had been gazing curiously at a great tree-fern which overshadowed the encampment. "I say, look at this," said he. "I believe it is meant for a sign-post."

A slip of hard wood had been nailed to the tree in such a way as to point to the westward.

"Most certainly a signpost," said Challenger. "What else? Finding himself upon a dangerous errand, our pioneer has left this sign so that any party which follows him may know the way he has taken. Perhaps we shall come upon some other indications as we proceed."

We did indeed, but they were of a terrible and most unexpected nature. Immediately beneath the cliff there grew a considerable patch of high bamboo, like that which we had traversed in our journey. Many of these stems were twenty feet high, with sharp, strong tops, so that even as they stood they made formidable spears. We were passing along the edge of this cover when my eye was caught by the gleam of something white within it. Thrusting in my head between the stems, I found myself gazing at a fleshless skull. The whole skeleton was there, but the skull had detached itself and lay some feet nearer to the open.

With a few blows from the machetes of our Indians we cleared the spot and were able to study the details of this old tragedy. Only a few shreds of clothes could still be distinguished, but there were the remains of boots upon the bony feet, and it was very clear that the dead man was a European. A gold watch by Hudson, of New York, and a chain which held a stylographic pen, lay among the bones. There was also a silver cigarette-case, with "J. C., from A. E. S.," upon the lid. The state of the metal seemed to show that the catastrophe had occurred no great time before.

"Who can he be?" asked Lord John. "Poor devil! every bone in his body seems to be broken."

"And the bamboo grows through his smashed ribs," said Summerlee. "It is a fast-growing plant, but it is surely inconceivable that this body could have been here while the canes grew to be twenty feet in length."

"As to the man's identity," said Professor Challenger, "I have no doubt whatever upon that point. As I made my way up the river before I reached you at the fazenda I instituted very particular inquiries about Maple White. At Para they knew nothing. Fortunately, I had a definite clue, for there was a particular picture in his sketchbook which showed him taking lunch with a certain ecclesiastic at Rosario. This priest I was able to find, and though he proved a very argumentative fellow, who took it absurdly amiss that I should point out to him the corrosive effect which modern science must have upon his beliefs, he none the less gave me some positive information. Maple White passed Rosario four years ago, or two years before I saw his dead body. He was not alone at the time, but there was a friend, an American named James Colver, who remained in the boat and did not meet this ecclesiastic. I think, therefore, that there can be no doubt that we are now looking upon the remains of this James Colver."

"Nor," said Lord John, "is there much doubt as to how he met his death. He has fallen or been chucked from the top, and so been impaled. How else could he come by his broken bones, and how could he have been stuck through by these canes with their points so high above our heads?"

A hush came over us as we stood round these shattered remains and realized the truth of Lord John Roxton's words. The beetling head of the cliff projected over the cane-brake. Undoubtedly he had fallen from above. But *had* he fallen? Had it been an accident? Or—— Already ominous and terrible possibilities began to form round that unknown land.

We moved off in silence, and continued to coast round the line of cliffs, which were as even and unbroken as some of those monstrous Antarctic ice-fields which I have seen depicted as stretching from horizon to horizon and towering high above the mast-heads of the exploring vessel. In five miles we saw no rift or break. And then suddenly we perceived something which filled us with new hope. In a hollow of the rock, protected from rain, there was drawn a rough arrow in chalk, pointing still to the westward.

"Maple White again," said Professor Challenger. "He had some presentiment that worthy footsteps would follow close behind him."

"He had chalk, then?"

"A box of colored chalks was among the effects I found in his knapsack. I remember that the white one was worn to a stump."

"That is certainly good evidence," said Summerlee. "We can only accept his guidance and follow on to the westward."

We had proceeded some five more miles when again we saw a white arrow upon the rocks. It was at a point where the face of the cliff was for the first time split into a narrow cleft. Inside the cleft was a second guidance mark, which pointed right up it with the tip somewhat elevated, as if the spot indicated were above the level of the ground.

It was a solemn place, for the walls were so gigantic and the slit of blue sky so narrow and so obscured by a double fringe of verdure that only a dim and shadowy light penetrated to the bottom. We had had no food for many hours, we were very weary with the stony and irregular journey, but our nerves were too strung to allow us to halt. We ordered the camp to be pitched, however, and, leaving the Indians to arrange it, we four, with the two half-breeds, proceeded up the narrow gorge.

It was not more than forty feet across at the mouth, but it rapidly closed until it ended in an acute angle, too straight and smooth for an ascent. Certainly it was not this which our pioneer had attempted to indicate. We made our way back—the whole gorge was not more than a quarter of a mile deep—and then suddenly the quick eyes of Lord John fell upon what we were seeking. High up above our heads, amid the dark shadows, there was one circle of deeper gloom. Surely it could only be the opening of a cave.

The base of the cliff was heaped with loose stones at the spot, and it was not difficult to clamber up. When we reached it, all doubt was removed. Not only was it an opening into the rock, but on the side of it was marked once again the sign of the arrow. Here was the point, and this the means by which Maple White and his ill-fated comrade had made their ascent.

We were too excited to return to the camp, but must make our first exploration at once. Lord John had an electric torch in his knapsack, and this had to serve us as light. He advanced, throwing his little clear circlet of yellow radiance before him, while in single file we followed at his heels.

The cave had evidently been water-worn, the sides being smooth and the floor covered with rounded stones. It was of such a size that a single man could just fit through by stooping. For fifty yards it ran almost straight into the rock, and then it ascended at an angle of forty-five. Presently this incline became even steeper, and we found ourselves climbing upon hands and knees among loose rubble which slid from beneath us. Suddenly an exclamation broke from Lord Roxton.

"It's blocked!" said he.

Clustering behind him we saw in the yellow field of light a wall of broken basalt which extended to the ceiling.

"The roof has fallen in!"

In vain we dragged out some of the pieces. The only effect was that the larger ones became detached and threatened to roll down the gradient and crush us. It was evident that the obstacle was far beyond any efforts which we could make to remove it. The road by which Maple White had ascended was no longer available.

Too much cast down to speak, we stumbled down the dark tunnel and made our way back to the camp.

One incident occurred, however, before we left the gorge, which is of importance in view of what came afterwards. We had gathered in a little group at the bottom of the chasm, some forty feet beneath the mouth of the cave, when a huge rock rolled suddenly downwards and shot past us with tremendous force. It was the narrowest escape for one or all of us. We could not ourselves see whence the rock had come, but our half-breed servants, who were still at the opening of the cave, said that it had flown past them, and must therefore have fallen from the summit. Looking upwards, we could see no sign of movement above us amidst the green jungle which topped the cliff. There could be little doubt, however, that the stone was aimed at us, so the incident surely pointed to humanity— and malevolent humanity—upon the plateau!

We withdrew hurriedly from the chasm, our minds full of this new development and its bearing upon our plans. The situation was difficult enough before, but if the obstructions of Nature were increased by the deliberate opposition of man, then our case was indeed a hopeless one. And yet, as we looked up at that beautiful fringe of verdure only a few hundreds of feet above our heads, there was not one of us who could conceive the idea of returning to London until we had explored it to its depths.

On discussing the situation, we determined that our best course was to continue to coast round the plateau in the hope of finding some other means of reaching the top. The line of cliffs, which had decreased considerably in height, had already begun to trend from west to north, and if we could take this as representing the arc of a circle, the whole circumference could not be very great. At the worst, then, we should be back in a few days at our starting-point.

We made a march that day which totalled some two-and-twenty miles, without any change in our prospects. I may mention that our aneroid shows us that in the continual incline which we have ascended since we abandoned our canoes we have risen to no less than three thousand feet above sea-level. Hence there is a considerable change both in the temperature and in the vegetation. We have shaken off some of that horrible insect life which is the bane of tropical travel. A few palms still survive, and many tree-ferns, but the Amazonian trees have been all left behind. It was pleasant to see the convolvulus, the passion-flower, and the begonia, all reminding me of home, here among these inhospitable rocks. There was a red begonia just the same color as one that is kept in a pot in the window of a certain villa in Streatham—but I am drifting into private reminiscence.

That night—I am still speaking of the first day of our circumnavigation of the plateau—a great experience awaited us, and one which for ever set at rest any doubt which we could have had as to the wonders so near us.

You will realize as you read it, my dear Mr. McArdle, and possibly for the first time, that the paper has not sent me on a wild-goose chase, and that there is conceivably fine copy waiting for the world whenever we have the Professor's leave to make use of it. I shall not dare to publish these articles unless I can bring back my proofs to England, or I shall be hailed as the journalistic Munchausen of all time. I have no doubt that you feel the same way yourself, and that you would not care to stake the whole credit of the *Gazette* upon this adventure until we can meet the chorus of criticism and scepticism which such articles must of necessity elicit. So this wonderful incident, which would make such a headline for the old paper, must still wait its turn in the editorial drawer.

And yet it was all over in a flash, and there was no sequel to it, save in our own convictions.

What occurred was this. Lord John had shot an ajouti—which is a small, pig-like animal—and, half of it having been given to the Indians, we were cooking the other half upon our fire. There is a chill in the air after dark, and we had all drawn close to the blaze. The night was moonless, but there were some stars, and one could see for a little distance across the plain. Well, suddenly out of the darkness, out of the night, there swooped something with a swish like an aeroplane. The whole group of us were covered for an instant by a canopy of leathery wings, and I had a momentary vision of a long, snake-like neck, a fierce, red, greedy eye, and a great snapping beak, filled, to my amazement, with little, gleaming teeth. The next instant it was gone—and so was our dinner. A huge black shadow, twenty feet across, skimmed up into the air; for an instant the monster wings blotted out the stars, and then it vanished over the brow of the cliff above us. We all sat in amazed silence round the fire, like the heroes of Virgil when the Harpies came down upon them. It was Summerlee who was the first to speak.

"Professor Challenger," said he, in a solemn voice, which quavered with emotion, "I owe you an apology. Sir, I am very much in the wrong, and I beg that you will forget what is past."

It was handsomely said, and the two men for the first time shook hands. So much we have gained by this clear vision of our first pterodactyl. It was worth a stolen supper to bring two such men together.

But if prehistoric life existed upon the plateau, it was not superabundant, for we had no further glimpse of it during the next three days. During this time we traversed a barren and forbidding country, which alternated between stony desert and desolate marshes full of many wildfowl, upon the north and east of the cliffs. From that direction the place is really inaccessible, and, were it not for a hardish ledge which runs at the very base of the precipice, we should have had to turn back. Many times we were up to our waists in the slime and blubber of an old, semi-tropical swamp. To make matters worse, the place seemed to be a favorite breeding place of the Jaracaca snake, the most venomous and aggressive in South America. Again and again these horrible creatures came writhing and springing towards us across the surface of this putrid bog, and it was only by keeping our shot guns for ever ready that we could feel safe from them. One funnel-shaped depression in the morass, of a livid green in color from some lichen which festered in it, will always remain as a nightmare memory in my mind. It seems to have been a special nest of these vermin, and the slopes were alive with them, all writhing in our direction, for it is a peculiarity of the Jaracaca that it will always attack man at first sight. There were too many for us to shoot, so we fairly took to our heels and ran until we were exhausted. I shall always remember as we looked back how far behind we could see the heads and necks of our horrible pursuers rising and falling amid the reeds. Jaracaca Swamp we named it in the map which we are constructing.

The cliffs upon the farther side had lost their ruddy tint, being chocolate-brown in color; the vegetation was more scattered along the top of them, and they had sunk to three or four hundred feet in height, but in no place did we find any point where they could be ascended. If anything, they were more impossible than at the first point where we had met them. Their absolute steepness is indicated in the photograph which I took over the stony desert.

"Surely," said I, as we discussed the situation, "the rain must find its way down somehow. There are bound to be water-channels in the rocks."

"Our young friend has glimpses of lucidity," said Professor Challenger, patting me upon the shoulder.

"The rain must go somewhere," I repeated.

"He keeps a firm grip upon actuality. The only drawback is that we have conclusively proved by ocular demonstration that there are *no* water channels down the rocks."

"Where, then, does it go?" I persisted.

"I think it may be fairly assumed that if it does not come outwards it must run inwards."

"Then there is a lake in the centre."

"So I should suppose."

"It is more than likely that the lake may be an old crater," said Summerlee. "The whole formation is, of course, highly volcanic. But however that may be, I should expect to find the surface of the plateau slope inwards with a considerable sheet of water in the center, which may drain off, by some subterranean channel, into the marshes of the Jaracaca Swamp."

"Or evaporation might preserve an equilibrium," remarked Challenger, and the two learned men wandered off into one of their usual scientific arguments, which were as comprehensible as Chinese to the layman.

On the sixth day we completed our circuit of the cliffs, and found ourselves back at the first camp, beside the isolated pinnacle of rock. We were a disconsolate party, for nothing could have been more minute than our investigation, and it was absolutely certain that there was no single point where the most active human being could possibly hope to scale the cliff. The place which Maple White's chalk-marks had indicated as his own means of access was now entirely impassable.

What were we to do now? Our stores of provisions, supplemented by our guns, were holding out well, but the day must come when they would need replenishment. In a couple of months the rains might be expected, and we should be washed out of our camp. The rock was harder than marble, and any attempt at cutting a path for so great a height was more than our time or resources would admit. No wonder that we looked gloomily at each other that night, and sought our blankets without hardly a word exchanged. I remember that as I dropped off to sleep my last recollection was that Challenger was squatting, like a monstrous bull-frog, by the fire, his huge head in his hands, sunk apparently in the deepest thought, and entirely oblivious to the good-night which I wished him.

But it was a very different Challenger who greeted us in the morning—a Challenger with contentment and self-congratulation shining from his whole person. He faced us as we assembled for breakfast with a deprecating false modesty in his eyes, as who should say, "I know that I deserve all that you can say, but I pray you to spare my blushes by not saying it." His beard bristled exultantly, his chest was thrown out, and his hand was thrust into the front of his jacket. So, in his fancy, may he see himself sometimes, gracing the vacant pedestal in Trafalgar Square, and adding one more to the horrors of the London streets.

"Eureka!" he cried, his teeth shining through his beard. "Gentlemen, you may congratulate me and we may congratulate each other. The problem is solved."

"You have found a way up?"

"I venture to think so."

"And where?"

For answer he pointed to the spire-like pinnacle upon our right.

Our faces—or mine, at least—fell as we surveyed it. That it could be climbed we had our companion's assurance. But a horrible abyss lay between it and the plateau.

"We can never get across," I gasped.

"We can at least all reach the summit," said he. "When we are up I may be able to show you that the resources of an inventive mind are not yet exhausted."

After breakfast we unpacked the bundle in which our leader had brought his climbing accessories. From it he took a coil of the strongest and lightest rope, a hundred and fifty feet in length, and climbing irons, clamps, and other devices. Lord John was an experienced mountaineer, and Summerlee had done some rough climbing at various times, so that I was really the novice at rock-work of the party; but my strength and activity may have made up for my want of experience.

It was not in reality a very stiff task, though there were moments which made my hair bristle upon my head. The first half was perfectly easy, but from there upwards it became continually steeper, until, for the last fifty feet, we were literally clinging with our fingers and toes to tiny ledges and crevices in the rock. I could not have accomplished it, nor could Summerlee, if Challenger had not gained the summit (it was extraordinary to see such activity in so unwieldly a creature) and there fixed the rope round the trunk of the considerable tree which grew there. With this as our support, we were soon able to scramble up the jagged wall until we found ourselves upon the small grassy platform, some twenty-five feet each way, which formed the summit.

The first impression which I received when I had recovered my breath was the extraordinary view over the country which we traversed. The whole Brazilian plain seemed to lie beneath us, extending away and away until it ended in dim blue mists upon the farthest skyline. In the foreground was the long slope, strewn with rocks and dotted with tree-ferns; farther off in the middle distance, looking over the saddle-back hill, I could just see the yellow and green mass of bamboos through which we had passed; and then, gradually, the vegetation increased until it formed the huge forest which extended as far as the eyes could reach, and for a good two thousand miles beyond.

I was still drinking in this wonderful panorama when the heavy hand of the Professor fell upon my shoulder.

"This way, my young friend," said he; "*vestigia nulla restrorsum.* Never look rearwards, but always to our glorious goal."

The level of the plateau, when I turned, was exactly that on which we stood, and the green bank of bushes, with occasional trees, was so near that it was difficult to realize how inaccessible it remained. At a rough guess the gulf was forty feet across, but, so far as I could see, it might as well have been forty miles. I placed one arm round the trunk of the tree and leaned over the abyss. Far down were the small dark figures of our servants, looking up at us. The wall was absolutely precipitous, as was that which faced me.

"This is indeed curious," said the creaking voice of Professor Summerlee.

I turned, and found that he was examining with great interest the tree to which I clung. That smooth bark and those small, ribbed leaves seemed familiar to my eyes. "Why," I cried, "it's a beech!"

"Exactly," said Summerlee. "A fellow-countryman in a far land."

"Not only a fellow-countryman, my good sir," said Challenger, "but also, if I may be allowed to enlarge your simile, an ally of the first value. This beech tree will be our savior."

"By George!" cried Lord John, "a bridge!"

"Exactly, my friends, a bridge! It is not for nothing that I expended an hour last night in focusing my mind upon the situation. I have some recollection of once remarking to our young friend here that G. E. C. is at his best when his back is to the wall. Last night you will admit that all our backs were to the wall. But where willpower and intellect go together, there is always a way out. A drawbridge had to be found which could be dropped across the abyss. Behold it!"

It was certainly a brilliant idea. The tree was a good sixty feet in height, and if it only fell the right way it would easily cross the chasm. Challenger had slung the camp axe over his shoulder when he ascended. Now he handed it to me.

"Our young friend has the thews and sinews," said he. "I think he will be most useful at this task. I must beg, however, that you will kindly refrain from thinking for yourself, and that you will do exactly what you are told."

Under his direction I cut such gashes in the sides of the tree as would ensure that it should fall as we desired. It had already a strong, natural tilt in the direction of the plateau, so that the matter was not difficult. Finally I set to work in earnest upon the trunk, taking turn and turn with Lord John. In a little over an hour there was a loud crack, the tree swayed forward, and then crashed over, burying its branches among the bushes on the farther side. The severed trunk rolled to the very edge of our platform, and for one terrible second we all thought that it was over. It balanced itself, however, a few inches from the edge, and there was our bridge to the unknown.

All of us, without a word, shook hands with Professor Challenger, who raised his straw hat and bowed deeply to each in turn.

"I claim the honor," said he, "to be the first to cross to the unknown land—a fitting subject, no doubt, for some future historical painting."

He had approached the bridge when Lord John laid his hand upon his coat.

"My dear chap," said he, "I really cannot allow it."

"Cannot allow it, sir!" The head went back and the beard forward.

"When it is a matter of science, don't you know, I follow your lead because you are by way of bein' a man of science. But it's up to you to follow me when you come into my department."

"Your department, sir?"

"We all have our professions, and soldierin' is mine. We are, accordin' to my ideas, invadin' a new country, which may or may not be chock-full of enemies of sorts. To barge blindly into it for want of a little common sense and patience isn't my notion of management."

The remonstrance was too reasonable to be disregarded. Challenger tossed his head and shrugged his heavy shoulders.

"Well, sir, what do you propose?"

"For all I know there may be a tribe of cannibals waitin' for lunch-time among those very bushes," said Lord John, looking across the bridge. "It's better to learn wisdom before you get into a cookin'-pot; so we will content ourselves with hopin' that there is no trouble waitin' for us, and at the same time we will act as if there were. Malone and I will go down again, therefore, and we will fetch up the four rifles, together with Gomez and the other. One man can then go across and the rest will cover him with guns, until he sees that it is safe for the whole crowd to come along."

Challenger sat down upon the cut stump and groaned his impatience; but Summerlee and I were of one mind that Lord John was our leader when such practical details were in question. The climb was a more simple thing now that the rope dangled down the face of the worst part of the ascent. Within an hour we had brought up the rifles and a shot-gun. The half-breeds had ascended also, and under Lord John's orders they had carried up a bale of provisions in case our first exploration should be a long one. We had each bandoliers of cartridges.

"Now, Challenger, if you really insist upon being the first man in," said Lord John, when every preparation was complete.

"I am much indebted to you for your gracious permission," said the angry Professor; for never was a man so intolerant of every form of authority. "Since you are good enough to allow it, I shall most certainly take it upon myself to act as pioneer upon this occasion."

Seating himself with a leg overhanging the abyss on each side, and his hatchet slung upon his back, Challenger hopped his way across the trunk and was soon at the other side. He clambered up and waved his arms in the air.

"At last!" he cried; "at last!"

I gazed anxiously at him, with a vague expectation that some terrible fate would dart at him from the curtain of green behind him. But all was quiet, save that a strange, many-colored bird flew up from under his feet and vanished among the trees.

Summerlee was the second. His wiry energy is wonderful in so frail a frame. He insisted upon having two rifles slung upon his back, so that both Professors were armed when he had made his transit. I came next, and tried not to look down into the horrible gulf over which I was passing. Summerlee held out the butt-end of his rifle, and an instant later I was able to grasp his hand. As to Lord John, he walked across—actually walked, without support! He must have nerves of iron.

And there we were, the four of us, upon the dreamland, the lost world, of Maple White. To all of us it seemed the moment of our supreme triumph. Who could have guessed that it was the prelude to our supreme disaster? Let me say in a few words how the crushing blow fell upon us.

We had turned away from the edge, and had penetrated about fifty yards of close brushwood, when there came a frightful rending crash from behind us. With one impulse we rushed back the way we had come. The bridge was gone!

Far down at the base of the cliff I saw, as I looked over, a tangled mass of branches and splintered trunk. It was our beech tree. Had the edge of the platform crumbled and let it through? For a moment this explanation was in all our minds. The next, from the farther side of the rocky pinnacle before us a swarthy face, the face of Gomez the halfbreed, was slowly protruded. Yes, it was Gomez, but no longer the Gomez of the demure smile and the mask-like expression. Here was a face with flashing eyes and distorted features, a face convulsed with hatred and with the mad joy of gratified revenge.

"Lord Roxton!" he shouted. "Lord John Roxton!"

"Well," said our companion, "here I am."

A shriek of laughter came across the abyss.

"Yes, there you are, you English dog, and there you will remain! I have waited and waited, and now has come my chance. You found it hard to get up; you will find it harder to get down. You cursed fools, you are trapped, every one of you!"

We were too astounded to speak. We could only stand there staring in amazement. A great broken bough upon the grass showed whence he had gained his leverage to tilt over our bridge. The face had vanished, but presently it was up again, more frantic than before.

"We nearly killed you with a stone at the cave," he cried, "but this is better. It is slower and more terrible. Your bones will whiten up there, and none will know where you lie or come to cover them. As you lie dying, think of Lopez, whom you shot five years ago on the

Putomayo River. I am his brother, and, come what will I die happy now, for his memory has been avenged." A furious hand was shaken at us, and then all was quiet.

Had the half-breed simply wrought his vengeance and then escaped, all might have been well with him. It was that foolish, irresistible Latin impulse to be dramatic which brought his own downfall. Roxton, the man who had earned himself the name of the Flail of the Lord through three countries, was not one who could be safely taunted. The half-breed was descending on the farther side of the pinnacle; but before he could reach the ground Lord John had run along the edge of the plateau and gained a point from which he could see his man. There was a single crack of his rifle, and, though we saw nothing, we heard the scream and then the distant thud of the falling body. Roxton came back to us with a face of granite.

"I have been a blind simpleton," said he, bitterly. "It's my folly that has brought you all into this trouble. I should have remembered that these people have long memories for blood-feuds, and have been more upon my guard."

"What about the other one? It took two of them to lever that tree over the edge."

"I could have shot him, but I let him go. He may have had no part in it. Perhaps it would have been better if I had killed him, for he must, as you say, have lent a hand."

Now that we had the clue to his action, each of us could cast back and remember some sinister act upon the part of the half-breed—his constant desire to know our plans, his arrest outside our tent when he was overhearing them, the furtive looks of hatred which from time to time one or other of us had surprised. We were still discussing it, endeavoring to adjust our minds to these new conditions, when a singular scene in the plain below arrested our attention.

A man in white clothes, who could only be the surviving half-breed, was running as one does run when Death is the pacemaker. Behind him, only a few yards in his rear, bounded the huge ebony figure of Zambo, our bearer. Even as we looked, he sprang upon the back of the fugitive and flung his arms round his neck. They rolled on the ground together. An instant afterwards Zambo rose, looked at the prostrate man, and then, waving his hand joyously to us, came running in our direction. The white figure lay motionless in the middle of the great plain.

Our two traitors had been destroyed, but the mischief that they had done lived after them. By no possible means could we get back to the pinnacle. We had been natives of the world; now we were natives of the plateau. The two things were separate and apart. There was the plain which led to the canoes. Yonder, beyond the violet, hazy horizon, was the stream which led back to civilization. But the link between was missing. No human ingenuity could suggest a means of bridging the chasm which yawned between ourselves and our past lives. One instant had altered the whole conditions of our existence.

It was at such a moment that I learned the stuff of which my three comrades were composed. They were grave, it is true, and thoughtful, but of an invincible serenity. For the moment we could only sit among the bushes in patience and wait the coming of Zambo. Presently his honest black face topped the rocks and his Herculean figure emerged upon the top of the pinnacle.

"What I do now?' he cried. "You tell me and I do it."

It was a question which it was easier to ask than to answer. One thing only was clear. He was our one trusty link with the outside world. On no account must he leave us.

"No, no!" he cried. "I not leave you. Whatever come, you always find me here. But no able to keep Indians. Already they say too much, Curupuri live on this place, and they go home. Now you leave them me no able to keep them."

"Make them wait till to-morrow, Zambo," I shouted; "then I can send letter back by them."

"Very good, sarr! I promise they wait till tomorrow," said Zambo. "But what I do for you now?"

There was plenty for him to do, and admirably the faithful fellow did it. First of all, under our directions, he undid the rope from the tree-stump and threw one end of it across to us. It was not thicker than a clothesline, but it was of great strength, and though we could not make a bridge of it, we might well find it invaluable if we had any climbing to do. He then fastened his end of the rope to the package of supplies which had been carried up, and we were able to drag it across. This gave us the means of life for at least a week, even if we found nothing else. Finally he descended and carried up two other packets of mixed goods—a box of ammunition and a number of other things, all of which we got across by throwing our rope to him and hauling it back. It was evening when he at last climbed down, with a final assurance that he would keep the Indians till next morning.

And so it is that I have spent nearly the whole of this our first night upon the plateau writing up our experiences by the light of a single candle-lantern.

We supped and camped at the very edge of the cliff, quenching our thirst with two bottles of Apollinaris which were in one of the cases. It is vital to us to find water, but I think even Lord John himself had had adventures enough for one day, and none of us felt inclined to make the first push into the unknown. We forbore to light a fire or to make any unnecessary sound.

Tomorrow (or today, rather, for it is already dawn as I

write) we shall make our first venture into this strange land. When I shall be able to write again—or if I ever shall write again—I know not. Meanwhile, I can see that the Indians are still in their place, and I am sure that the faithful Zambo will be here presently to get my letter. I only trust that it will come to hand.

P.S.—The more I think the more desperate does our position seem. I see no possible hope of our return. If there were a high tree near the edge of the plateau we might drop a return bridge across, but there is none within fifty yards. Our united strength could not carry a trunk which would serve our purpose. The rope, of course, is far too short that we could descend by it. No, our position is hopeless—hopeless!

10

The Most Wonderful Things Have Happened

THE MOST WONDERFUL THINGS HAVE HAPPENED AND ARE CON-
tinually happening to us. All the paper that I possess consists of five old notebooks and a lot of scraps, and I have
only the one stylographic pencil; but so long as I can
move my hand I will continue to set down our experiences
and impressions, for, since we are the only men of the
whole human race to see such things, it is of enormous importance that I should record them whilst they are fresh in
my memory and before that fate which seems to be con-
stantly impending does actually overtake us. Whether
Zambo can at last take these letters to the river, or whether
I shall myself in some miraculous way carry them back
with me, or, finally, whether some daring explorer, coming
upon our tracks, with the advantage, perhaps, of a per-
fected monoplane, should find this bundle of manuscript,
in any case I can see that what I am writing is destined to
immortality as a classic of true adventure.

On the morning after our being trapped upon the plateau
by the villainous Gomez we began a new stage in our ex-

periences. The first incident in it was not such as to give me a very favorable opinion of the place to which we had wandered. As I roused myself from a short nap after day had dawned, my eyes fell upon a most singular appearance upon my own leg. My trouser had slipped up, exposing a few inches of skin above my sock. On this there rested a large, purplish grape. Astonished at the sight, I leaned forward to pick it off, when, to my horror, it burst between my finger and thumb, squirting blood in every direction. My cry of disgust had brought the two Professors to my side.

"Most interesting," said Summerlee, bending over my skin. "An enormous blood-tick, as yet I believe, unclassified."

"The firstfruits of our labors," said Challenger in his booming, pedantic fashion. "We cannot do less than call it *Ixodes Maloni*. The very small inconvenience of being bitten, my young friend, cannot, I am sure, weigh with you as against the glorious privilege of having your name inscribed in the deathless roll of zoology. Unhappily you have crushed this fine specimen at the moment of satiation."

"Filthy vermin!" I cried.

Professor Challenger raised his great eyebrows in protest, and placed a soothing paw upon my shoulder.

"You should cultivate the scientific eye and the detached scientific mind," said he. "To a man of philosophic temperament like myself the blood-tick, with its lancet-like proboscis and its distending stomach, is as beautiful a work of Nature as the peacock, or, for that matter, the aurora borealis. It pains me to hear you speak of it in so unappreciative a fashion. No doubt, with due diligence, we can secure some other specimen."

"There can be no doubt of that," said Summerlee,

grimly, "for one has just disappeared behind your shirt-collar."

Challenger sprang into the air bellowing like a bull, and tore frantically at his coat and shirt to get them off. Summerlee and I laughed so that we could hardly help him. At last we exposed that monstrous torso (fifty-four inches, by the tailor's tape). His body was all matter with black hair, out of which jungle we picked the wandering tick before it had bitten him. But the bushes round were full of the horrible pests, and it was clear that we must shift our camp.

But first of all it was necessary to make our arrangements with Zambo, who appeared presently on the pinnacle with a number of tins of cocoa and biscuits, which he tossed over to us. Of the stores which remained below he was ordered to retain as much as would keep him for two months. The Indians were to have the remainder as a reward for their services and as payment for taking our letters back to the Amazon. Some hours later we saw them in a single file far out upon the plain, each with a bundle on his head, making their way back along the path we had come. Zambo occupied our little tent at the base of the pinnacle, and there he remained, our one link with the world below.

And now we had to decide upon our immediate movements. We shifted our position from among the tick-laden bushes until we came to a small clearing thickly surrounded by trees upon all sides. There were some flat slabs of rock in the center, with an excellent well close by, and there we sat in cleanly comfort while we made our first plans for the invasion of this new country. Birds were calling among the foliage—especially one with a peculiar whooping cry which was new to us—but beyond these sounds there were no signs of life.

Our first care was to make some sort of list of our own stores, so that we might know what we had to rely upon. What with the things we had ourselves brought up and those which Zambo had sent across on the rope, we were fairly well supplied. Most important of all, in view of the dangers which might surround us, we had our four rifles and one thousand three hundred rounds, also a shot-gun, but not more than a hundred and fifty medium pellet cartridges. In the matter of provisions we had enough to last for several weeks, with a sufficiency of tobacco and a few scientific implements, including a large telescope and a good field glass. All these things we collected together in the clearing, and as a first precaution, we cut down with our hatchet and knives a number of thorny bushes, which we piled round in a circle some fifteen yards in diameter. This was to be our headquarters for the time—our place of refuge against sudden danger and the guardhouse for our stores. Fort Challenger, we called it.

It was midday before we had made ourselves secure, but the heat was not oppressive, and the general character of the plateau, both in its temperament and in its vegetation, was almost temperate. The beech, the oak, and even the birch were to be found among the tangle of trees which girt us in. One huge gingko tree, topping all the others, shot its great limbs and maidenhair foliage over the fort which we had constructed. In its shade we continued our discussion, while Lord John, who had quickly taken command in the hour of action, gave us his views.

"So long as neither man nor beast has seen or heard us, we are safe," said he. "From the time they know we are here our troubles begin. There are no signs that they have found us out as yet. So our game surely is to lie low for time and spy out the land. We want to have a good look at our neighbors before we get on visitin' terms."

"But we must advance," I ventured to remark.

"By all means, sonny my boy! We will advance. But with common sense. We must never go so far that we can't get back to our base. Above all, we must never, unless it is life or death, fire off our guns."

"But *you* fired yesterday," said Summerlee.

"Well, it couldn't be helped. However, the wind was strong and blew outwards. It is not likely that the sound could have travelled far into the plateau. By the way, what shall we call this place? I suppose it is up to us to give it a name?"

There were several suggestions, more or less happy, but Challenger's was final.

"It can only have one name," said he. "It is called after the pioneer who discovered it. It is Maple White Land."

Maple White Land it became, and so it is named in that chart which has become my special task. So it will, I trust, appear in the atlas of the future.

The peaceful penetration of Maple White Land was the pressing subject before us. We had the evidence of our own eyes that the place was inhabited by some unknown creatures, and there was that of Maple White's sketchbook to show that more dreadful and more dangerous monsters might still appear. That there might also prove to be human occupants and that they were of a malevolent character was suggested by the skeleton impaled upon the bamboos, which could not have got there had it not been dropped from above. Our situation, stranded without possibility of escape in such a land, was clearly full of danger, and our reason endorsed every measure of caution which Lord John's experience could suggest. Yet it was surely impossible that we should halt on the edge of this world of mystery when our very souls were tingling with impatience to push forward and to pluck the heart from it.

We therefore blocked the entrance to our zareba by filling it up with several thorny bushes, and left our camp with the stores entirely surrounded by this protecting hedge. We then slowly and cautiously set forth into the unknown, following the course of the little stream which flowed from our spring, as it should always serve us as a guide on our return.

Hardly had we started when we came across signs that there were indeed wonders awaiting us. After a few hundred yards of thick forest, containing many trees which were quite unknown to me, but which Summerlee, who was the botanist of the party, recognized as forms of conifera and of cycadaceous plants which have long passed away in the world below, we entered a region where the stream widened out and formed a considerable bog. High reeds of a peculiar type grew thickly before us, which were pronounced to be equisetacea, or mare's-tails, with tree-ferns scattered amongst them, all of them swaying in a brisk wind. Suddenly Lord John, who was walking first, halted with uplifted hand.

"Look at this!" said he. "By George, this must be the trail of the father of all birds!"

An enormous three-toed track was imprinted in the soft mud before us. The creature, whatever it was, had crossed the swamp and had passed on into the forest. We all stopped to examine that monstrous spoor. If it were indeed a bird—and what animal could leave such a mark?—its foot was so much larger than an ostrich's that its height upon the same scale must be enormous. Lord John looked eagerly round him and slipped two cartridges into his elephant-gun.

"I'll stake my good name as a shikaree," said he, "that the track is a fresh one. The creature has not passed ten minutes. Look how the water is still oozing into that deeper print! By Jove! See, here is the mark of a little one!"

Sure enough, smaller tracks of the same general form were running parallel to the large ones.

"But what do you make of this?" cried Professor Summerlee, triumphantly, pointing to what looked like the huge print of a five-fingered human hand appearing among the three-toed marks.

"Wealden!" cried Challenger, in an ecstasy. "I've seen them in the Wealden clay. It is a creature walking erect upon three-toed feet, and occasionally putting one of its five-fingered fore-paws upon the ground. Not a bird, my dear Roxton—not a bird."

"A beast?"

"No; a reptile—a dinosaur. Nothing else could have left such a track. They puzzled a worthy Sussex doctor some ninety years ago; but who in the world could have hoped—hoped—to have seen a sight like that?"

His words died away into a whisper, and we all stood in motionless amazement. Following the tracks, we had left the morass and passed through a screen of brushwood and trees. Beyond was an open glade, and in this were five of the most extraordinary creatures that I have ever seen. Crouching down among the bushes, we observed them at our leisure.

There were, as I say, five of them, two being adults and three young ones. In size they were enormous. Even the babies were as big as elephants, while the two large ones were far beyond all creatures I have ever seen. They had slate-colored skin, which was scaled like a lizard's and shimmered where the sun shone upon it. All five were sitting up, balancing themselves upon their broad, powerful tails and their huge three-toed hind-feet, while with their small five-fingered front-feet they pulled down the branches upon which they browsed. I do not know that I can bring their appearance home to you better than by saying that they looked like monstrous kangaroos, twenty feet in length, and with skins like black crocodiles.

I do not know how long we stayed motionless gazing at this marvellous spectacle. A strong wind blew towards us and we were well concealed, so there was no chance of discovery. From time to time the little ones played round their parents in unwieldy gambols, the great beasts bounding into the air and falling with dull thuds upon the earth. The strength of the parents seemed to be limitless, for one of them, having some difficulty in reaching a bunch of foliage which grew upon a considerable-sized tree, put his fore-legs round the trunk and tore it down as if it had been a sapling. The action seemed, as I thought, to show not only the great development of its muscles, but also the small one of its brain, for the whole weight came crashing down upon the top of it, and it uttered a series of shrill yelps to show that, big as it was, there was a limit to what it could endure. The incident made it think, apparently, that the neighborhood was dangerous, for it slowly lurched off through the wood, followed by its mate and its three enormous infants. We saw the shimmering slatey gleam of their skins between the tree-trunks, and their heads undulating high above the brushwood. Then they vanished from our sight.

I looked at my comrades. Lord John was standing at gaze with his finger on the trigger of his elephant-gun, his eager hunter's soul shining from his fierce eyes. What would he not give for one such head to place between the two crossed oars above the mantelpiece in his snuggery at the Albany! And yet his reason held him in, for all our exploration of the wonders of this unknown land depended upon our presence being concealed from its inhabitants.

The two professors were in silent ecstasy. In their excitement they had unconsciously seized each other by the hand, and stood like two little children in the presence of a marvel, Challenger's cheeks bunched up into a seraphic smile, and Summerlee's sardonic face softening for the moment into wonder and reverence.

"*Nunc dimittis!*" he cried at last. "What will they say in England of this?"

"My dear Summerlee, I will tell you with great confidence exactly what they will say in England," said Challenger. "They will say that you are an infernal liar and a scientific charlatan, exactly as you and others said of me."

"In the face of photographs?"

"Faked, Summerlee! Clumsily faked!"

"In the face of specimens?"

"Ah, there we may have them! Malone and his filthy Fleet Street crew may be all yelping our praises yet. August the twenty-eight—the day we saw five live iguanodons in a glade of Maple White Land. Put it down in your diary, my young friend, and send it to your rag."

"And be ready to get the toe-end of the editorial boot in return," said Lord John. "Things look a bit different from the latitude of London, young fellah-my-lad. There's many a man who never tells his adventures for he can't hope to be believed. Who's to blame them? For this will seem a bit of a dream to ourselves in a month or two. *What* did you say they were?"

"Iguanodons," said Summerlee. "You'll find their footmarks all over the Hastings sands, in Kent, and in Sussex. The South of England was alive with them when there was plenty of good lush greenstuff to keep them going. Conditions have changed, and the beasts died. Here it seems that the conditions have not changed, and the beasts have lived."

"If ever we get out of this alive, I must have a head with me," said Lord John. "Lord, how some of that Somaliland-Uganda crowd would turn a beautiful pea-green if they saw it! I don't know what you chaps think, but it strikes me that we are on mighty thin ice all this time."

I had the same feeling of mystery and danger around us. In the gloom of the trees there seemed a constant menace, and as we looked up into their shadowy foliage vague terrors crept into one's heart. It is true that these monstrous creatures which we had seen were lumbering, inoffensive brutes which were unlikely to hurt anyone, but in this world of wonders what other survival might there not be— what fierce, active horrors ready to pounce upon us from their lair among the rocks or brushwood? I knew little of prehistoric life, but I had a clear remembrance of one book which I had read in which it spoke of creatures who would live upon our lions and tigers as a cat lives upon mice. What if these also were to be found in the woods of Maple White Land!

It was destined that on this very morning—our first in the new country—we were to find out what strange hazards lay around us. It was a loathsome adventure, and one of which I hate to think. If, as Lord John said, the glade of the iguanodons will remain with us as a dream, then surely the swamp of the pterodactyls will for ever be our nightmare. Let me set down exactly what occurred.

We passed very slowly through the woods, partly because Lord John acted as scout before he would let us advance, and partly because at every second step one or other of our professors would fall, with a cry of wonder, before some flower or insect which presented him with a new type. We may have traveled two or three miles in all, keeping to the right of the line of the stream, when we came upon a considerable opening in the trees. A belt of brushwood led up to a tangle of rocks—the whole plateau was strewn with boulders. We were walking slowly towards these rocks, among bushes which reached over our waists, when we became aware of a strange low gabbling and whistling sound, which filled the air with a constant clamor and appeared to come from some spot immediately before us. Lord John held up his hand as a signal for us to stop, and he made his way swiftly, stooping and running, to the line of rocks. We saw him peep over them and give a gesture of amazement. Then he stood staring as if forgetting us, so utterly entranced was he by what he saw. Finally he waved us to come on, holding up his hand as a signal for caution. His whole bearing made me feel that something wonderful but dangerous lay before us.

Creeping to his side, we looked over the rocks. The place into which we gazed was a pit, and may, in the early days, have been one of the smaller volcanic blow-holes of the plateau. It was bowl-shaped, and at the bottom, some hundreds of yards from where we lay, were pools of green-scummed stagnant water, fringed with bulrushes. It was a weird place in itself, but its occupants made it seem like a scene from the Seven Circles of Dante. The place was a rookery of pterodactyls. There were hundreds of them congregated within view. All the bottom area round the water-edge was alive with their young ones, and with hideous mothers brooding upon their leathery, yellowish eggs. From this crawling flapping mass of obscene reptilian life came the shocking clamor which filled the air and the mephitic, horrible, musty odor which turned us sick. But above, perched each upon its own stone, tall, grey, and withered, more like dead and dried specimens than actual living creatures, sat the horrible males, absolutely motionless save for the rolling of their red eyes or an occasional snap of their rat-trap beaks as a dragonfly went past them. Their huge, membranous wings were closed by folding their forearms, so that they sat like gigantic old women, wrapped in hideous web-colored shawls, and with their ferocious heads protruding above them. Large and small, not less than a thousand of these filthy creatures lay in the hollow before us.

Our professors would gladly have stayed there all day, so entrances were they by this opportunity of studying the life of a prehistoric age. They pointed out the fish and dead birds lying about among the rocks as proving the nature of the food of these creatures, and I heard them congratulating each other on having cleared up the point why the bones of this flying dragon are found in such great numbers in certain well-defined areas, as in the Cambridge Green-sand, since it was now seen that, like penguins, they lived in gregarious fashion.

Finally, however, Challenger, bent upon proving some point which Summerlee had contested, thrust his head over the rock and nearly brought destruction upon us all. In an instant the nearest male gave a shrill, whistling cry, and flapped its twenty-foot span of leathery wings as it soared up into the air. The females and young ones huddled together beside the water, while the whole circle of sentinels rose one after the other and sailed off into the sky. It was a wonderful sight to see at least a hundred creatures of such enormous size and hideous appearance all swooping like swallows with swift, shearing wing-strokes above us; but soon we realized that it was not one on which we could afford to linger. At first the great brutes flew round in a huge ring, as if to make sure what the exact extent of the danger might be. Then, the flight grew lower and the circle narrower, until they were whizzing round and round us, the dry, rustling flap of their huge slate-colored wings filling the air with a volume of sound that made me think of Hendon aerodrome upon a race day.

"Make for the wood and keep together," cried Lord John, clubbing his rifle. "The brutes mean mischief."

The moment we attempted to retreat the circle closed in upon us, until the tips of the wings of those nearest to us nearly touched our faces. We beat at them with the stocks of our guns, but there was nothing solid or vulnerable to strike. Then suddenly out of the whizing, slate-colored circle a long neck shot out, and a fierce beak made a thrust at us. Another and another followed. Summerlee gave a cry and put his hand to his face, from which the blood was streaming. I felt a prod at the back of my neck, and turned dizzy with the shock. Challenger fell, and as I stooped to pick him up I was again struck from behind and dropped on the top of him. At the same instant I heard the crash of Lord John's elephant-gun, and, looking up, saw one of the creatures with a broken wing struggling upon the ground, spitting and gurgling at us with a wide-opened beak and bloodshot, goggled eyes, like some devil in a mediaeval picture. Its comrades had flown higher at the sudden sound, and were circling above our heads.

"Now," cried Lord John, "now for our lives!"

We staggered through the brushwood, and even as we reached the trees the harpies were on us again. Summerlee was knocked down, but we tore him up and rushed among the trunks. Once there we were safe, for those huge wings had no space for their sweep beneath the branches. As we limped homewards, sadly mauled and discomfited, we saw them for a long time flying at a great height against the deep blue sky above our heads, soaring round and round, no bigger than wood-pigeons, with their eyes no doubt still following our progress. At last, however, as we reached the thicker woods they gave up the chase, and we saw them no more.

"A most interesting and convincing experience," said Challenger, as we halted beside the brook and he bathed a swollen knee. "We are exceptionally well informed, Summerlee, as to the habits of the enraged pterodactyl."

Summerlee was wiping the blood from a cut in his forehead, while I was tying up a nasty stab in the muscle of the neck. Lord John had the shoulder of his coat torn away, but the creature's teeth had only grazed the flesh.

"It is worth noting," Challenger continued, "that our young friend has received an undoubted stab, while Lord John's coat could only have been torn by a bite. In my own case, I was beaten about the head by their wings, so we have had a remarkable exhibition of their various methods of offense."

"It has been touch and go for our lives," said Lord John gravely, "and I could not think of a more rotten sort of death than to be outed by such filthy vermin. I was sorry to fire my rifle, but, by Jove! there was no great choice."

"We should not be here if you hadn't," said I, with conviction.

"It may do no harm," said he. "Among these woods there must be many loud cracks from splitting or falling trees which would be just like the sound of a gun. But now, if you are of my opinion, we have had thrills enough for one day, and had best get back to the surgical box at the camp for some carbolic. Who knows what venom these beasts may have in their hideous jaws?"

But surely no men ever had just such a day since the world began. Some fresh surprise was ever in store for us. When, following the course of our brook, we at last reached our glade and saw the thorny barricade of our camp, we thought that our adventures were at an end. But we had something more to think of before we could rest. The gate of Fort Challenger had been untouched, the walls were unbroken, and yet it had been visited by some strange and powerful creature in our absence. No footmark showed a trace of its nature, and only the overhanging branch of the enormous gingko tree suggested how it might have come and gone; but of its malevolent strength there was ample evidence in the condition of our stores. They were strewn at random all over the ground, and one tin of meat had been crushed into pieces so as to extract the contents. A case of cartridges had been shattered into matchwood, and one of the brass shells lay shredded into pieces beside it. Again the feeling of vague horror came upon our souls, and we gazed round with frightened eyes at the dark shadows which lay around us, in all of which some fearsome shape might be lurking. How good it was when we were hailed by the voice of Zambo, and, going to the edge of the plateau, saw him sitting grinning at us upon the top of the opposite pinnacle.

"All well, Mr. Challenger, all well!" he cried. "Me stay here. No fear. You always find me when you want."

His honest face, and the immense view before us, which carried us half-way back to the affluent of the Amazon, helped us to remember that we really were upon this earth in the twentieth century, and had not by some magic been conveyed to some raw planet in its earliest and wildest state. How difficult it was to realise that the violet line upon the far horizon was well advanced to that great river upon which huge steamers ran, and folk talked of the small affairs of life, while we, marooned among the creatures of a bygone age, could but gaze towards it and yearn for all that it meant!

One other memory remains with me of this wonderful day, and with it I will close this letter. The two professors, their tempers aggravated no doubt by their injuries, had fallen out as to whether our assailants were of the genus pterodactylus or dimorphodon, and high words had ensued. To avoid their wrangling I moved some little way apart, and was seated smoking upon the trunk of a fallen tree, when Lord John strolled over in my direction.

"I say, Malone," said he, "do you remember that place where those beasts were?"

"Very clearly."

"A sort of volcanic pit, was it not?"

"Exactly," said I.

"Did you notice the soil?"

"Rocks."

"But round the water—where the reeds were?"

"It was a bluish soil. It looked like clay."

"Exactly. A volcanic tube full of blue clay."

"What of that?" I asked.

"Oh, nothing, nothing," said he, and strolled back to where the voices of the contending men of science rose in a prolonged duet, the high, strident note of Summerlee rising and falling to the sonorous bass of Challenger. I should have thought no more of Lord John's remark were it not that once again that night I heard him mutter to himself; "Blue clay—clay in a volcanic tube!" They were the last words I heard before I dropped into an exhausted sleep.

11

For Once I Was the Hero

LORD JOHN ROXTON WAS RIGHT WHEN HE THOUGHT THAT some specially toxic quality might lie in the bite of the horrible creatures which had attacked us. On the morning after our first adventure upon the plateau, both Summerlee and I were in great pain and fever, while Challenger's knee was so bruised that he could hardly limp. We kept to our camp all day, therefore. Lord John busying himself, with such help as we could give him, in raising the height and thickness of the thorny walls which were our only defense. I remember that during the whole long day I was haunted by the feeling that we were closely observed, though by whom or whence I could give no guess.

So strong was the impression that I told Professor Challenger of it, who put it down to the cerebral excitement caused by my fever. Again and again I glanced round swiftly, with the conviction that I was about to see something, but only to meet the dark tangle of our hedge or the solemn and cavernous gloom of the great trees which arched above our heads. And yet the feeling grew ever stronger in my own mind that something observant and something malevolent was at our very elbow. I thought of the Indian superstition of the Curupuri—the dreadful, lurking spirit of the woods—and I could have imagined that his terrible presence haunted those who have invaded his most remote and sacred retreat.

That night (our third in Maple White Land) we had an experience which left a fearful impression upon our minds, and made us thankful that Lord John had worked so hard in making our retreat impregnable. We were all sleeping round our dying fire when we were aroused—or, rather, I should say, shot out of our slumber—by a succession of the most frightful cries and screams to which I have ever listened. I know no sound to which I could compare this amazing tumult, which seemed to come from some spot within a few hundred yards of our camp. It was as ear-splitting as any whistle of a railway-engine; but whereas the whistle is a clear, mechanical, sharp-edged sound, this was far deeper in volume and vibrant with the uttermost strain of agony and horror. We clapped our hands to our ears to shut out that never-shaking appeal. A cold sweat broke out over my body, and my heart turned sick at the misery of it. All the woes of tortured life, all its stupendous indictment of high heaven, its innumerable sorrows, seemed to be centered and condensed into that one dreadful, agonized cry. And then, under this high-pitched, ringing sound there was another, more intermittent, a low, deep-chested laugh, a growling, throaty gurgle of merriment which formed a grotesque accompaniment to the shriek with which it was blended. For three or four minutes on end the fearsome duet continued, while all the foliage rustled with the rising of startled birds. Then it shut off as suddenly as it began. For a long time we sat in horrified silence. Then Lord John threw a bundle of twigs upon the fire, and their red glare lit up the intent faces of my companions and flickered over the great boughs above our heads.

"What was it?" I whispered.

"We shall know in the morning," said Lord John. "It was close to us—not farther than the glade."

"We have been privileged to overhear a prehistoric tragedy, the sort of drama which occurred among the reeds upon the border of some Jurassic lagoon, when the greater dragon pinned the lesser among the slime," said Challenger, with more solemnity than I had ever heard in his voice. "It was surely well for man that he came late in the order of creation. There were powers abroad in earlier days which no courage and no mechanism of his could have met. What could his sling, his throwing-stick, or his arrow avail him against such forces as have been loose to-night? Even with a modern rifle it would be all odds on the monster."

"I think I should back my little friend," said Lord John, caressing his Express. "But the beast would certainly have a good sporting chance."

Summerlee raised his hand.

"Hush!" he cried. "Surely I hear something?"

From the utter silence there emerged a deep, regular pat-pat. It was the tread of some animal—the rhythm of soft but heavy pads placed cautiously upon the ground. It stole slowly round the camp, and then halted near our gateway. There was a low, sibilant rise and fall—the breathing of the creature. Only our feeble hedge separated us from this horror of the night. Each of us had seized his rifle, and Lord John had pulled out a small bush to make an embrasure in the hedge.

"By George!" he whispered. "I think I can see it!"

I stooped and peered over his shoulder through the gap.

Yes, I could see it, too. In the deep shadow of the tree there was a deeper shadow yet, black, inchoate, vague—a crouching form full of savage vigor and menace. It was no higher than a horse, but the dim outline suggested vast bulk and strength. That hissing pant, as regular and full-volumed as the exhaust of an engine, spoke of a monstrous organism. Once, as it moved, I thought I saw the glint of two terrible, greenish eyes. There was an uneasy rustling, as if it were crawling slowly forward.

"I believe it is going to spring!" said I, cocking my rifle.

"Don't fire! Don't fire!" whispered Lord John. "The crash of a gun in this silent night would be heard for miles. Keep it as a last card."

"If it gets over the hedge we're done," said Summerlee, and his voice crackled into a nervous laugh as he spoke.

"No, it must not get over," cried Lord John; "but hold your fire to the last. Perhaps I can make something of the fellow. I'll chance it, anyhow."

It was as brave an act as ever I saw a man do. He stooped to the fire, picked up a blazing branch, and slipped in an instant through a sallyport which he had made in our gateway. The thing moved forward with a dreadful snarl, Lord John never hesitated, but, running towards it with a quick, light step, he dashed the flaming wood into the brute's face. For one moment I had a vision of a horrible mask like a giant toad's, of a warty, leprous skin, and of a loose mouth all be-slobbered with fresh blood. The next, there was a crash in the underwood and our dreadful visitor was gone.

"I thought he wouldn't face the fire," said Lord John, laughing, as he came back and threw his branch among the faggots.

"You should not have taken such a risk!" we all cried.

"There was nothing else to be done. If he had got among us we should have shot each other in tryin' to down him. On the other hand, if we had fired through the hedge and wounded him he would soon have been on the top of us—to say nothin' of giving ourselves away. On the whole, I think that we are jolly well out of it. What was he, then?"

Our learned men looked at each other with some hesitation.

"Personally, I am unable to classify the creature with any certainty," said Summerlee, lighting his pipe from the fire.

"In refusing to commit yourself you are but showing a proper scientific reserve," said Challenger, with massive condescension. "I am not myself prepared to go farther than to say in general terms that we have almost certainly been in contact tonight with some form of carnivorous dinosaur. I have already expressed my anticipation that something of the sort might exist upon this plateau."

"We have to bear in mind," remarked Summerlee, "that there are many prehistoric forms which have never come down to us. It would be rash to suppose that we can give a name to all that we are likely to meet."

"Exactly. A rough classification may be the best that we can attempt. Tomorrow some further evidence may help us to an identification. Meantime we can only renew our interrupted slumbers."

"But not without a sentinel," said Lord John, with decision. "We can't afford to take chances in a country like this. Two-hour spells in the future, for each of us."

"Then I'll just finish my pipe in starting the first one," said Professor Summerlee; and from that time onwards we never trusted ourselves again without a watchman.

In the morning it was not long before we discovered the

source of the hideous uproar which had aroused us in the night. The iguanodon glade was the scene of a horrible butchery. From the pools of blood and the enormous lumps of flesh scattered in every direction over the green sward we imagined at first that a number of animals had been killed, but on examining the remains more closely we discovered that all this carnage came from one of these unwieldy monsters, which had been literally torn to pieces by some creature not larger, perhaps, but far more ferocious, than itself.

Our two professors sat in absorbed argument, examining piece after piece, which showed the marks of savage teeth and of enormous claws.

"Our judgment must still be in abeyance," said Professor Challenger, with a huge slab of whitish-colored flesh across his knee. "The indications would be consistent with the presence of a sabre-toothed tiger, such as are still found among the breccia of our caverns; but the creature actually seen was undoubtedly of a larger and more reptilian character. Personally, I should pronounce for allosaurus."

"Or megalosaurus," said Summerlee.

"Exactly. Any one of the larger carnivorous dinosaurs would meet the case. Among them are to be found all the most terrible types of animal-life that have ever cursed the earth or blessed a museum." He laughed sonorously at his own conceit, for, though he had little sense of humor, the crudest pleasantry from his own lips moved him always to roars of appreciation.

"The less noise the better," said Lord John, curtly. "We don't know who or what may be near us. If this fellah comes back for his breakfast and catches us here we won't have so much to laugh at. By the way, what is this mark upon the iguanodon's hide?"

On the dull, scaly, slate-colored skin, somewhere above the shoulder, there was a singular black circle of some substance which looked like asphalt. None of us could suggest what it meant, though Summerlee was of opinion that he had seen something similar upon one of the young ones two days before. Challenger said nothing, but looked pompous and puffy, as if he could if he would, so that finally Lord John asked his opinion direct.

"If your lordship will graciously permit me to open my mouth, I shall be happy to express my sentiments," said he, with elaborate sarcasm. "I am not in the habit of being taken to task in the fashion which seems to be customary with your lordship. I was not aware that it was necessary to ask your permission before smiling at a harmless pleasantry."

It was not until he had received his apology that our touchy friend would suffer himself to be appeased. When at last his ruffled feelings were at ease, he addressed us at some length from his seat upon a fallen tree, speaking, as his habit was, as if he were imparting most precious information to a class of a thousand.

"With regard to the marking," said he, "I am inclined to agree with my friend and colleague, Professor Summerlee, that the stains are from asphalt. As this plateau is, in its very nature, highly volcanic, and as asphalt is a substance which one associates with Plutonic forces, I cannot doubt that it exists in the free liquid state, and that the creatures may have come in contact with it. A much more important problem is the question as to the existence of the carnivorous monster which has left its traces in this glade. We know roughly that this plateau is not larger than an average English county. Within this confined space a certain number of creatures, mostly types which have passed away in the world below, have lived together for innumerable years. Now, it is very clear to me that in so long a period one would have expected that the carnivorous creatures, multiplying unchecked, would have exhausted their food supply and have been compelled to either modify their flesh-eating habits or die of hunger. This we see has not been so. We can only imagine therefore, that the balance of Nature is preserved by some check which limits the numbers of these ferocious creatures. One of the many interesting problems, therefore, which await our solution is to discover what that check may be and how it operates. I venture to trust that we may have some future opportunity for the closer study of the carnivorous dinosaurs."

"And I venture to trust that we may not," I observed.

The Professor only raised his great eyebrows, as the schoolmaster meets the irrelevant observation of the naughty boy.

"Perhaps Professor Summerlee may have an observation to make," he said, and the two *savants* ascended together into some rarified scientific atmosphere, where the possibilities of a modification of the birth-rate were weighed against the decline of the food supply as a check in the struggle for existence.

That morning we mapped out a small portion of the plateau, avoiding the swamp of the pterodactyls, and keeping to the east of our brook instead of to the west. In that direction the country was still thickly wooded, with so much undergrowth that our progress was very slow.

I have dwelt up to now upon the terrors of Maple White Land; but there was another side to the subject, for all that morning we wandered among lovely flowers—mostly, as I observed, white or yellow in color, these being, as our professors explained, the primitive flower-shades. In many places the ground was absolutely covered with them, and as we walked ankle-deep on that wonderful yielding carpet, the scent was almost intoxicating in its sweetness and intensity. The homely English bee buzzed everywhere around us. Many of the trees under which we passed had their branches bowed down with fruit, some of which were of familiar sorts, while other varieties were new. By observing which of them were pecked by the birds we avoided all danger of poison and added a delicious variety to our food reserve. In the jungle which we traversed were numerous hard-trodden paths made by the wild beasts, and in the more marshy places we saw a profusion of strange footmarks, including many of the iguanodon. Once in a grove we observed several of these great creatures grazing, and Lord John, with his glass, was able to report that they also were spotted with asphalt, though in a different place to the one which we had examined in the morning. What this phenomenon meant we could not imagine.

We saw many small animals, such as porcupines, a scaly ant-eater, and a wild pig, piebald in colour and with long curved tusks. Once, through a break in the trees, we saw a clear shoulder of green hill some distance away, and across this a large dun-colored animal was traveling at a considerable pace. It passed so swiftly that we were unable to say what it was; but if it were a deer, as was claimed by Lord John, it must have been as large as those monstrous Irish elks which are still dug up from time to time in the bogs of my native land.

Ever since the mysterious visit which had been paid to our camp we always returned to it with some misgivings. However, on this occasion we found everything in order. That evening we had a grand discussion upon our present situation and future plans, which I must describe at some length as it led to a new departure by which we were enabled to gain a more complete knowledge of Maple White Land than might have come in many weeks of exploring.

It was Summerlee who opened the debate. All day he had been querulous in manner, and now some remark of Lord John's as to what we should do on the morrow brought all his bitterness to a head.

"What we ought to be doing today, tomorrow, and all the time," said he, "is finding some way out of the trap into which we have fallen. You are all turning your brains towards getting into this country. I say that we should be scheming how to get out of it."

"I am surprised, sir," boomed Challenger, stroking his majestic beard, "that any man of science should commit himself to so ignoble a sentiment. You are in a land which offers such an inducement to the ambitious naturalist as none ever has since the world began, and you suggest leaving it before we have acquired more than the most superficial knowledge of it or of its contents. I expected better things of you, Professor Summerlee."

"You must remember," said Summerlee, sourly, "that I have a large class in London who are at present at the mercy of an extremely inefficient *locum tenens*. This makes my situation different from yours, Professor Challenger, since, so far as I know, you have never been entrusted with any responsible educational work."

"Quite so," said Challenger. "I have felt it to be a sacrilege to divert a brain which is capable of the highest original research to any lesser object. That is why I have sternly set my face against any proffered scholastic appointment."

"For example?" asked Summerlee, with a sneer; but Lord John hastened to change the conversation.

"I must say," said he, "that I think it would be a mighty poor thing to go back to London before I know a great deal more of this place than I do at present."

"I could never dare to walk into the back office of my

paper and face old McArdle," said I. (You will excuse the frankness of this report, will you not, sir?) "He'd never forgive me for leaving such unexhausted copy behind me. Besides, so far as I can see, it is not worth discussing, since we can't get down, even if we wanted."

"Our young friend makes up for many obvious mental lacunae by some measure of primitive common sense," remarked Challenger. "The interests of his deplorable profession are immaterial to us; but, as he observes, we cannot get down in any case, so it is a waste of energy to discuss it."

"It is a waste of energy to do anything else," growled Summerlee from behind his pipe. "Let me remind you that we came here upon a perfectly definite mission, entrusted to us at the meeting of the Zoological Institute in London. That mission was to test the truth of Professor Challenger's statements. Those statements, as I am bound to admit, we are now in a position to endorse. Our ostensible work is therefore done. As to the detail which remains to be worked out upon this plateau, it is so enormous that only a large expedition, with a very special equipment, could hope to cope with it. Should we attempt to do so ourselves, the only possible result must be that we shall never return with the important contribution to science which we have already gained. Professor Challenger has devised means for getting us on to this plateau when it appeared to be inaccessible; I think that we should now call upon him to use the same ingenuity in getting us back to the world from which we came."

I confess that as Summerlee stated his view it struck me as altogether reasonable. Even Challenger was affected by the consideration that his enemies would never stand confuted if the confirmation of his statements should never reach those who had doubted them.

"The problem of the descent is at first sight a formidable one," said he, "and yet I cannot doubt that the intellect can solve it. I am prepared to agree with our colleague that a protracted stay in Maple White Land is at present inadvisable, and that the question of our return will soon have to be faced. I absolutely refuse to leave, however, until we have made at least a superficial examination of this country, and are able to take back with us something in the nature of a chart."

Professor Summerlee gave a snort of impatience.

"We have spent two long days in exploration," said he, "and we are no wiser as to the actual geography of the place than when we started. It is clear that it is all thickly wooded, and it would take months to penetrate it and to learn the relations of one part to another. If there were some central peak it would be different, but it all slopes downwards, so far as we can see. The farther we go the less likely it is that we will get any general view."

It was at that moment that I had an inspiration. My eyes chanced to light upon the enormous gnarled trunk of the gingko tree which cast its huge branches over us. Surely, if its bole exceeded that of all the others, its height must do the same. If the rim of the plateau was indeed the highest point, then why should this mighty tree not prove to be a watch-tower which commanded the whole country? Now, ever since I ran wild as a lad in Ireland I have been a bold and skilled tree-climber. My comrades might be masters on the rocks, but I knew that I would be supreme among those branches. Could I only get my legs on to the lowest of the giant off-shoots, then it would be strange indeed if I could not make my way to the top. My comrades were delighted at my idea.

"Our young friend," said Challenger, bunching up the red apples of his cheeks, "is capable of acrobatic exertions which would be impossible to a man of a more solid, though possibly of a more commanding, appearance. I applaud his resolution."

"By George, young fellah, you've put your hand on it!" said Lord John, clapping me on the back. "How we never came to think of it before I can't imagine! There's not more than an hour of daylight left, but if you take your notebook you may be able to get some rough sketch of the place. If we put these three ammunition cases under the branch, I will soon hoist you on to it."

He stood on the boxes while I faced the trunk, and was gently raising me when Challenger sprang forward and gave me such a thrust with his huge hand that he fairly shot me into the tree. With both arms clasping the branch, I scrambled hard with my feet until I had worked, first my body, and then my knees, on to it. There were three excellent off-shoots, like huge rungs of a ladder, above my head, and a tangle of convenient branches beyond, so that I clambered onwards with such speed that I soon lost sight of the ground and had nothing but foliage beneath me. Now and then I encountered a check, and once I had to shin up a creeper for eight or ten feet, but I made excellent progress, and the booming of Challenger's voice seemed to be a great distance beneath me. The tree was, however, enormous, and, looking upwards, I could see no thinning of the leaves above my head There was some thick, bush-like clump which seemed to be a parasite upon a branch up which I was swarming. I leaned my head round it in order to see what was beyond, and I nearly fell out of the tree in my surprise and horror at what I saw.

A face was gazing into mine—at the distance of only a foot or two. The creature that owned it had been crouching behind the parasite, and had looked round it at the same instant that I did. It was a human face—or at least it was far more human than any monkey's that I have ever seen. It was long, whitish, and blotched with pimples, the nose flattened, and the lower jaw projecting, with a bristle of coarse whiskers round the chin. The eyes, which were under thick and heavy brows, were bestial and ferocious, and as it opened its mouth to snarl what sounded like a curse at me I observed that it had curved, sharp canine teeth. For an instant I read hatred and menace in the evil eyes. Then, as quick as a flash, came an expression of overpowering fear. There was a crash of broken boughs as it dived wildly down into the tangle of green. I caught a glimpse of a hairy body like that of a reddish pig, and then it was gone amid a swirl of leaves and branches.

"What's the matter?" shouted Roxton from below. "Anything wrong with you?"

"Did you see it?" I cried with my arms round the branch and all my nerves tingling.

"We heard a row, as if your foot had slipped. What was it?"

I was so shocked at the sudden and strange appearance of this ape-man that I hesitated whether I should not climb down again and tell my experience to my companions. But I was already so far up the great tree that it seemed a humiliation to return without having carried out my mission.

After a long pause therefore, to recover my breath and my courage, I continued my ascent. Once I put my weight upon a rotten branch and swung for a few seconds by my hands, but in the main it was all easy climbing. Gradually the leaves thinned around me, and I was aware, from the wind upon my face, that I had topped all the trees of the forest. I was determined, however, not to look about me before I had reached the very highest point, so I scrambled on until I had got so far that the topmost branch was bending beneath my weight. There I settled into a convenient fork, and, balancing myself securely, I found myself looking down at a most wonderful panorama of this strange country in which we found ourselves.

The sun was just above the western skyline, and the evening was a particularly bright and clear one, so that the whole extent of the plateau was visible beneath me. It was, as seen from this height, of an oval contour, with a breadth of about thirty miles and a width of twenty. Its general shape was that of a shallow funnel, all the sides sloping down to a considerable lake in the center. This lake may have been ten miles in circumference, and lay very green and beautiful in the evening light, with a thick fringe of reeds at its edges, and with its surface broken by several yellow sandbanks, which gleamed golden in the mellow sunshine. A number of long dark objects, which were too large for alligators and too long for canoes, lay upon the edges of these patches of sand. With my glass I could clearly see that they were alive, but what their nature might be I could not imagine.

From the side of the plateau on which we were, slopes of woodland, with occasional glades, stretched down for five or six miles to the central lake. I could see at my very feet the glade of the iguanodons, and farther off was a round opening in the trees which marked the swamp of the pterodactyls. On the side facing me, however, the plateau presented a very different aspect. There the basalt cliffs of the outside were reproduced upon the inside, forming an escarpment about two hundred feet high, with a woody slope beneath it. Along the base of these red cliffs, some distance above the ground, I could see a number of dark holes through the glass, which I conjectured to be the mouths of the caves. At the opening of one of these something white was shimmering, but I was unable to make out what it was. I sat charting the country until the sun had set and it was so dark that I could no longer distinguish details. Then I climbed down to my companions waiting for me so eagerly at the bottom of the great tree. For once I was the hero of the expedition. Alone I had thought of it, and alone I had done it; and here was the chart which would save us a month's blind groping among unknown dangers. Each of them shook me solemnly by the hand. But before they discussed the details of my map I had to tell them of my encounter with the ape-man among the branches.

"He has been there all the time," said I.

"How do you know that?" asked Lord John.

"Because I have never been without that feeling that something malevolent was watching us. I mentioned it to you, Professor Challenger."

"Our young friend certainly said something of the kind. He is also the one among us who is endowed with that Celtic temperament which would make him sensitive to such impressions."

"The whole theory of telepathy—" began Summerlee filling his pipe.

"Is too vast to be now discussed," said Challenger, with decision. "Tell me, now," he added, with the air of a bishop addressing a Sunday school, "did you happen to observe whether the creature could cross its thumb over its palm?"

"No, indeed."

"Had it a tail?"

"No."

"Was the foot prehensile?"

"I do not think it could have made off so fast among the branches if it could not get a grip with its feet."

"In South America there are, if my memory serves me— you will check the observation, Professor Summerlee—

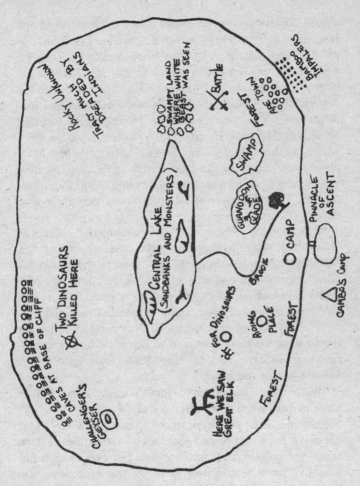

ROUGH CHART OF MAPLE-WHITE LAND

some thirty-six species of monkeys, but the anthropoid ape is unknown. It is clear, however, that he exists in this country, and that he is not the hairy, gorilla-like variety, which is never seen out of Africa or the East." (I was inclined to interpolate, as I looked at him, that I had seen his first cousin in Kensington.) "This is a whiskered and colorless type, the latter characteristic pointing to the fact that he spends his days in arboreal seclusion. The question which we have to face is whether he approaches more closely to the ape or the man. In the latter case, he may well approximate to what the vulgar have called the 'missing link.' The solution of this problem is our immediate duty."

"It is nothing of the sort," said Summerlee, abruptly. "Now that, through the intelligence and activity of Mr. Malone" (I cannot help quoting the words), "we have got our chart, our one and only immediate duty is to get ourselves safe and sound out of this awful place."

"The fleshpots of civilization," groaned Challenger.

"The ink-pots of civilization, sir. It is our task to put on record what we have seen, and to leave the further exploration to others. You all agreed as much before Mr. Malone got us the chart."

"Well," said Challenger, "I admit that my mind will be more at ease when I am assured that the result of our expedition has been conveyed to our friends. How we are to get down from this place I have not as yet an idea. I have never yet encountered any problem, however, which my inventive brain was unable to solve, and I promise you that tomorrow I will turn my attention to the question of our descent."

And so the matter was allowed to rest. But that evening, by the light of the fire and of a single candle, the first map of the lost world was elaborated. Every detail which I had roughly noted from my watchtower was drawn out in its relative place. Challenger's pencil hovered over the great blank which marked the lake.

"What shall we call it?" he asked.

"Why should you not take the chance of perpetuating your own name?" said Summerlee, with his usual touch of acidity.

"I trust, sir, that my name will have other and more personal claims upon posterity," said Challenger, severely. "Any ignoramus can hand down his worthless memory by imposing a mountain or a river. I need no such monument."

Summerlee, with a twisted smile, was about to make some fresh assault when Lord John hastened to intervene.

"It's up to you, young fellah, to name the lake," said he. "You saw it first, and, by George, if you choose to put 'Lake Malone' on it, no one has a better right."

"By all means. Let our young friend give it a name," said Challenger.

"Then," said I, blushing, I dare say, as I said it, "let it be named Lake Gladys."

"Don't you think the Central Lake would be more descriptive?" remarked Summerlee.

"I should prefer Lake Gladys."

Challenger looked at me sympathetically, and shook his great head in mock disapproval. "Boys will be boys," said he. "Lake Gladys let it be."

12

It Was Dreadful in the Forest

I HAVE SAID—OR PERHAPS I HAVE NOT SAID, FOR MY MEMORY plays me sad tricks these days—that I glowed with pride when three such men as my comrades thanked me for having saved, or at least greatly helped, the situation. As the youngster of the party, not merely in years, but in experience, character, knowledge, and all that goes to make a man, I had been overshadowed from the first. And now I was coming into my own. I warmed at the thought. Alas! for the pride which goes before a fall! That little glow of self-satisfaction, that added measure of self-confidence, were to lead me on that very night to the most dreadful experience of my life, ending with a shock which turns my heart sick when I think of it.

It came about in this way. I had been unduly excited by the adventure of the tree, and sleep seemed to be impossible. Summerlee was on guard, sitting hunched over our small fire, a quaint, angular figure, his rifle across his knees and his pointed, goat-like beard wagging with each weary nod of his head. Lord John lay silent, wrapped in the South American poncho which he wore, while Challenger snored with a roll and rattle which reverberated through the woods. The full moon was shining brightly, and the air was crisply cold. What a night for a walk! And then suddenly came the thought, "Why not?" Suppose I stole softly away, suppose I made my way down to the central lake, suppose I was back at breakfast with some record of the place—would I not in that case be thought an even more worthy associate? Then, if Summerlee carried the day and some means of escape were found, we should return to London with firsthand knowledge of the central mystery of the plateau, to which I alone, of all men, would have penetrated. I thought of Gladys, with her "There are heroisms all round us." I seemed to hear her voice as she said it. I thought also of McArdle. What a three-column article for the paper! What a foundation for a career! A correspondentship in the next great war might be within my reach. I clutched at a gun—my pockets were full of cartridges—and, parting the thorn bushes at a gate of our zareba, I quickly slipped out. My last glance showed me the unconscious Summerlee, most futile of sentinels, still nodding away like a queer mechanical toy in front of the smouldering fire.

I had not gone a hundred yards before I deeply repented my rashness. I may have said somewhere in this chronicle that I am too imaginative to be a really courageous man, but that I have an overpowering fear of seeming afraid. This was the power which now carried me onwards. I simply could not sink back with nothing done. Even if my comrades should not have missed me, and should never know of my weakness, there would still remain some intolerable self-shame in my own soul. And yet I shuddered at the position in which I found myself, and would have given all I possessed at that moment to have been honorably free of the whole business.

It was dreadful in the forest. The trees grew so thickly and their foliage spread so widely that I could see nothing of the moonlight save that here and there the high branches made a tangled filigree against the starry sky. As the eyes became more used to the obscurity one learned that there were different degrees of darkness among the trees—that some were dimly visible, while between and among them there were coal-black shadowed patches, like the mouths of caves, from which I shrank in horror as I passed. I thought of the despairing yell of the tortured iguanodon—that dreadful cry which had echoed through the woods. I thought, too, of the glimpse I had in the light of Lord John's torch of that bloated, warty, blood-slavering muzzle. Even now I was on its hunting-ground. At any instant it might spring upon me from the shadows—this nameless and horrible monster. I stopped, and, picking a cartridge from my pocket, I opened the breech of my gun. As I touched the lever my heart leaped within me. It was the shotgun, not the rifle, which I had taken!

Again the impulse to return swept over me. Here, surely, was a most excellent reason for my failure—one for which no one would think the less of me. And again the foolish pride fought against that very word. I could not—must not—fail. After all, my rifle would probably have been as useless as a shotgun against such dangers as I might meet. If I were to go back to camp to change my weapon I could hardly expect to enter and to leave again without being seen. In that case there would be explanations, and my attempt would no longer be all my own. After a little hesitation, then, I screwed up my courage and continued upon my way, my useless gun under my arm.

The darkness of the forest had been alarming, but even

worse was the white, still flood of moonlight in the open glade of iguanodons. Hid among the bushes, I looked out at it. None of the great brutes were in sight. Perhaps the tragedy which had befallen one of them had driven them from their feeding ground. In the misty, silvery night I could see no sign of any living thing. Taking courage, therefore, I slipped rapidly across it, and among the jungle on the farther side I picked up once again the brook which was my guide. It was a cheery companion, gurgling and chuckling as it ran, like the dear old trout stream in the West Country where I have fished at night in my boyhood. So long as I followed it down I must come to the lake, and so long as I followed it back I must come to the camp. Often I had to lose sight of it on account of the tangled brushwood but I was always within earshot of its tinkle and splash.

As one descended the slope the woods became thinner, and bushes, with occasional high trees, took the place of the forest. I could make good progress, therefore, and I could see without being seen. I passed close to the ptero-dactyl swamp, and as I did so, with a dry, crisp, leathery rattle of wings, one of these great creatures—it was twenty feet at least from tip to tip—rose up from somewhere near me and soared into the air. As it passed across the face of the moon the light shone clearly through the membranous wings, and it looked like a flying skeleton against the white, tropical radiance. I crouched low among the bushes, for I knew from past experience that with a single cry the creature could bring a hundred of its loathsome mates about my ears. It was not until it had settled again that I dared to steal onwards upon my journey.

The night had been exceedingly still, but as I advanced I became conscious of a low, rumbling sound, a continuous murmur somewhere in front of me. This grew louder as I proceeded, until at last it was clearly quite close to me. When I stood still the sound was constant, so that it seemed to me to come from some stationary cause. It was like a boiling kettle or the bubbling of some great pot. Soon I came upon the source of it, for in the center of a small clearing I found a lake—or a pool, rather, for it was not larger than the basin of the Trafalgar Square fountain—of some black, pitch-like stuff, the surface of which rose and fell in great blisters of bursting gas. The air above it was shimmering with heat, and the ground round was so hot that I could hardly bear to lay my hand on it. It was clear that the great volcanic outburst which had raised this strange plateau so many years ago had not yet entirely spent its forces. Blackened rocks and mounds of lava I had already seen everywhere peeping out from amid the luxuriant vegetation which draped them, but this asphalt pool in the jungle was the first sign that we had of actual existing activity on the slopes of the ancient crater. I had no time to examine it further, for I had need to hurry if I was to be back in camp in the morning.

It was a fearsome walk, and one which will be with me so long as memory holds. In the great moonlit clearings I slunk along among the shadows on the margin. In the jungle I crept forward, stopping with a beating heart whenever I heard, as I often did, the crash of breaking branches as some wild beast went past. Now and then great shadows loomed up for an instant and were gone—great, silent shadows which seemed to prowl upon padded feet. How often I stopped with the intention of returning, and yet every time my pride conquered my fear, and sent me on again until my object should be attained.

At last (my watch showed that it was one in the morning) I saw the gleam of water amid the openings of the jungle, and ten minutes later I was among the reeds upon the borders of the central lake. I was exceedingly dry, so I lay down and took a long draught of its waters, which were fresh and cold. There was a broad pathway with many tracks upon it at the spot which I had found, so that it was clearly one of the drinking places of the animals. Close to the water's edge there was a huge isolated block of lava. Up this I climbed, and, lying on the top, I had an excellent view in every direction.

The first thing which I saw filled me with amazement. When I described the view from the summit of the great tree, I said that on the farther cliff I could see a number of dark spots, which appeared to be the mouths of caves. Now as I looked up at the same cliffs, I saw discs of light in every direction, ruddy, clearly-defined patches, like the port-holes of a liner in the darkness. For a moment I thought it was the lava-glow from some volcanic action; but this could not be so. Any volcanic action would surely be down in the hollow, and not high among the rocks. What, then, was the alternative? It was wonderful, and yet it must surely be. These ruddy spots must be the reflection of fires within the caves—fires which could only be lit by the hand of man. There were human beings, then, upon the plateau. How gloriously my expedition was justified! Here was news indeed for us to bear back with us to London!

For a long time I lay and watched these red, quivering blotches of light. I suppose they were ten miles off from me, yet even at that distance one could observe how, from time to time, they twinkled or were obscured as someone passed before them. What would I not have given to be able to crawl up to them, to peep in, and to take back some word to my comrades as to the appearance and character of the race who lived in so strange a place! It was out of the question for the moment, and yet surely we could not leave the plateau until we had some definite knowledge upon the point.

Lake Gladys—my own lake—lay like a sheet of quicksilver before me, with a reflected moon shining brightly in the center of it. It was shallow, for in many places I saw low sandbanks protruding above the water. Everywhere upon the still surface I could see signs of life, sometimes mere rings and ripples in the water, sometimes the gleam of a great silver-sided fish in the air, sometimes the arched, slate-colored back of some passing monster. Once upon a yellow sandbank I saw a creature like a huge swan, with a clumsy body and a high, flexible neck, shuffling about upon the margin. Presently it plunged in, and for some time I could see the arched neck and darting head undulating over the water. Then it dived, and I saw it no more.

My attention was soon drawn away from these distant sights and brought back to what was going on at my very feet. Two creatures like large armadillos had come down to the drinking place, and were squatting at the edge of the water, their long, flexible tongues like red ribbons shooting in and out as they lapped. A huge deer, with branching horns, a magnificent creature which carried itself like a king, came down with its doe and two fawns and drank beside the armadillos. No such deer exists anywhere else upon earth, for the moose or elks which I have seen would hardly have reached its shoulders. Presently it gave a warning snort and was off with its family among the reeds, while the armadillos also scuttled for shelter. A newcomer, a most monstrous animal, was coming down the path.

For a moment I wondered where I could have seen that ungainly shape, that arched back with triangular fringes along it, that strange bird-like head held close to the ground. Then it came back to me. It was the stegosaurus—the very creature which Maple White had preserved in his sketch-book, and which had been the first object which arrested the attention of Challenger! There he was—perhaps the very specimen which the American artist had encountered. The ground shook beneath his tremendous weight, and his gulpings of water resounded through the still night. For five minutes he was so close to my rock that by stretching out my hand I could have touched the hideous waving hackles upon his back. Then he lumbered away and was lost among the boulders.

Looking at my watch, I saw that it was half-past two o'clock, and high time, therefore, that I started upon my homeward journey. There was no difficulty about the direction in which I should return, for all along I had kept the little brook upon my left, and it opened to the lake within a stone's-throw of the boulder upon which I had been lying. I set off, therefore, in high spirits, for I felt that I had done good work and was bringing back a fine budget of news for my companions. Foremost of all, of course, were the sight of the fiery caves and the certainty that some troglodytic race inhabited them. But besides that I could speak from experience of the central lake. I could testify that it was full of strange creatures, and I had seen several land forms of primeval life which we had not before encountered. I reflected as I walked that few men in the world could have spent a stranger night or added more to human knowledge in the course of it.

I was plodding up the slope, turning these thoughts over in my mind, and had reached a point which may have been halfway to home, when my mind was brought back to my own position by a strange noise behind me. It was something between a snore and a growl, low, deep, and exceedingly menacing. Some strange creature was evidently near me, but nothing could be seen, so I hastened more rapidly upon my way. I had traversed half a mile or so when suddenly the sound was repeated, still behind me, but louder and more menacing than before. My heart stood still within me as it flashed across me that the beast, whatever it was, must surely be after *me*. My skin grew cold and my hair rose at the thought. That these monsters should tear each other to pieces was a part of the strange struggle for existence, but that they should turn upon modern man, that they should deliberately track and hunt down the predominant human, was a staggering and fearsome thought. I remembered again the blood-slobbered face which we had seen in the glare of Lord John's torch, like some horrible vision from the deepest circle of Dante's hell. With my knees shaking beneath me, I stood and glared with starting eyes down the moonlit path which lay behind me. All was quiet as in a dream landscape. Silver clearings and the black patches of the bushes—nothing else could I see. Then from out of the silence, imminent and threatening, there came once more that low, throaty croaking, far louder and closer than before. There could no longer be a doubt. Something was on my trail, and was closing in upon me every minute.

I stood like a man paralyzed, still staring at the ground which I had traversed. Then suddenly I saw it. There was movement among the bushes at the far end of the clearing which I had just traversed. A great dark shadow disengaged itself and hopped out into the clear moonlight. I say "hopped" advisedly, for the beast moved like a kangaroo, springing along in an erect position upon its powerful hind-legs, while its front ones were held bent in front of it. It was of enormous size and power, like an erect elephant, but its movements, in spite of its bulk, were exceedingly alert. For a moment, as I saw its shape, I hoped that it was an iguanodon, which I knew to be harmless, but, ignorant as I was, I soon saw that this was a very different creature. Instead of the gentle, deer-shaped head of the great three-toed leaf-eater, this beast had a broad, squat, toad-like face like that which had alarmed us in our camp. His ferocious cry and the horrible energy of his pursuit both assured me that this was surely one of the great flesh-eating dinosaurs, the most terrible beasts which have ever walked this earth. As the huge brute loped along it dropped forward upon its fore paws and brought its nose to the ground every twenty yards or so. It was smelling out my trail. Sometimes, for an instant, it was at fault. Then it would catch it up again and come bounding swiftly along the path I had taken.

Even now when I think of that nightmare the sweat breaks out upon my brow. What could I do? My useless fowling-piece was in my hand. What help could I get from that? I looked desperately round for some rock or tree, but I was in a bushy jungle with nothing higher than a sapling within sight, while I knew that the creature behind me could tear down an ordinary tree as though it were a reed. My only possible chance lay in flight. I could not move swiftly over the rough, broken ground, but as I looked round me in despair I saw a well-marked, hard-beaten path which ran across in front of me. We had seen several of the sort, the runs of various wild beasts, during our expeditions. Along this I could perhaps hold my own, for I was a fast runner, and in excellent condition. Flinging away my useless gun, I set myself to do such a half mile as I have never done before or since. My limbs ached, my chest heaved, I felt that my throat would burst for want of air, and yet with that horror behind me I ran and ran and ran. At last I paused, hardly able to move. For a moment I thought that I had thrown him off. The path lay still behind me. And then suddenly, with a crashing and a rending, a thudding of giant feet and a panting of monster lungs, the beast was upon me once more. He was at my very heels. I was lost.

Madman that I was to linger so long before I fled! Up to then he had hunted by scent, and his movement was slow. But he had actually seen me as I started to run. From then onwards he had hunted by sight, for the path showed him where I had gone. Now, as he came round the curve, he was springing in great bounds. The moonlight shone upon his huge projecting eyes, the row of enormous teeth in his open mouth, and the gleaming fringe of claws upon his short, powerful forearms. With a scream of terror, I turned and rushed wildly down the path. Behind me the thick, gasping breathing of the creature sounded louder and louder. His heavy footfall was beside me. Every instant I expected to feel his grip upon my back. And then suddenly there was a crash—I was falling through space, and everything beyond was darkness and rest.

As I emerged from my unconsciousness—which could not, I think, have lasted more than a few minutes—I was aware of a most dreadful and penetrating smell. Putting out my hand in the darkness I came upon something which felt like a huge lump of meat, while my other hand closed upon a large bone. Up above me there was a circle of starlit sky, which showed me that I was lying at the bottom of a deep pit. Slowly I staggered to my feet and felt myself all over. I was stiff and sore from head to foot, but there was no limb which would not move, no joint which would not bend. As the circumstances of my fall came back into my confused brain, I looked up in terror, expecting to see that dreadful head silhouetted against the paling sky. There was no sign of the monster, however, nor could I hear any sound from above. I began to walk slowly round, therefore, feeling in every direction to find out what this strange place could be into which I had been so opportunely precipitated.

It was, as I have said, a pit, with sharply-sloping walls and a level bottom about twenty feet across. This bottom was littered with great gobbets of flesh, most of which was in the last state of putridity. The atmosphere was poisonous and horrible. After tripping and stumbling over these lumps of decay, I came suddenly against something hard, and I found that an upright post was firmly fixed in the centre of the hollow. It was so high that I could not reach the top of it with my hand, and it appeared to be covered with grease.

Suddenly I remembered that I had a tin box of wax-vestas in my pocket. Striking one of them, I was able at last to form some opinion of this place into which I had fallen. There could be no question as to its nature. It was a trap—made by the hand of man. The post in the center, some nine feet long, was sharpened at the upper end, and was black with the stale blood of the creatures who had been impaled upon it. The remains scattered about were fragments of the victims, which had been cut away in order to clear the stake for the next who might blunder in. I remembered that Challenger had declared that man could not exist upon the plateau, since with his feeble weapons he could not hold its own against the monsters who roamed over it. But now it was clear enough how it could be done. In their narrow-mouthed caves the natives, whoever they might be, had refuges into which the huge saurians could not penetrate, while with their developed brains they were capable of setting such traps, covered with branches, across the paths which marked the run of the animals as would destroy them in spite of all their strength and activity. Man was always the master.

The sloping wall of the pit was not difficult for an active man to climb, but I hesitated long before I trusted myself within reach of the dreadful creature which had so nearly destroyed me. How did I know that he was not lurking in the nearest clump of bushes, waiting for my reappearance? I took heart, however, as I recalled a conversation between Challenger and Summerlee upon the habits of the great saurians. Both were agreed that the monsters were practically brainless, that there was no room for reason in their tiny cranial cavities, and that if they have disappeared from the rest of the world it was assuredly on account of their own stupidity, which made it impossible for them to adapt themselves to changing conditions.

To lie in wait for me now would mean that the creature had appreciated what had happened to me, and this in turn would argue some power connecting cause and effect. Surely it was more likely that a brainless creature, acting solely by vague predatory instinct, would give up the chase when I disappeared, and, after a pause of astonishment, would wander away in search of some other prey? I clambered to the edge of the pit and looked over. The stars were fading, the sky was whitening, and the cold wind of morning blew pleasantly upon my face. I could see or hear nothing of my enemy. Slowly I climbed out and sat for a while upon the ground, ready to spring back into my refuge if any danger should appear. Then, reassured by the absolute stillness and by the growing light, I took my courage in both hands and stole back along the path which I had come. Some distance down it I picked up my gun, and shortly afterwards struck the brook which was my guide. So, with many a frightened backward glance, I made for home.

And suddenly there came something to remind me of my absent companions. In the clear, still morning air there sounded far away the sharp, hard note of a rifle-shot. I paused and listened, but there was nothing more. For a moment I was shocked at the thought that some sudden danger might have befallen them. But then a simpler and more natural explanation came to my mind. It was now broad daylight. They had imagined that I was lost in the woods, and had fired this shot to guide me home. It is true that we had made a strict resolution against firing, but if it seemed to them that I might be in danger they would not hesitate. It was for me now to hurry on as fast as possible, and so to reassure them.

I was weary and spent, so my progress was not as fast as I wished; but at last I came into regions which I knew. There was the swamp of the pterodactyls upon my left; there in front of me was the glade of the iguanodons. Now I was in the last belt of trees which separated me from Fort Challenger. I raised my voice in a cheery shout to allay their fears. My heart sank at that ominous stillness. I quickened my pace into a run. The zareba rose before me, even as I had left it, but the gate was open. I rushed in. In the cold morning light it was a fearful sight which met my eyes. Our effects were scattered in wild confusion over the ground; my comrades had disappeared, and close to the smoldering ashes of our fire the grass was stained crimson with a hideous pool of blood.

I was so stunned by this sudden shock that for a time I must have nearly lost my reason. I have a vague recollection, as one remembers a bad dream, of rushing about through the woods all round the empty camp, calling wildly for my companions. No answer came back from the silent shadows. The horrible thought that I might never see them again, that I might find myself abandoned all alone in that dreadful place, with no possible way of descending into the world below, that I might live and die in that nightmare country, drove me to desperation. I could have torn my hair and beaten my head in my despair. Only now did I realize how I had learned to lean upon my companions, upon the serene self-confidence of Challenger, and upon the masterful, humorous coolness of Lord Roxton. Without them I was like a child in the dark, helpless and powerless. I did not know which way to turn or what I should do first.

After a period, during which I sat in bewilderment, I set myself to try and discover what sudden misfortune could have befallen my companions. The whole disordered appearance of the camp showed that there had been some sort of attack, and the rifle shot no doubt marked the time when it had occurred. That there should have been only one shot showed that it had been all over in an instant. The rifles still lay upon the ground, and one of them—Lord John's—had the empty cartridge in the breech. The blankets of Challenger and of Summerlee beside the fire suggested that they had been asleep at the time. The cases of ammunition and of food were scattered about in a wild litter, together with our unfortunate cameras and plate-carriers, but none of them were missing. On the other hand, all the exposed provisions—and I remembered that there were a considerable quantity of them—were gone. They were animals, then, and not natives, who had made the inroad, for surely the latter would have left nothing behind.

But if animals, or some single terrible animal, then what had become of my comrades? A ferocious beast would surely have destroyed them and left their remains. It is true that there was that one hideous pool of blood, which told of violence. Such a monster as had pursued me during the night could have carried away a victim as easily as a cat could a mouse. In that case the others would have followed in pursuit. But then they would assuredly have taken their rifles with them. The more I tried to think it out with my confused and weary brain the less could I find any plausible explanation. I searched round in the forest, but could see no tracks which could help me to a conclusion. Once I lost myself, and it was only by good luck, and after an hour of wondering, that I found the camp once more.

Suddenly a thought came to me and brought some little comfort to my heart. I was not absolutely alone in the world. Down at the bottom of the cliff, and within call of me, was waiting the faithful Zambo. I went to the edge of the plateau and looked over. Sure enough, he was squatting among his blankets beside his fire in his little camp. But, to my amazement, a second man was seated in front of him. For an instant my heart leaped for joy, as I thought that one of my comrades had made his way safely down. But a second glance dispelled the hope. The rising sun shone red upon the man's skin. He was an Indian. I shouted loudly and waved my handkerchief. Presently Zambo looked up, waved his hand, and turned to ascend the pinnacle. In a short time he was standing close to me and listening with deep distress to the story which I told him.

"Devil got them sure, Mr. Malone," said he. "You got into the devil's country, sah, and he take you all to himself. You take advice, Mr. Malone, and come down quick, else he get you as well."

"How can I come down, Zambo?"

"You get creepers from trees, Mr. Malone. Throw them over here. I make fast to this stump, and so you have bridge."

"We have thought of that. There are no creepers here which could bear us."

"Send for ropes, Mr. Malone."

"Who can I send, and where?"

"Send to Indian village, sah. Plenty hide-rope in Indian village. Indian down below; send him."

"Who is he?"

"One of our Indians. Other ones beat him and take away his pay. He come back to us. Ready now to take letter, bring rope—anything."

To take a letter! Why not? Perhaps he might bring help; but in any case he would ensure that our lives were not spent for nothing, and that news of all that we had won for Science should reach our friends at home. I had two completed letters already waiting. I would spend the day in writing a third, which would bring my experiences absolutely up to date. The Indian could bear this back tot he world. I ordered Zambo, therefore, to come again in the evening, and I spent my miserable and lonely day in recording my own adventures of the night before. I also drew up a note, to be given to any white merchant or captain of a steamboat whom the Indian could find, imploring them to see that ropes were sent to us, since our lives must depend upon it. These documents I threw to Zambo in the evening, and also my purse, which contained three English sovereigns. These were to be given to the Indian, and he was promised twice as much if he returned with the ropes.

So now you will understand, my dear Mr. McArdle, how this communication reaches you, and you will also know the truth, in case you never hear again from your unfortunate correspondent. Tonight I am too weary and too depressed to make my plans. Tomorrow I must think out some way by which I shall keep in touch with this camp, and yet search round for any traces of my unhappy friends.

13

A Sight I Shall Never Forget

JUST AS THE SUN WAS SETTING UPON THAT MELANCHOLY NIGHT
I saw the lonely figure of the Indian upon the vast plain
beneath me, and I watched him, our one faint hope of sal-
vation, until he disappeared in the rising mists of evening
which lay, rose-tinted from the setting sun, between the
far-off river and me.

It was quite dark when I at last turned back to our
stricken camp, and my last vision as I went was the red
gleam of Zambo's fire, the one point of light in the wide
world below, as was his faithful presence in my own shadowed soul. And yet I felt happier than I had done since
this crushing blow had fallen upon me, for it was good to
think that the world should know what we had done, so
that at the worst our names should not perish with our
bodies, but should go down to posterity associated with
the result of our labors.

It was an awesome thing to sleep in that ill-fated camp;
and yet it was even more unnerving to do so in the jungle.
One or the other it must be. Prudence, on the one hand,

warned me that I should remain on guard, but exhausted Nature, on the other, declared that I should do nothing of the kind. I climbed up on to a limb of the great gingko tree, but there was no secure perch on its rounded surface, and I should certainly have fallen off and broken my neck the moment I began to doze. I got down, therefore, and pondered over what I should do. Finally, I closed the door of the zareba, lit three separate fires in a triangle, and having eaten a hearty supper dropped off into a profound sleep, from which I had a strange and most welcome awakening. In the early morning, just as day was breaking, a hand was laid upon my arm, and starting up, with all my nerves in a tingle and my hand feeling for a rifle, I gave a cry of joy as in the cold grey light I saw Lord John kneeling beside me.

It was he—and yet it was not he. I had left him calm in his bearing, correct in his person, prim in his dress. Now he was pale and wild-eyed, gasping as he breathed like one who has run far and fast. His gaunt face was scratched and bloody, his clothes were hanging in rags, and his hat was gone. I stared in amazement, but he gave me no chance for questions. He was grabbing at our stores all the time he spoke.

"Quick, young fellah! Quick!" he cried. "Every moment counts. Get the rifles, both of them. I have the other two. Now, all the cartridges you can gather. Fill up your pockets. Now, some food. Half a dozen tins will do. That's all right! Don't wait to talk or think. Get a move on, or we are done!"

Still half-awake, and unable to imagine what it all might mean, I found myself hurrying madly after him through the wood, a rifle under each arm and a pile of various stores in my hands. He dodged in and out through the thickest of the scrub until he came to a dense clump of brushwood. Into this he rushed, regardless of thorns, and threw himself into the heart of it, pulling me down by his side.

"There!" he panted. "I think we are safe here. They'll make for the camp as sure as fate. It will be their first idea. But this should puzzle 'em."

"What is it all?" I asked, when I had got my breath. "Where are the professors? And who is it that is after us?"

"The ape-men," he cried. "My God, what brutes! Don't raise your voice, for they have long ears—sharp eyes, too, but no power of scent, so far as I could judge, so I don't think they can sniff us out. Where have you been, young fellah? You were well out of it."

In a few sentences I whispered what I had done.

"Pretty bad," said he, when he had heard of the dinosaur and the pit. "It isn't quite the place for a rest cure. What? But I had no idea what its possibilities were until those devils got hold of us. The man-eatin' Papuans had me once, but they are Chesterfields compared to this crowd."

"How did it happen?" I asked.

"It was in the early mornin'." Our learned friends were just stirrin'. Hadn't even begun to argue yet. Suddenly it rained apes. They came down thick as apples out of a tree. They had been assemblin' in the dark, I suppose, until that great tree over our heads was heavy with them. I shot one of them through the belly, but before we knew where we were they had us spread-eagled on our backs. I call them apes, but they carried sticks and stones in their hands and jabbered talk to each other, and ended up by tyin' our hands with creepers, so they are ahead of any beast that I have seen in my wanderin's. Ape-men—that's what they are—Missin' Links, and I wished they had stayed missin.' They carried off their wounded comrade—he was bleedin' like a pig—and then they sat around us, and if ever I saw frozen murder it was in their faces. They were big fellows, as big as a man and a deal stronger. Curious glassy grey eyes they have, under red tufts, and they just sat and gloated and gloated. Challenger is no chicken, but even he was cowed. He managed to struggle on to his feet, and yelled out at them to have done with it and get it over. I think he had gone a bit off his head at the suddenness of it; for he raged and cursed at them like a lunatic. If they had been a row of his favorite Pressmen he could not have slanged them worse."

"Well, what did they do?" I was enthralled by the strange story which my companion was whispering into my ear, while all the time his keen eyes were shooting in every direction and his hand grasping his cocked rifle.

"I thought it was the end of us, but instead of that it started them on a new line. They all jabbered and chattered together. Then one of them stood out beside Challenger. You'll smile, young fellah, but 'pon my word they might have been kinsmen. I couldn't have believed it if I hadn't seen it with my own eyes. This old ape-man—he was their chief—was a sort of red Challenger, with every one of our friend's beauty points, only just a trifle more so. He had the short body, the big shoulders, the round chest, no neck, a great ruddy frill of a beard, the tufted eyebrows, the 'What do *you* want, damn you!' look about the eyes, and the whole catalog. When the ape-man stood by Challenger and put his paw on his shoulder, the thing was complete. Summerlee was a bit hysterical, and he laughed till he cried. The ape-men laughed too—or at least they put up the devil of a cacklin'—and then they set to work to drag us off through the forest. They wouldn't touch the guns and things—thought them dangerous, I expect—but they carried away all our loose food. Summerlee and I got some rough handlin' on the way—

there's my skin and my clothes to prove it—for they took us a bee-line through the brambles, and their own hides are like leather. But Challenger was all right. Four of them carried him shoulder high, and he went like a Roman emperor. What's that?"

It was a strange clicking noise in the distance, not unlike castanets.

"There they go!" said my companion, slipping cartridges into the second double-barrelled "Express." "Load them all up, young fellah-my-lad, for we're not going to be taken alive, and don't you think it! That's the row they make when they are excited. By George! they'll have something to excite them if the put us up. The 'Last Stand of the Greys' won't be in it. 'With their rifles grasped in their stiffened hands, 'mid a ring of the dead and dyin',' as some fathead sings. Can you hear them now?"

"Very far away."

"That little lot will do no good, but I expect their search parties are all over the wood. Well, I was tellin' you my tale of woe. They got us soon to this town of theirs—about a thousand huts of branches and leaves in a great grove of trees near the edge of the cliff. It's three or four miles from here. The filthy beasts fingered me all over, and I feel as if I should never be clean again. They tied us up—the fellow who handled me could tie like a bo'sun—and there we lay with our toes up, beneath a tree, while a great brute stood guard over us with a club in his hand. When I say 'we' I mean Summerlee and myself. Old Challenger was up a tree, eatin' pines and havin' the time of his life. I'm bound to say that he managed to get some fruit to us, and with his own hands he loosened our bonds. If you'd seen him sittin' up in that tree hob-nobbin' with his twin brother—and singin' in that rollin' bass of his, 'Ring out wild bells,' 'cause music of any kind seemed to put 'em in a good humor, you'd have smiled; but we weren't in much mood for laughin', as you guess. They were inclined, within limits, to let him do what he liked, but they drew the line pretty sharply at us. It was a mighty consolation to us all to know that you were runnin' loose and had the archives in your keepin'.'

"Well now, young fellah, I'll tell you what will surprise you. You say you saw signs of men, and fires, traps, and the like. Well, we have seen the natives themselves. Poor devils they were, down-faced little chaps, and had enough to make them so. It seems that the humans hold one side of this plateau—over yonder, where you saw the caves—and the ape-men hold this side, and there is bloody war between them all the time. That's the situation, so far as I could follow it. Well, yesterday the ape-men got hold of a dozen of the humans and brought them in as prisoners. You never heard such a jabberin' and shriekin' in your life. The men were little red fellows, and had been bitten and clawed so that they could hardly walk. The ape-men put two of them to death there and then—fairly pulled the arm off one of them—it was perfectly beastly. Plucky little chaps they are, and hardly gave a squeak. But it turned us absolutely sick. Summerlee fainted, and even Challenger had as much as he could stand. I think they have cleared, don't you?"

We listened intently, but nothing save the calling of the birds broke the deep peace of the forest. Lord John went on with his story.

"I think you have had the escape of your life, young fellah-my-lad. It was catchin' those Indians that put *you* clean out of their heads, else they would have been back to the camp for you as sure as fate and gathered you in. Of course, as you said, they have been watchin' us from the beginnin' out of that tree, and they knew perfectly well that we were one short. However, they could think only of this new haul; so it was I, and not a bunch of apes, that dropped in on you in the morning. Well, we had a horrid business afterwards. My God! what a nightmare the whole thing is! You remember the great bristle of sharp canes down below where we found the skeleton of the American? Well, that is just under ape-town, and that's the jumpin'-off place of their prisoners. I expect there's heaps of skeletons there, if we looked for 'em. They have a sort of clear parade ground on the top, and they make a proper ceremony about it. One by one the poor devils have to jump, and the game is to see whether they are merely dashed to pieces or whether they get skewered on the canes. They took us out to see it, and the whole tribe lined up on the edge. Four of the Indians jumped, and the canes went through 'em like knitting needles through a pat of butter. No wonder we found that poor Yankee's skeleton with the canes growin' between his ribs. It was horrible— but it was doocedly interestin' too. We were all fascinated to see them take the dive, even when we thought it would be our turn next on the spring-board.

"Well, it wasn't. They kept six of the Indians up for today—that's how I understood it—but I fancy we were to be the star performers in the show. Challenger might get off, but Summerlee and I were in the bill. Their language is more than half signs, and it was not hard to follow them. So I thought it was time we made a break for it. I had been plottin' it out a bit, and had one or two things clear in my mind. It was all on me, for Summerlee was useless and Challenger not much better. The only time they got together they got slangin,' because they couldn't agree upon the scientific classification of these red-headed devils that had got hold of us. One said it was the dryopithecus of Java, the other said it was pithecanthropus. Madness, I call it—loonies—both. But, as I say, I had thought out one or two points that were helpful. One was that these brutes could not run as fast as a man in the open. They have short, bandy legs, you see, and heavy bodies. Even Challenger could give a few yards in a hundred to the best of them, and you or I would be a perfect Shrubb. Another point was that they knew nothin' about guns. I don't believe they ever understood how the fellow I shot came by his hurt. If we could get at our guns there was no sayin' what we could do.

"So I broke away early this mornin',' gave my guard a kick in the tummy that laid him out, and sprinted for the camp. There I got you and the guns, and here we are."

"But the professors!" I cried, in consternation.

"Well, we must just go back and fetch 'em. I couldn't bring 'em with me. Challenger was up the tree, and Summerlee was not fit for the effort. The only chance was to get the guns and try a rescue. Of course they may scupper them at once in revenge. I don't think they would touch Challenger, but I wouldn't answer for Summerlee. But they would have had him in any case. Of that I am certain. So I haven't made matters any worse by boltin.' But we are honor bound to go back and have them out or see it through with them. So you can make up your soul, young fellah-my-lad, for it will be one way or the other before evenin'."

I have tried to imitate her Lord Roxton's jerky talk, his short, strong sentences, the half-humorous, half-reckless tone that ran through it all. But he was a born leader. As danger thickened his jaunty manner would increase, his speech become more racy, his cold eyes glitter into ardent life, and his Don Quixote moustache bristle with joyous excitement. His love of danger, his intense appreciation of the drama of an adventure—all the more intense for being held tightly in—his consistent view that every peril in life is a form of sport, a fierce game betwixt you and Fate, with Death as a forfeit, made him a wonderful companion at such hours. If it were not for our fears as to the fate of our companions, it would have been a positive joy to throw myself with such a man into such an affair. We were rising from our brushwood hiding-place when suddenly I felt his grip upon my arm.

"By George!" he whispered, "here they come!"

From where we lay we could look down a brown aisle, arched with green, formed by the trunks and branches. Along this a party of the ape-men were passing. They went in single file, with bent legs and rounded backs, their hands occasionally touching the ground, their heads turning to left and right as they trotted along. Their crouching gait took away from their height, but I should put them at five feet or so, with long arms and enormous chests. Many of them carried sticks, and at the distance they looked like a line of very hairy and deformed human beings. For a moment I caught this clear glimpse of them. Then they were lost among the bushes.

"Not this time," said Lord John, who had caught up his rifle. "Our best chance is to lie quiet until they have given up the search. Then we shall see whether we can't get back to their town and hit 'em where it hurts most. Give 'em an hour and we'll march."

We filled in the time by opening one of our food tins and making sure of our breakfast. Lord Roxton had had nothing but some fruit since the morning before and ate like a starving man. Then, at last, our pockets bulging with cartridges and a rifle in each hand, we started off upon our mission of rescue. Before leaving it we carefully marked our little hiding-place among the brushwood and its bearing to Fort Challenger, that we might find it again if we needed it. We slunk through the bushes in silence until we came to the very edge of the cliff, close to the old camp. Then we halted, and Lord John gave me some idea of his plans.

"So long as we are among the thick trees these swine are our masters," said he. "They can see us and we cannot see them. But in the open it is different. There we can move faster than they. So we must stick to the open all we can. The edge of the plateau has fewer large trees than further inland. So that's our line of advance. Go slowly, keep your eyes open and your rifle ready. Above all, never let them get you prisoner while there is a cartridge left—that's my last word to you, young fellah."

When we reached the edge of the cliff I looked over and saw our good Zambo sitting smoking on a rock below us. I would have given a great deal to have hailed him and told him how we were placed, but it was too dangerous, lest we should be heard. The woods seemed to be full of the ape-men; again and again we heard their curious clicking chatter. At such times we plunged into the nearest clump of bushes and lay still until the sound had passed away. Our advance, therefore, was very slow, and two hours at least must have passed before I saw by Lord John's cautious movements that we must be close to our destination. He motioned to me to lie still, and he crawled forward himself. In a minute he was back again, his face quivering with eagerness.

"Come!" said he. "Come quick! I hope to the Lord we are not too late already!"

I found myself shaking with nervous excitement as I scrambled forward and lay down beside him, looking out through the bushes at a clearing which stretched before us.

It was a sight which I shall never forget until my dying days—so weird, so impossible, that I do not know how I am to make you realize it, or how in a few years I shall bring myself to believe in it if I live to sit once more on a lounge in the Savage Club and look out on the drab solidity of the Embankment. I know that it will seem then to be some wild nightmare, some delirium of fever. Yet I will set it down now, while it is still fresh in my memory, and one at least, the man who lay in the damp grasses by my side, will know if I have lied.

A wide, open space lay before us—some hundreds of yards across—all green turf and low bracken growing to the very edge of the cliff. Round this clearing there was a semicircle of trees with curious huts built of foliage piled one above the other among the branches. A rookery, with every nest a little house, would best convey the idea. The openings of these huts and the branches of the trees were thronged with a dense mob of ape-people, whom from their size I took to be the females and infants of the tribe. They formed the background of the picture, and were all looking out with eager interest at the same scene which fascinated and bewildered us.

In the open, and near the edge of the cliff, there had assembled a crowd of some hundred of these shaggy red-haired creatures, many of them of immense size, and all of them horrible to look upon. There was a certain discipline among them, for none of them attempted to break the line which had been formed. In front there stood a small group of Indians—little, clean-limbed, red fellows, whose skins glowed like polished bronze in the strong sunlight. A tall, thin white man was standing beside them, his head bowed, his arms folded, his whole attitude expressive of his horror and dejection. There was no mistaking the angular form of Professor Summerlee.

In front of and around this dejected group of prisoners were several ape-men who watched them closely and made all escape impossible. Then, right out from all the others and close to the edge of the cliff, were two figures, so strange, and under other circumstances so ludicrous, that they absorbed my attention. The one was our comrade, Professor Challenger. The remains of his coat still hung from his shoulders, but his shirt had been all torn out, and his great beard merged itself in the black tangle which covered his mighty chest. He had lost his hat, and his hair, which had grown long in our wanderings, was flying in wild disorder. A single day seemed to have changed him from the highest product of modern civilization to the most desperate savage in South America. Beside him stood his master the king of the ape-men. In all things he was, as Lord John had said, the very image of our Professor, save that his coloring was red instead of black. The same short, broad figure, the same heavy shoulders, the same forward hang of the arms, the same bristling beard merging itself in the hairy chest. Only above the eyebrows, where the sloping forehead and low, curved skull of the ape-man were in sharp contrast to the broad brow and magnificent cranium of the European, could one see any marked difference. At every other point the king was an absurd parody of the Professor.

All this, which takes me so long to describe, impressed itself upon me in a few seconds. Then we had very different things to think of, for an active drama was in progress. Two of the ape-men had seized one of the Indians out of the group and dragged him forward to the edge of the cliff. The king raised his hand as a signal. They caught the man up by his leg and arm, and swung him three times backwards and forwards with tremendous violence. Then, with a frightful heave they shot the poor wretch over the precipice. With such force did they throw him that he curved high in the air before beginning to drop. As he vanished from sight, the whole assembly, except the guards, rushed forward to the edge of the precipice, and there was a long pause of absolute silence, broken by a mad yell of delight. They sprang about, tossing their long, hairy arms in the air and howling with exultation. Then they fell back from the edge, formed themselves again into line, and waited for the next victim.

This time it was Summerlee. Two of his guards caught him by the wrists and pulled him brutally to the front. His thin figure and long limbs struggled and fluttered like a chicken being dragged from a coop. Challenger had turned to the king and waved his hands frantically before him. He was begging, pleading, imploring for his comrade's life. The ape-man pushed him roughly aside and shook his head. It was the last conscious movement he was to make upon earth. Lord John's rifle cracked, and the king sank down, a tangled red sprawling thing, upon the ground.

"Shoot into the thick of them! Shoot! sonny, shoot!" cried my companion.

There are strange red depths in the soul of the most commonplace man. I am tender-hearted by nature, and have found my eyes moist many a time over the scream of a wounded hare. Yet the blood lust was on me now. I found myself on my feet emptying one magazine, then the other, clicking open the breech to re-load, snapping it to again, while cheering and yelling with pure ferocity and joy of slaughter as I did so. With our four guns the two of us made a horrible havoc. Both the guards who held Summerlee were down, and he was staggering about like a drunken man in his amazement, unable to realize that he was a free man. The dense mob of ape-men ran about in bewilderment, marveling whence this storm of death was coming or what it might mean. They waved, gesticulated, screamed, and tripped up over those who had fallen. Then, with a sudden impulse, they all rushed in a howling crowd to the trees for shelter, leaving the ground behind them spotted with their stricken comrades. The prisoners were left for the moment standing alone in the middle of the clearing.

Challenger's quick brain had grasped the situation. He seized the bewildered Summerlee by the arm, and they both ran towards us. Two of their guards bounded after them and fell to two bullets from Lord John. We ran forward into the open to meet our friends, and pressed a loaded rifle into the hands of each. But Summerlee was at the end of his strength. He could hardly totter. Already the ape-men were recovering from their panic. They were coming through the brushwood and threatening to cut us off. Challenger and I ran Summerlee along, one at each of his elbows, while Lord John covered our retreat, firing again and again as savage heads snarled at us out of the bushes. For a mile or more the chattering brutes were at our very heels. Then the pursuit slackened, for they learned our power and would no longer face that unerring rifle. When we had at last reached the camp, we looked back and found ourselves alone.

So it seemed to us; and yet we were mistaken. We had hardly closed the thorn-bush door of our zareba, clasped each other's hands, and thrown ourselves panting upon the ground beside our spring, when we heard a patter of feet and then a gentle, plaintive crying from outside our entrance. Lord Roxton rushed forward, rifle in hand, and threw it open. There, prostrate upon their faces, lay the little red figures of the four surviving Indians, trembling with fear of us and yet imploring our protection. With an expressive sweep of his hands one of them pointed to the woods around them, and indicated that they were full of danger. Then, darting forward, he threw his arms round Lord John's legs and rested his face upon them.

"By George!" cried Lord John, pulling at his moustache in great perplexity, "I say—what the dooce are we to do with these people? Get up, little chappie, and take your face off my boots."

Summerlee was sitting up and stuffing some tobacco into his old briar.

"We've got to see them safe," said he. "You've pulled us all out of the jaws of death. My word! it was a good bit of work!"

"Admirable!" cried Challenger. "Admirable! Not only we as individuals, but European science collectively, owe you a deep debt of gratitude for what you have done. I do not hesitate to say that the disappearance of your Professor Summerlee and myself would have left an appreciable gap in modern zoological history. Our young friend here and you have done most excellently well."

He beamed at us with the old paternal smile, but European science would have been somewhat amazed could they have seen their chosen child, the hope of the future, with his tangled, unkempt head, his bare chest, and his tattered clothes. He had one of the meat tins between his knees, and sat with a large piece of cold Australian mutton between his fingers. The Indian looked up at him, and then, with a little yelp, cringed to the ground and clung to Lord John's leg.

"Don't you be scared, my bonnie boy," said Lord John, patting the matted head in front of him. "He can't stick your appearance, Challenger; and, by George! I don't wonder. All right, little chap, he's only a human, just the same as the rest of us."

"Really, sir!" cried the Professor.

"Well, it's lucky for you, Challenger, that you *are* a little out of the ordinary. If you hadn't been so like the king—"

"Upon my word, Lord John Roxton, you allow yourself great latitude."

"Well, it's a fact."

"I beg, sir, that you will change the subject. Your remarks are irrelevant and unintelligible. The question before us is what are we to do with these Indians? The obvious thing is to escort them home, if we knew where their home was."

"There is no difficulty about that," said I. "They live in the caves on the other side of the central lake."

"Our young friend here knows where they live. I gather that it is some distance."

"A good twenty miles," said I.

Summerlee gave a groan.

"I, for one, could never get there. Surely I hear those brutes still howling upon our track."

As he spoke, from the dark recesses of the woods we heard far away the jibbering cry of the ape-men. The Indians once more set up a feeble wail of fear.

"We must move, and move quick!" said Lord John. "You help Summerlee, young fellah. These Indians will carry stores. Now, then, come along before they can see us."

In less than half an hour we had reached our brushwood retreat and concealed ourselves. All day we heard the excited calling of the ape-men in the direction of our old camp, but none of them came our way, and the tired fugitives, red and white, had a long, deep sleep. I was dozing myself in the evening when someone plucked my sleeve, and I found Challenger kneeling beside me.

"You keep a diary of these events, and you expect eventually to publish it, Mr. Malone," said he, with solemnity.

"I am only here as a Press reporter," I answered.

"Exactly. You may have heard some rather fatuous remarks of Lord John Roxton's which seemed to imply that there was some—some resemblance—"

"Yes, I heard them."

"I need not say that any publicity given to such an idea—any levity in your narrative of what occurred—would be exceedingly offensive to me."

"I will keep well within the truth."

"Lord John's observations are frequently exceedingly fanciful, and he is capable of attributing the most absurd reasons to the respect which is always shown by the most undeveloped races to dignity and character. You follow my meaning?"

"Entirely."

"I leave the matter to your discretion." Then, after a long pause, he added: "The king of the ape-men was really a creature of great distinction—a most remarkably handsome and intelligent personality. Did it not strike you?"

"A most remarkable creature," said I.

And the Professor, much eased in his mind, settled down to his slumber once more.

14

Those Were
the Real Conquests

WE HAD IMAGINED THAT OUR PURSUERS, THE APE-MEN, KNEW nothing of our brushwood hiding place, but we were soon to find out our mistake. There was no sound in the woods—not a leaf moved upon the trees and all was peace around us—but we should have been warned by our first experience how cunningly and how patiently these creatures can watch and wait until their chance comes. Whatever fate may be mine through life, I am very sure that I shall never be nearer death than I was that morning. But I will tell you the thing in its due order.

We all awoke exhausted after the terrific emotions and scanty food of yesterday. Summerlee was still so weak that it was an effort for him to stand; but the old man was full of a sort of surly courage which would never admit defeat. A council was held, and it was agreed that we should wait quietly for an hour or two where we were, have our much-needed breakfast, and then make our way across the plateau and round the central lake to the caves where my observations had shown that the Indians lived. We relied

upon the fact that we could count upon the good word of
those whom we had rescued to ensure a warm welcome
with their fellows. Then, with our mission accomplished
and possessing a fuller knowledge of the secrets of Maple
White Land, we should turn our whole thoughts to the vital problem of our escape and return. Even Challenger was
ready to admit that we should then have done all for which
we had come, and that our first duty from that time onwards was to carry back to civilization the amazing discoveries we had made.

We were able now to take a more leisurely view of the
Indians whom we had rescued. They were small men,
wiry, active, and well-built, with lank black hair tied up in
a bunch behind their heads with a leathern thong, and
leathern also were their loin-cloths. Their faces were hair-
less, well formed, and good-humored. The lobes of their
ears, hanging ragged and bloody, showed that they had
been pierced for some ornaments which their captors had
torn out. Their speech, though unintelligible to us, was flu-
ent among themselves, and as they pointed to each other
and uttered the word "Accala" many times over, we gathered that this was the name of their nation. Occasionally,
with faces which were convulsed with fear and hatred,
they shook their clenched hands at the woods round and
cried: "Doda! Doda!" which was surely their term for their
enemies.

"What do you make of them, Challenger?" asked Lord
John. "One thing is very clear to me, and that is that the
little chap with the front of his head shaved is a chief
among them."

It was indeed evident that this man stood apart from the
others, and that they never ventured to address him without every sign of deep respect. He seemed to be the youn-
gest of them all, and yet, so proud and high was his spirit,

that upon Challenger laying his great hand upon his head he started like a spurred horse and, with a quick flash of his dark eyes, moved further away from the Professor. Then, placing his hand upon his breast and holding himself with great dignity, he uttered the word "Maretas" several times. The Professor, unabashed, seized the nearest Indian by the shoulder and proceeded to lecture upon him as if he were a potted specimen in a class-room.

"The type of these people," said he in his sonorous fashion, "whether judged by cranial capacity, facial angle, or any other test, cannot be regarded as a low one; on the contrary, we must place it as considerably higher in the scale than many South American tribes which I can mention. On no possible supposition can we explain the evolution of such a race in this place. For that matter, so great a gap separates these ape-men from the primitive animals which have survived upon this plateau, that it is inadmissible to think that they could have developed where we find them."

"Then where the dooce did they drop from?" asked Lord John.

"A question which will, no doubt, be eagerly discussed in every scientific society in Europe, and America," the Professor answered. "My own reading of the situation for what it is worth"—he inflated his chest enormously and looked insolently around him at the words—"is that evolution has advanced under the peculiar conditions of this country up to the vertebrate stage, the old types surviving and living on in company with the newer ones. Thus we find such modern creatures as the tapir—an animal with quite a respectable length of pedigree—the great deer, and the anteater in the companionship of reptilian forms of Jurassic type. So much is clear. And now come the ape-men and the Indian. What is the scientific mind to think of their presence? I can only account for it by an invasion from outside. It is probable that there existed an anthropoid ape in South America, who in past ages found his way to this place, and that he developed into the creatures we have seen, some of which"—here he looked hard at me—"were of an appearance and shape which if it had been accompanied by corresponding intelligence, would, I do not hesitate to say, have reflected credit upon any living race. As to the Indians I cannot doubt that they are more recent immigrants from below. Under the stress of famine or of conquest they have made their way up here. Faced by ferocious creatures which they had never before seen, they took refuge in the caves which our young friend has described, but they have no doubt had a bitter fight to hold their own against wild beasts, and especially against the ape-men who would regard them as intruders, and wage a merciless war upon them with a cunning which the larger beasts would lack. Hence the fact that their numbers appear to be limited. Well, gentlemen, have I read you the riddle aright, or is there any point which you would query?"

Professor Summerlee for once was too depressed to argue, though he shook his head violently as a token of general disagreement. Lord John merely scratched his scanty locks with the remark that he couldn't put up a fight as he wasn't in the same weight or class. For my own part I performed my usual *rôle* of bringing things down to a strictly prosaic and practical level by the remark that one of the Indians was missing.

"He has gone to fetch some water," said Lord Roxton. "We fitted him up with an empty beef tin and he is off."

"To the old camp?" I asked.

"No, to the brook. It's among the trees there. It can't be

more than a couple of hundred yards. But the beggar is certainly taking his time."

"I'll go and look after him," said I. I picked up my rifle and strolled in the direction of the brook, leaving my friends to lay out the scanty breakfast. It may seem to you rash that even for so short a distance I should quit the shelter of our friendly thicket, but you will remember that we were many miles from Ape-town, that so far as we knew the creatures had not discovered our retreat, and that in any case with a rifle in my hands I had no fear of them. I had not yet learned their cunning or their strength.

I could hear the murmur of our brook somewhere ahead of me, but there was a tangle of trees and brushwood between me and it. I was making my way through this at a point which was just out of sight of my companions, when, under one of the trees, I noticed something red huddled among the bushes. As I approached it, I was shocked to see that it was the dead body of the missing Indian. He lay upon his side, his limbs drawn up, and his head screwed round at a most unnatural angle, so that he seemed to be looking straight over his own shoulder. I gave a cry to warn my friends that something was amiss, and running forward I stooped over the body. Surely my guardian angel was very near to me then, for some instinct of fear, or it may have been some faint rustle of leaves, made me glance upwards. Out of the thick green foliage which hung low over my head, two long muscular arms covered with reddish hair were slowly descending. Another instant and the great stealthy hands would have been round my throat. I sprang backwards, but quick as I was, those hands were quicker still. Through my sudden spring they missed a fatal grip, but one of them caught the back of my neck and the other my face. I threw my hands up to protect my throat, and the next moment the huge paw had slid down my face and closed over them. I was lifted lightly from the ground, and I felt an intolerable pressure forcing my head back and back until the strain upon the cervical spine was more than I could bear. My senses swam, but I still tore at the hand and forced it out from my chin. Looking up I saw a frightful face with cold inexorable light blue eyes looking down into mine. There was something hypnotic in those terrible eyes. I could struggle no longer. As the creature felt me grow limp in his grasp, two white canines gleamed for a moment at each side of the vile mouth, and the grip tightened still more upon my chin, forcing it always upwards and back. A thin, opal-tinted mist formed before my eyes and little silvery bells tinkled in my ears. Dully and far off I heard the crack of a rifle and was feebly aware of the shock as I was dropped to the earth, where I lay without sense or motion.

I awoke to find myself on my back upon the grass in our lair within the thicket. Someone had brought the water from the brook, and Lord John was sprinkling my head with it, while Challenger and Summerlee were propping me up, with concern in their faces. For a moment I had a glimpse of the human spirits behind their scientific masks. It was really shock, rather than any injury, which had prostrated me, and in half an hour, in spite of aching head and stiff neck, I was sitting up and ready for anything.

"But you've had the escape of your life, young fellah-my-lad," said Lord John. "When I heard your cry and ran forward, and saw your head twisted half-off and your stoh-wassers kickin' in the air, I thought we were one short. I missed the beast in my flurry, but he dropped you all right and was off like a streak. By George! I wish I had fifty men with rifles. I'd clear out the whole infernal gang of them and leave this country a bit cleaner than we found it."

It was clear now that the ape-men had in some way marked us down, and that we were watched on every side. We had not so much to fear from them during the day, but they would be very likely to rush us by night; so the sooner we got away from their neighborhood the better. On three sides of us was absolute forest, and there we might find ourselves in an ambush. But on the fourth side—that which sloped down in the direction of the lake—there was only low scrub, with scattered trees and occasional open glades. It was, in fact, the route which I had myself taken in my solitary journey, and it led us straight for the Indian caves. This then must for every reason be our road.

One great regret we had, and that was to leave our old camp behind us, not only for the sake of the stores which remained there, but even more because we were losing touch with Zambo, our link with the outside world. However, we had a fair supply of cartridges and all our guns, so, for a time at least, we could look after ourselves, and we hoped soon to have a chance of returning and restoring our communications with Zambo. He had faithfully promised to stay where he was, and we had not a doubt that he would be as good as his word.

It was in the early afternoon that we started upon our journey. The young chief walked at our head as our guide, but refused indignantly to carry any burden. Behind him came the two surviving Indians with our scanty possession upon their backs. We four white men walked in the rear with rifles loaded and ready. As we started there broke from the thick silent woods behind us a sudden great ululation of the ape-men, which may have been a cheer of triumph at our departure or a jeer of contempt at our flight. Looking back we saw only the dense screen of trees, but that long-drawn yell told us how many of our enemies lurked among them. We saw no sign of pursuit, however, and soon we had got into more open country and beyond their power.

As I tramped along, the rearmost of the four, I could not help smiling at the appearance of my three companions in front. Was this the luxurious Lord John Roxton who had sat that evening in the Albany amidst his Persian rugs and his pictures in the pink radiance of the tinted lights? And was this the imposing Professor who had swelled behind the great desk in his massive study at Enmore Park? and finally, could this be the austere and prim figure which had risen before the meeting at the Zoological Institute? No three tramps that one could have met in a Surrey lane could have looked more hopeless and bedraggled. We had, it is true, been only a week or so upon the top of the plateau, but all our spare clothing was in our camp below, and the one week had been a severe one upon us all, though least to me who had not to endure the handling of the ape-men. My three friends had all lost their hats, and had not bound handkerchiefs round their heads, their clothes hung in ribbons about them, and their unshaven grimy faces were hardly to be recognized. Both Summerlee and Challenger were limping heavily, while I still dragged my feet from weakness after the shock of the morning, and my neck was as stiff as a board from the murderous grip that held it. We were indeed a sorry crew, and I did not wonder to see our Indian companions glance back at us occasionally with horror and amazement on their faces.

In the late afternoon we reached the margin of the lake, and as we emerged from the bush and saw the sheet of water stretching before us our native friends set up a shrill cry of joy and pointed eagerly in front of them. It was indeed a wonderful sight which lay before us. Sweeping over the glassy surface was a great flotilla of canoes coming straight for the shore upon which we stood. They were some miles out when first we saw them, but they shot forward with great swiftness, and were soon so near that the rowers could distinguish our persons. Instantly a thunderous shout of delight burst from them, and we saw them rise from their seats, waving their paddles and spears madly in the air. Then, bending to their work once more, they flew across the intervening water, beached their boats upon the sloping sand, and rushed up to us, prostrating themselves with loud cries of greeting before the young chief. Finally one of them, an elderly man, with a necklace and bracelet of great lustrous glass beads and the skin of some beautiful mottled amber-colored animal slung over his shoulders, ran forward and embraced most tenderly the youth whom we had saved. He then looked at us and asked some questions, after which he stepped up with much dignity and embraced us also each in turn. Then, at his order, the whole tribe lay down upon the ground before us in homage. Personally I felt shy and uncomfortable at this obsequious adoration, and I read the same feeling in the faces of Lord John and Summerlee, but Challenger expanded like a flower in the sun.

"They may be undeveloped types," said he, stroking his beard and looking round at them, "but their deportment in the presence of their superiors might be a lesson to some of our more advanced Europeans. Strange how correct are the instincts of the natural man!"

It was clear that the natives had come out upon the warpath, for every man carried his spear—a long bamboo tipped with bone—his bow and arrows, and some sort of club or stone battle-axe slung at his side. Their dark, angry glances at the woods from which we had come, and the frequent repetition of the word "Doda," made it clear enough that this was a rescue party who had set forth to save or revenge the old chief's son, for such we gathered that the youth must be. A council was now held by the whole tribe squatting in a circle, whilst we sat near on a slab of basalt and watched their proceedings. Two or three warriors spoke, and finally our young friend made a spirited harangue with such eloquent features and gestures that we could understand it all as clearly as if we had known the language.

"What is the use of returning?" he said. "Sooner or later the thing must be done. Your comrades have been murdered. What if I have returned safe? These others have been done to death. There is no safety for any of us. We are assembled now and ready." Then he pointed to us. "These strange men are our friends. They are great fighters, and they hate the ape-men even as we do. They command," here he pointed up to heaven, "the thunder and the lightning. When shall we have such a chance again? Let us go forward, and either die now or live for the future in safety. How else shall we go back unashamed to our women?"

The little red warriors hung upon the words of the speaker, and when he had finished they burst into a roar of applause, waving their rude weapons in the air. The old chief stepped forward to us, and asked us some question, pointing at the same time to the woods. Lord John made a sign to him that he should wait for an answer and then he turned to us.

"Well, it's up to you to say what you will do," said he; "for my part I have a score to settle with these monkey-folk, and if it ends by wiping them off the face of the earth I don't see that the earth need fret about it. I'm goin' with our little red pals and I mean to see them through the scrap. What do you say, young fellah?"

"Of course I will come."

"And you, Challenger?"

"I will assuredly cooperate."

"And you, Summerlee?"

"We seem to be drifting very far from the object of this expedition, Lord John. I assure you that I little thought when I left my professorial chair in London that it was for the purpose of heading a raid of savages upon a colony of anthropoid apes."

"To such base uses do we come," said Lord John, smiling. "But we are up against it, so what's the decision?"

"It seems a most questionable step," said Summerlee, argumentative to the last, "but if you are all going, I hardly see how I can remain behind."

"Then it is settled," said Lord John, and turning to the chief he nodded and slapped his rifle. The old fellow clasped our hands, each in turn, while his men cheered louder than ever. It was too late to advance that night, so the Indians settled down into a rude bivouac. On all sides their fires began to glimmer and smoke. Some of them who had disappeared into the jungle came back presently driving a young iguanodon before them. Like the others, it had a daub of asphalt upon its shoulder, and it was only when we saw one of the natives step forward with the air of an owner and give his consent to the beast's slaughter that we understood at last that these great creatures were as much private property as a herd of cattle, and that these symbols which had so perplexed us were nothing more than the marks of the owner. Helpless, torpid, and vegetarian, with great limbs and a minute brain, they could be rounded up and driven by a child. In a few minutes the huge beast had been cut up and slabs of him were hanging over a dozen camp fires, together with great scaly ganoid fish which had been speared in the lake.

Summerlee had lain down and slept upon the sand, but we others roamed round the edge of the water, seeking to learn something more of this strange country. Twice we found pits of blue clay, such as we had already seen in the swamp of the pterodactyls. These were old volcanic vents, and for some reason excited the greatest interest in Lord John. What attracted Challenger, on the other hand, was a bubbling, gurgling mud geyser, where some strange gas formed great bursting bubbles upon the surface. He thrust a hollow reed into it and cried out with delight like a schoolboy when he was able, on touching it with a lighted match to cause a sharp explosion and a blue flame at the far end of the tube. Still more pleased was he when, inverting a leathern pouch over the end of the reed, and so filling it with the gas, he was able to send it soaring up into the air.

"An inflammable gas, and one markedly lighter than the atmosphere. I should say beyond doubt that it contains a considerable proportion of free hydrogen. The resources of G. E. C. are not yet exhausted, my young friend. I may yet show you how a great mind moulds all Nature to its use." He swelled with some secret purpose, but would say no more.

There was nothing which we could see upon the shore which seemed to me so wonderful as the great sheet of water before us. Our numbers and our noise had frightened all living creatures away, and save for a few pterodactyls, which soared round high above our heads while they waited for the carrion, all was still around the camp. But it was different out upon the rose-tinted waters of the Central Lake. It boiled and heaved with strange life. Great slate-colored backs and high serrated dorsal fins shot up with a fringe of silver, and then rolled down into the depths again. The sandbanks far out were spotted with uncouth crawling forms, huge turtles, strange saurians, and one great flat creature like a writhing palpitating mat of black greasy leather, which flopped its way slowly to the lake. Here and there high serpent heads projected out of the water, cutting swiftly through it with a little collar of foam in front, and a long swirling wake behind, rising and falling in graceful, swan-like undulations as they went. It was not until one of these creatures wriggled on to a sandbank within a few hundred yards of us, and exposed a barrel-shaped body and huge flippers behind the long serpent neck that Challenger and Summerlee, who had joined us, broke out into their duet of wonder and admiration.

"Plesiosaurus! A fresh-water Plesiosaurus!" cried Summerlee. "That I should have lived to see such a sight! We are blessed, my dear Challenger, above all zoologists since the world began!"

It was not until the night had fallen, and the fires of our savage allies glowed red in the shadows, that our two men of science could be dragged away from the fascinations of that primeval lake. Even in the darkness as we lay upon the strand, we heard from time to time the snort and plunge of the huge creatures who lived therein.

At earliest dawn our camp was astir and an hour later we had started upon our memorable expedition. Often in my dreams have I thought that I might live to be a war correspondent. In what wildest one could I have conceived the nature of the campaign which it should be my lot to report? Here then is my first despatch from a field of battle:

Our numbers had been reinforced during the night by a fresh batch of natives from the caves, and we may have been four or five hundred strong when we made our advance. A fringe of scouts was thrown out in front, and behind them the whole force in a solid column made their way up the long slope of the bush country until we were near the edge of the forest. Here they spread out into a long straggling line of spearmen and bowmen. Roxton and Summerlee took their position upon the right flank, while Challenger and I were on the left. It was a host of the stone age that we were accompanying to battle—we with the last word of the gunsmith's art from St. James's Street and the Strand.

We had not long to wait for our enemy. A wild shrill clamor rose from the edge of the wood and suddenly a body of ape-men rushed out with clubs and stones, and made for the center of the Indian line. It was a valiant move but a foolish one, for the great bandy-legged creatures were slow of foot, while their opponents were as active as cats. It was horrible to see the fierce brutes with foaming mouths and glaring eyes, rushing and grasping, but forever missing their elusive enemies, while arrow after arrow buried itself in their hides. One great fellow ran past me roaring with pain, with a dozen darts sticking from his chest and ribs. In mercy I put a bullet through his skull, and he fell sprawling among the aloes. But this was the only shot fired, for the attack had been on the center of the line, and the Indians there had needed no help of ours in repulsing it. Of all the ape-men who had rushed out into the open, I do not think that one got back to cover.

But the matter was more deadly when we came among the trees. For an hour or more after we entered the wood, there was a desperate struggle in which for a time we hardly held our own. Springing out from among the scrub the ape-men with huge clubs broke in upon the Indians and often felled three or four of them before they could be speared. Their frightful blows shattered everything upon which they fell. One of them knocked Summerlee's rifle to matchwood and the next would have crushed his skull had an Indian not stabbed the beast to the heart. Other ape-men in the trees above us hurled down stones and logs of wood, occasionally dropping bodily on to our ranks and fighting furiously until they were felled. Once our allies broke under the pressure, and had it not been for the execution done by our rifles they would certainly have taken to their heels. But they were gallantly rallied by their old chief and came on with such a rash that the ape-men began in turn to give way. Summerlee was weaponless, but I was emptying my magazine as quick as I could fire, and on the further flank we heard the continuous cracking of our companions' rifles. Then in a moment came the panic and the collapse. Screaming and howling, the great creatures rushed away in all directions through the brushwood, while our allies yelled in their savage delight, following swiftly after their flying enemies. All the feuds of countless generations, all the hatreds and cruelties of their narrow history, all the memories of ill-usage and persecution were to be purged that day. At last man was to be supreme and the man-beast to find for ever his allotted place. Fly as they would the fugitives were too slow to escape from the active savages, and from every side in the tangled woods we heard the exultant yells, the twanging of bows, and the crash and thud as ape-men were brought down from their hiding-places in the trees.

I was following the others, when I found that Lord John and Summerlee had come across to join us.

"It's over," said Lord John. "I think we can leave the tidying up to them. Perhaps the less we see of it the better we shall sleep."

Challenger's eyes were shinning with the lust of slaughter.

"We have been privileged," he cried, strutting about like a gamecock, "to be present at one of the typical decisive battles of history—the battles which have determined the fate of the world. What, my friends, is the conquest of one nation by another? It is meaningless. Each produces the same result. But those fierce fights, when in the dawn of the ages the cave-dwellers held their own against the tiger folk, or the elephants first found that they had a master, those were the real conquests—the victories that count. By this strange turn of fate we have seen and helped to decide even such a contest. Now upon this plateau the future must ever be for man."

It needed a robust faith in the end to justify such tragic means. As we advanced together through the woods we found the ape-men lying thick, transfixed with spears or arrows. Here and there a little group of shattered Indians marked where one of the anthropoids had turned to bay, and sold his life dearly. Always in front of us we heard the yelling and roaring which showed the direction of the pursuit. The ape-men had been driven back to their city, they had made a last stand there, once again they had been broken, and now we were in time to see the final fearful scene of all. Some eighty or a hundred males, the last survivors, had been driven across that same little clearing which led to the edge of the cliff, the scene of our own exploit two days before. As we arrived the Indians, a semi-circle of spearmen, had closed in on them, and in a minute it was over. Thirty or forty died where they stood. The others, screaming and clawing, were thrust over the precipice, and went hurtling down, as their prisoners had of old, on to the sharp bamboos six hundred feet below. It was as Challenger had said, and the reign of man was assured for ever in Maple White Land. The males were exterminated, Ape Town was destroyed, the females and young were driven away to live in bondage, and the long rivalry of untold centuries had reached its bloody end.

For us the victory brought much advantage. Once again

we were able to visit our camp and get at our stores. Once more also we were able to communicate with Zambo, who had been terrified by the spectacle from afar of an avalanche of apes falling from the edge of the cliff.

"Come away, come away!" he cried, his eyes starting from his head. "The debbil get you sure if you stay up there."

"It is the voice of sanity!" said Summerlee with conviction. "We have had adventures enough and they are neither suitable to our character or our position. I hold you to your word, Challenger. From now onwards you devote your energies to getting us out of this horrible country and back once more to civilization."

15

Our Eyes Have Seen
Great Wonders

I WRITE THIS FROM DAY TO DAY, BUT I TRUST THAT BEFORE I come to the end of it, I may be able to say that the light shines, at last, through our clouds. We are held here with no clear means of making our escape, and bitterly we chafe against it. Yet, I can well imagine that the day may come when we may be glad that we were kept, against our will, to see something more of the wonders of this singular place, and of the creatures who inhabit it.

The victory of the Indians and the annihilation of the ape-men marked the turning point of our fortunes. From then onwards, we were in truth masters of the plateau, for the natives looked upon us with a mixture of fear and gratitude, since by our strange powers we had aided them to destroy their hereditary foe. For their own sakes they would, perhaps, be glad to see the departure of such formidable and incalculable people, but they have not themselves suggested any way by which we may reach the plains below. There had been, so far as we could follow their signs, a tunnel by which the place could be approached, the lower exit of which we had seen from below. By this, no doubt, both ape-men and Indians had at different epochs reached the top, and Maple White with his companion had taken the same way. Only the year before, however, there had been a terrific earthquake, and the upper end of the tunnel had fallen in and completely disappeared. The Indians now could only shake their heads and shrug their shoulders when we expressed by signs our desire to descend. It may be that they cannot, but it may also be that they will not help us to get away.

At the end of the victorious campaign the surviving apefolk were driven across the plateau (their wailings were horrible) and established in the neighborhood of the Indian caves, where they would, from now onwards, be a servile race under the eyes of their masters. It was a rude, raw, primeval version of the Jews in Babylon or the Israelites in Egypt. At night we could hear from amid the trees the long-drawn cry, as some primitive Ezekiel mourned for fallen greatness and recalled the departed glories of Ape Town. Hewers of wood and drawers of water, such were they from now onwards.

We had returned across the plateau with our allies two days after the battle, and made our camp at the foot of their cliffs. They would have had us share their caves with them, but Lord John would by no means consent to it, considering that to do so would put us in their power if they were treacherously disposed. We kept our independence therefore, and had our weapons ready for any emergency, while preserving the most friendly relations. We also continually visited their caves, which were most remarkable places, though whether made by man or by Nature we have never been able to determine. They were all on the one stratum, hollowed out of some soft rock which lay between the volcanic basalt forming the ruddy cliffs above them, and the hard granite which formed their base.

The openings were about eighty feet above the ground, and were led up to by long stone stairs, so narrow and steep that no large animal could mount them. Inside they were warm and dry, running in straight passages of varying length into the side of the hill, with smooth grey walls decorated with many excellent pictures done with charred sticks and representing the various animals of the plateau. If every living thing were swept from the country the future explorer would find upon the walls of these caves ample evidence of the strange fauna—the dinosaurs, iguanodons and fish lizards—which had lived so recently upon earth.

Since we have learned that the huge iguanodons were kept as tame herds by their owners, and were simply walking meat-stores, we had conceived that man, even with his primitive weapons, had established his ascendancy upon the plateau. We were soon to discover that it was not so, and that he was still there upon tolerance. It was on the third day after our forming our camp near the Indian caves that the tragedy occurred. Challenger and Summerlee had gone off together that day to the lake, where some of the natives, under their direction, were engaged in harpooning specimens of the great lizards. Lord John and I had remained in our camp, while a number of the Indians were scattered about upon the grassy slope in front of the caves engaged in different ways. Suddenly there was a shrill cry of alarm, with the word "Stoa" resounding from a hundred tongues. From every side men, women and children were rushing wildly for shelter, swarming up the staircases and into the caves in a mad stampede.

Looking up, we could see them waving their arms from the rocks above and beckoning to us to join them in their refuge. We had both seized our magazine rifles and ran out to see what the danger could be. Suddenly from the near belt of trees there broke forth a group of twelve or fifteen Indians, running for their lives, and at their very heels two of those frightful monsters which had disturbed our camp and pursued me upon my solitary journey. In shape they were like horrible toads, and moved in a succession of springs, but in size they were of an incredible bulk, larger than the largest elephant. We had never before seen them save at night, and indeed they are nocturnal animals save when disturbed in their lairs, as these had been. We now stood amazed at the sight, for their blotched and warty skins were of a curious fish-like iridescence, and the sunlight struck them with an ever-varying rainbow bloom as they moved.

We had little time to watch them, however, for in an instant they had overtaken the fugitives and were making a dire slaughter among them. Their method was to fall forward with their full weight upon each in turn, and, leaving him crushed and mangled, to bound on after the others. The wretched Indians screamed with terror, but were helpless, run as they would, before the relentless purpose and horrible activity of these monstrous creatures. One after another they went down, and there were not half a dozen surviving by the time my companion and I could come to their help. But our aid was of little avail and only involved us in the same peril. At the range of a couple of hundred yards we emptied our magazines, firing bullet after bullet into the beasts, but with no more effect than if we were pelting them with pellets of paper. Their slow reptilian natures cared nothing for wounds, and the springs of their lives, with no special brain center but scattered throughout their spinal cords, could not be tapped by any modern weapons. The most that we could do was to check their progress by distracting their attention with the flash and roar of our guns, and so to give both the natives and ourselves time to reach the steps which led to safety. But where the conical explosive bullets of the twentieth century were of no avail the poisoned arrows of the natives, dipped in the juice of strophanthus and steeped afterwards in decayed carrion, could succeed. Such arrows were of little avail to the hunter who attacked the beast, because their action in that torpid circulation was slow, and before its powers failed it could certainly overtake and slay its assailant. But now, as the two monsters hounded us to the very foot of the stairs, a drift of darts came whistling from every chink in the cliff above them. In a minute they were feathered with them, and yet with no sign of pain they clawed and slobbered with impotent rage at the steps which would lead them to their victims, mounting clumsily up for a few yards and then sliding again to the ground. But at last the poison worked. One of them gave a deep rumbling groan and dropped his huge squat head on to the earth. The other bounded round in an eccentric circle with shrill, wailing cries, and then lying down writhed in agony for some minutes before it also stiffened and lay still. With yells of triumph the Indians came flocking down from their caves and danced a frenzied dance of victory round the dead bodies, in mad joy that two more of the most dangerous of all their enemies had been slain. That night they cut up and removed the bodies, not to eat—for the poison was still active—but lest they should breed a pestilence. The great reptilian hearts, however, each as large as a cushion, still lay there, beating slowly and steadily, with a gentle rise and fall, in horrible independent life. It was upon the third day that the ganglia ran down and the dreadful things were still.

Some day, when I have a better desk than a meat-tin and

more helpful tools than a worn stub of pencil and a last, tattered notebook, I will write some fuller account of the Accala Indians—of our life amongst them, and of the glimpses which we had of the strange conditions of wondrous Maple White Land. Memory, at least, will never fail me, for so long as the breath of life is in me every hour and every action of that period will stand out as hard and clear as do the first strange happenings of our childhood. No new impressions could efface those which are so deeply cut. When the time comes I will describe that wondrous moonlit night upon the great lake when a young ichthyosaurus—a strange creature, half seal, half fish, to look at, with bone-covered eyes on each side of his snout, and a third eye fixed upon the top of his head—was entangled in an Indian net, and nearly upset our canoe before we towed it ashore; the same night that a green water-snake shot out from the rushes and carried off in its coils the steersman of Challenger's canoe. I will tell, too, of the great nocturnal white thing—to this day we do not know whether it was beast or reptile—which lived in a vile swamp to the east of the lake, and flitted about with a faint phosphorescent glimmer in the darkness. The Indians were so terrified of it that they would not go near the place, and, though we twice made expeditions and saw it each time, we could not make our way through the deep marsh in which it lived. I can only say that it seemed to be larger than a cow and had the strangest musky odor. I will tell also of the huge bird which chased Challenger to the shelter of the rocks one day—a great running bird, far taller than an ostrich, with a vulture-like neck and cruel head which made it a walking death. As Challenger climbed to safety one dart of that savage curving beak shore off the heel of his boot as if it had been cut with a chisel. This time at least modern weapons prevailed and the great creature, twelve feet from head to foot—phororachus its name, according to our panting but exultant Professor—went down before Lord Roxton's rifle in a flurry of waving feathers and kicking limbs, with two remorseless yellow eyes glaring up from the midst of it. May I live to see that flattened vicious skull in its own niche amid the trophies of the Albany. Finally, I will surely give some account of the toxodon, the giant ten-foot guinea pig, with projecting chisel teeth, which we killed as it drank in the gray of the morning by the side of the lake.

All this I shall some day write at fuller length, and amidst these more stirring days I would tenderly sketch in those lovely summer evenings, when with the deep blue sky above us we lay in good comradeship among the long grasses by the wood and marveled at the strange fowl that swept over us and the quaint new creatures which crept from their burrows to watch us, while above us the boughs of the bushes were heavy with luscious fruit, and below us strange and lovely flowers peeped at us from among the herbage; or those long moonlit nights when we lay out upon the shimmering surface of the great lake and watched with wonder and awe the huge circles rippling out from the sudden splash of some fantastic monster; or the greenish gleam, far down in the deep water, of some strange creature upon the confines of darkness. These are the scenes which my mind and my pen will dwell upon in every detail at some future day.

But, you will ask, why these experiences and why this delay, when you and your comrades should have been occupied day and night in the devising of some means by which you could return to the outer world? My answer is, that there was not one of us who was not working for this end, but that our work had been in vain. One fact we had very speedily discovered: The Indians would do nothing to help us. In every other way they were our friends, but when it was suggested that they should help us to make and carry a plank which would bridge the chasm, or when we wished to get from them thongs of leather or liana to weave ropes which might help us, we were met by a good-humored, but an invincible, refusal. They would smile, twinkle their eyes, shake their heads, and there was the end of it. Even the old chief met us with the same obstinate denial, and it was only Maretas, the youngster whom we had saved, who looked wistfully at us and told us by his gestures that he was grieved for our thwarted wishes. Ever since their crowning triumph with the ape-men they looked upon us as supermen, who bore victory in the tubes of strange weapons, and they believed that so long as we remained with them good fortune would be theirs. A little red-skinned wife and a cave of our own were freely offered to each of us if we would but forget our own people and dwell for ever upon the plateau. So far all had been kindly, however far apart our desires might be; but we felt well assured that our actual plans of a descent must be kept secret, for we had reason to fear that at the last they might try to hold us by force.

In spite of the danger from dinosaurs (which is not great save at night, for as I may have said before they are nocturnal in their habits) I have twice in the last three weeks been over to our old camp in order to see Zambo who still kept watch and ward below the cliff. My eyes strained eagerly across the great plain in the hope of seeing afar off the help for which we had prayed. But the long cactus-strewn levels still stretched away, empty and bare, to the distant line of the cane-brake.

"They will come soon now, Mr. Malone. Before another week pass Indian come back and bring rope and fetch you down." Such was the cheery cry of our excellent Zambo.

I had one strange experience as I came from this second visit which had involved my being away for a night from my companions. I was returning along the well-remembered route, and had reached a spot within a mile or so of the marsh of the pterodactyls, when I saw an extraordinary object approaching me. It was a man who walked inside a framework of bent canes so that he was enclosed on all sides in a bell-shaped cage. As I drew nearer I was more amazed still to see that it was Lord John Roxton. When he saw me he slipped from under his curious protection and came towards me laughing, and yet, as I thought, with some confusion in his manner.

"Well, young fellah," said he, "who would have thought of meetin' you up here?"

"What in the world are you doing?" I asked.

"Visitin' my friends, the pterodactyls," said he.

"But why?"

"Interestin' beasts, don't you think? But unsociable! Nasty rude ways with strangers, as you may remember. So I rigged this framework which keeps them from bein' too pressin' in their attentions."

"But what do you want in the swamp?"

He looked at me with a very questioning eye, and I read hesitation in his face.

"Don't you think other people besides Professors can want to know things?" he said at last. "I'm studyin' the pretty dears. That's enough for you."

"No offense," said I.

His good-humor returned and he laughed.

"No offense, young fellah. I'm goin' to get a young devil chick for Challenger. That's one of my jobs. No, I don't want your company. I'm safe in this cage, and you are not. So long, and I'll be back in camp by nightfall."

He turned away and I left him wandering on through the wood with his extraordinary cage around him.

If Lord John's behavior at this time was strange, that of Challenger was more so. I may say that he seemed to possess an extraordinary fascination for the Indian women, and that he always carried a large spreading palm branch with which he beat them off as if they were flies, when their attentions became too pressing. To see him walking, like a comic opera Sultan, with this badge of authority in his hand, his black beard bristling in front of him, his toes pointing at each step, and a train of wide-eyed Indian girls behind him, clad in their slender drapery of bark cloth, is one of the most grotesque of all the pictures which I will carry back with me. As to Summerlee, he was absorbed in the insect and bird life of the plateau, and spent his whole time (save that considerable portion which was devoted to abusing Challenger for not getting us out of our difficulties) in cleaning and mounting his specimens.

Challenger had been in the habit of walking off by himself every morning and returning from time to time with looks of portentous solemnity, as one who bears the full weight of a great enterprise upon his shoulders. One day, palm branch in hand, and his crowd of adoring devotees behind him, he led us down to his hidden workshop and took us into the secret of his plans.

The place was a small clearing in the center of a palm grove. In this was one of those boiling mud geysers which I have already described. Around its edge were scattered a number of leathern thongs cut from iguanodon hide, and a large collapsed membrane which proved to be the dried and scraped stomach of one of the great fish lizards from the lake. This huge sack had been sewn up at one end and only a small orifice left at the other. Into this opening several bamboo canes had been inserted and the other ends of these canes were in contact with conical clay funnels which collected the gas bubbling up through the mud of the geyser. Soon the flaccid organ began to slowly expand and show such a tendency to upward movements that Challenger fastened the cords which held it to the trunks of the surrounding trees. In half an hour a good-sized gasbag had been formed, and the jerking and straining upon the thongs showed that it was capable of considerable lift. Challenger, like a glad father in the presence of his firstborn, stood smiling and stroking his beard in silent, self-satisfied content as he gazed at the creation of his brain. It was Summerlee who first broke the silence.

"You don't mean us to go up in that thing, Challenger?" said he, in an acid voice.

"I mean, my dear Summerlee, to give you such a demonstration of its powers that after seeing it you will, I am sure, have no hesitation in trusting yourself to it."

"You can put it right out of your head now, at once," said Summerlee with decision; "nothing on earth would induce me to commit such a folly. Lord John, I trust that you will not countenance such madness?"

"Dooced ingenious I call it," said our peer. "I'd like to see how it works."

"So you shall," said Challenger. "For some days I have exerted my whole brain force upon the problem of how we shall descend these cliffs. We have satisfied ourselves that we cannot climb down and that there is no tunnel. We are also unable to construct any kind of bridge which may take us back to the pinnacle from which we came? How then shall I find a means to convey us? Some little time ago I had remarked to our young friend here that free hydrogen was evolved from the geyser. The idea of a balloon naturally followed. I was, I will admit, somewhat baffled by the difficulty of discovering an envelope to contain the gas, but the contemplation of the immense entrails of these reptiles supplied me with a solution to the problem. Behold the result!"

He put one hand in the front of his ragged jacket and pointed proudly with the other.

By this time the gas-bag had swollen to a goodly rotundity and was jerking strongly upon its lashings.

"Midsummer madness!" snorted Summerlee.

Lord John was delighted with the whole idea. "Clever old dear, ain't he?" he whispered to me, and then louder to Challenger. "What about a car?"

"The car will be my next care. I have already planned how it is to be made and attached. Meanwhile I will simply show you how capable my apparatus is of supporting the weight of each of us."

"All of us, surely?"

"No, it is part of my plan that each in turn shall descend as in a parachute, and the balloon be drawn back by means which I shall have no difficulty in perfecting. If it will support the weight of one and let him gently down, it will have done all that is required of it. I will show you its capacity in that direction."

He brought out a lump of basalt of a considerable size, constructed in the middle so that a cord could be easily attached to it. This cord was the one which we had brought with us on the plateau after we had used it for climbing the pinnacle. It was over a hundred feet long, and though it was thin it was very strong. He had prepared a sort of collar with many straps depending from it. This collar was placed over the dome of the balloon, and the hanging thongs were gathered together below, so that the pressure of any weight would be diffused over a considerable surface. Then the lump of basalt was fastened to the thongs and the rope was allowed to hang from the end of it, being passed three times round the Professor's arm.

"I will now," said Challenger, with a smile of pleased anticipation, "demonstrate the carrying power of my balloon." As he said so he cut with a knife the various lashings that held it.

Never was our expedition in more imminent danger of complete annihilation. The inflated membrane shot up with frightful velocity into the air. In an instant Challenger was pulled off his feet and dragged after it. I had just time to throw my arms round his ascending waist when I was myself whipped up into the air. Lord John had me with a rat-trap grip round the legs, but I felt that he also was coming off the ground. For a moment I had a vision of four adventurers floating like a string of sausages over the land that they had explored. But, happily, there were limits to the strain which the rope would stand, though none apparently to the lifting powers of this infernal machine. There was a sharp crack, and we were in a heap upon the ground with coils of rope all over us. When we were able to stagger to our feet we saw far off in the deep blue sky one dark spot where the lump of basalt was speeding upon its way.

"Splendid!" cried the undaunted Challenger, rubbing his injured arm. "A most thorough and satisfactory demonstration! I could not have anticipated such a success. Within a week, gentlemen, I promise that a second balloon will be prepared, and that you can count upon taking in safety and comfort the first stage of our homeward journey."

So far I have written each of the foregoing events as it occurred. Now I am rounding off my narrative from the old camp, where Zambo has waited so long, with all our difficulties and dangers left like a dream behind us upon the summit of those vast ruddy crags which tower above our heads. We have descended in safety, though in a most unexpected fashion, and all is well with us. In six weeks or two months we shall be in London, and it is possible that this letter may not reach you much earlier than we do ourselves. Already our hearts yearn and our spirits fly towards the great mother city which holds so much that is dear to us.

It was on the very evening of our perilous adventure with Challenger's home-made balloon that the change came in our fortunes. I have said that the one person from whom we had had some sign of sympathy in our attempts to get away was the young chief whom we rescued. He alone had no desire to hold us against our will in a strange land. He had told us as much by his expressive language of signs. That evening, after dusk, he came down to our little camp, handed me (for some reason he had always shown his attentions to me, perhaps because I was the one who was nearest his age) a small roll of the bark of a tree, and then pointing solemnly up at the row of caves above him, he had put his finger to his lips as a sign of secrecy and had stolen back again to his people.

I took the slip of bark to the firelight and we examined it together. It was about a foot square, and on the inner side there was a singular arrangement of lines, which I here reproduce:

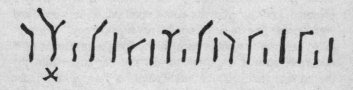

They were neatly done in charcoal upon the white surface, and looked to me at first sight like some sort of rough musical score.

"Whatever it is, I can swear that it is of importance to us," said I. "I could read that on his face as he gave it."

"Unless we have come upon a primitive practical joker," Summerlee suggested, "which I should think would be one of the most elementary developments of man."

"It is clearly some sort of script," said Challenger.

"Looks like a guinea puzzle competition," remarked Lord John, craning his neck to have a look at it. When suddenly he stretched out his hand and seized the puzzle.

"By George!" he cried, "I believe I've got it. The boy guessed right the very first time. See here! How many marks are on that paper? Eighteen. Well, if you come to think of it there are eighteen cave openings on the hill-side above us."

"He pointed up to the caves when he gave it to me," said I.

"Well, that settles it. This is a chart of the caves. What! Eighteen of them all in a row, some short, some deep, some branching, same as we saw them. It's a map, and here's a cross on it. What's the cross for? It is placed to mark one that is much deeper than the others."

"One that goes through," I cried.

"I believe our young friend has read the riddle," said Challenger. "If the cave does not go through I do not understand why this person, who has every reason to mean us well, should have drawn our attention to it. But if it *does* go through and comes out at the corresponding point on the other side, we should not have more than a hundred feet to descend."

"A hundred feet!" grumbled Summerlee.

"Well, our rope is still more than a hundred feet long," I cried. "Surely we could get down."

"How about the Indians in the cave?" Summerlee objected.

"There are no Indians in any of the caves above our heads," said I. "They are all used as barns and storehouses. Why should we not go up now at once and spy out the land?"

There is a dry bituminous wood upon the plateau—a species of araucaria, according to our botanist—which is always used by the Indians for torches. Each of us picked up a faggot of this, and we made our way up weed-covered steps to the particular cave which was marked in the drawing. It was, as I had said, empty, save for a great number of enormous bats, which flapped round our heads as we advanced into it. As we had no desire to draw the attention of the Indians to our proceedings, we stumbled along in the dark until we had gone round several curves and penetrated a considerable distance into the cavern. Then, at last, we lit our torches. It was a beautiful dry tunnel, with smooth gray walls covered with native symbols, a curved roof which arched over our heads, and white glistening sand beneath our feet. We hurried eagerly along it until, with a deep groan of bitter disappointment, we were brought to a halt. A sheer wall of rock had appeared before us, with no chink through which a mouse could have slipped. There was no escape for us there.

We stood with bitter hearts staring at this unexpected obstacle. It was not the result of any convulsion, as in the case of the ascending tunnel. It was, and had always been, a *cul-de-sac*.

"Never mind, my friends," said the indomitable Challenger. "You have still my promise of a balloon."

Summerlee groaned.

"Can we be in the wrong cave?" I suggested.

"No use, young fellah," said Lord John, with his finger on our chart. "Seventeen from the right and second from the left. This is the cave sure enough."

I looked at the mark to which his finger pointed, and I gave a sudden cry of joy.

"I believe I have it! Follow me! Follow me!"

I hurried back along the way we had come, my torch in my hand. "Here," said I, pointing to some matches upon the ground, "is where we lit up."

"Exactly."

"Well, it is marked as a forked cave, and in the darkness we passed the fork before the torches were lit. On the right side as we go out we should find the longer arm."

It was as I had said. We had not gone thirty yards before a great black opening loomed in the wall. We turned into it to find that we were in a much larger passage than before. Along it we hurried in breathless impatience for many hundreds of yards. Then, suddenly, in the black darkness of the arch in front of us we saw a gleam of dark red light. We stared in amazement. A sheet of steady flame seemed to cross the passage and to bar our way. We hastened towards it. No sound, no heat, no movement came from it, but still the great luminous curtain glowed before us, silvering all the cave and turning the sand to powdered jewels, until we drew closer it discovered a circular edge.

"The moon, by George!" cried Lord John. "We are through boys! We are through!"

It was indeed the full moon which shone straight down the aperture which opened upon the cliffs. It was a small rift, not larger than a window, but it was enough for all our purposes. As we craned our necks through it we could see that the descent was not a very difficult one, and that the level ground was no very great way below us. It was no wonder that from below we had not observed the place, as the cliffs curved overhead and an ascent at the spot would have seemed so impossible as to discourage close inspection. We satisfied ourselves that with the help of our rope we could find our way down, and then returned, rejoicing, to our camp to make our preparations for the next evening.

What we did we had to do quickly and secretly, since even at this last hour the Indians might hold us back. Our stores we would leave behind us, save only our guns and cartridges. But Challenger had some unwieldy stuff which he ardently desired to take with him, and one particular package, of which I may not speak, which gave us more labor than any. Slowly the day passed, but when the darkness fell we were ready for our departure. With much labor we got our things up the steps, and then, looking back, took one last long survey of that strange land, soon I fear to be vulgarized, the prey of hunter and prospector, but to each of us a dreamland of glamor and romance, a land where we had dared much, suffered much, and learned much—*our* land, as we shall ever fondly call it. Along upon our left the neighboring caves each threw out its ruddy cheery firelight into the gloom. From the slope below us rose the voices of the Indians as they laughed and sang. Beyond was the long sweep of the woods, and in the center, shimmering vaguely through the gloom, was the great lake, the mother of strange monsters. Even as we looked, a high whickering cry, the call of some weird animal, rang clear out of the darkness. It was the very voice of Maple White Land bidding us good-bye. We turned and plunged into the cave which led to home.

Two hours later, we, our packages, and all we owned, were at the foot of the cliff. Save for Challenger's luggage we had never a difficulty. Leaving it all where we descended, we started at once for Zambo's camp. In the early morning we approached it, but only to find, to our amazement, not one fire but a dozen upon the plain. The rescue party had arrived. There were twenty Indians from the river, with stakes, ropes, and all that could be useful for bridging the chasm. At least we shall have no difficulty now in carrying our packages, when tomorrow we begin to make our way back to the Amazon.

And so, in humble and thankful mood, I close this account. Our eyes have seen great wonders and our souls are chastened by what we have endured. Each is in his own way a better and deeper man. It may be that when we reach Para we shall stop to refit. If we do, this letter will be a mail ahead. If not, it will reach London on the very day that I do. In either case, my dear Mr. McArdle, I hope very soon to shake you by the hand.

16

A Procession!
A Procession!

I SHOULD WISH TO PLACE UPON RECORD HERE OUR GRATITUDE to all our friends upon the Amazon for the very great kindness and hospitality which was shown to us upon our return journey. Very particularly would I thank Signor Penalosa and other officials of the Brazilian Government for the special arrangements by which we were helped upon our way, and Signor Pereira of Para, to whose forethought we owe the complete outfit for a decent appearance in the civilized world which we found ready for us at that town. It seemed a poor return for all the courtesy which we encountered that we should deceive our hosts and benefactors, but under the circumstances we had really no alternative, and I hereby tell them that they will only waste their time and their money if they attempt to follow upon our traces. Even the names have been altered in our accounts, and I am very sure that no one, from the most careful study of them, could come within a thousand miles of our unknown land.

The excitement which had been caused through those

parts of South America which we had to traverse was imagined by us to be purely local, and I can assure our friends in England that we had no notion of the uproar which the mere rumor of our experiences had caused through Europe. It was not until *Ivernia* was within five hundred miles of Southampton that the wireless messages from paper after paper and agency after agency, offering huge prices for a short return message as to our actual results, showed us how strained was the attention not only of the scientific world but of the general public. It was agreed among us, however, that no definite statement should be given to the Press until we had met the members of the Zoological Institute, since as delegates it was our clear duty to give our first report to the body from which we had received our commission of investigation. Thus, although we found Southampton full of Pressmen, we absolutely refused to give any information, which had the natural effect of focusing public attention upon the meeting which was advertised for the evening of November 7th. For this gathering, the Zoological Hall, which had been the scene of the inception of our task, was found to be far too small, and it was only in the Queen's Hall in Regent Street that accommodation could be found. It is now common knowledge that the promoters might have ventured upon the Albert Hall and still found their space too scanty.

It was for the second evening after our arrival that the great meeting had been fixed. For the first, we had each, no doubt, our own pressing personal affairs to absorb us. Of mine I cannot yet speak. It may be that as it stands further from me I may think of it, and even speak of it, with less emotion. I have shown the reader in the beginning of this narrative where lay the springs of my action. It is but right, perhaps, that I should carry on the tale and show also the results. And yet the day may come when I would not have it otherwise. At least I have been driven forth to take part in a wondrous adventure, and I cannot but be thankful to the force that drove me.

And now I turn to the last supreme eventful moment of our adventure. As I was racking my brain as to how I should best describe it, my eyes fell upon the issue of my own journal for the morning of the 8th of November with the full and excellent account of my friend and fellow-reporter Macdona. What can I do better than transcribe his narrative—headlines and all? I admit that the paper was exuberant in the matter, out of compliment to its own enterprise in sending a correspondent, but the other great dailies were hardly less full in their account. Thus, then, friend Mac in his report:

THE NEW WORLD
GREAT MEETING AT THE QUEEN'S HALL
SCENES OF UPROAR
EXTRAORDINARY INCIDENT
WHAT WAS IT?
NOCTURNAL RIOT IN REGENT STREET
(Special)

"The much-discussed meeting of the Zoological Institute, convened to hear the report of the Committee of Investigation sent out last year to South America to test the assertions made by Professor Challenger as to the continued existence of prehistoric life upon that continent, was held last night in the greater Queen's Hall, and it is safe to say that it is likely to be a red-letter date in the history of Science, for the proceedings were of so remarkable and sensational a character that no one present is ever likely to forget them." (Oh, brother scribe Macdona, what a mon-

strous opening sentence!) "The tickets were theoretically
confined to members and friends, but the latter is an elas-
tic term, and long before eight o'clock, the hour fixed for
the commencement of the proceedings, all parts of the
Great Hall were tightly packed. The general public, however, which most unreasonably entertained a grievance at
having been excluded, stormed at the doors at a quarter to
eight, after a prolonged *mêlée* in which several people
were injured, including Inspector Scoble of H Division,
whose leg was unfortunately broken. After this unwarrant-
able invasion, which not only filled every passage, but
even intruded upon the space set apart for the Press, it is
estimated that nearly five thousand people awaited the arrival of the travelers. When they eventually appeared, they
took their places in the front of a platform which already
contained all the leading scientific men, not only of this
country, but of France and of Germany. Sweden was also
represented, in the person of Professor Sergius, the famous
Zoologist of the University of Upsala. The entrance of the
four heroes of the occasion was the signal for a remarkable demonstration of welcome, the whole audience rising
and cheering for some minutes. An acute observer might,
however, have detected some signs of dissent amid the applause, and gathered that the proceedings were likely to
become more lively than harmonious. It may safely be
prophesied, however, that no one could have foreseen the
extraordinary turn which they were actually to take.

"Of the appearance of the four wanderers little need be
said, since their photographs have for some time been appearing in all the papers. They bear few traces of the hardships which they are said to have undergone. Professor
Challenger's beard may be more shaggy, Professor
Summerlee's features more ascetic. Lord John Roxton's
figure gaunt, and all three may be burned to a darker tint

than when they left our shores, but each appeared to be in most excellent health. As to our own representative, the well-known athlete and international Rugby football player, E. D. Malone, he looks trained to a hair, and as he surveyed the crowd a smile of good-humored contentment pervaded his honest but homely face." (All right, Mac, wait till I get you alone!)

"When quiet had been restored and the audience resumed their seats after the ovation which they had given to the travelers, the chairman, the Duke of Durham, addressed the meeting. 'He would not,' he said, 'stand for more than a moment between that vast assembly and the treat which lay before them. It was not for him to anticipate what Professor Summerlee, who was the spokesman of the committee, had to say to them, but it was common humor that their expedition had been crowned by extraordinary success.' (Applause.) 'Apparently the age of romance was not dead, and there was common ground upon which the wildest imaginings of the novelist could meet the actual scientific investigations of the searcher for truth. He would only add, before he sat down, that he rejoiced—and all of them would rejoice—that these gentlemen had returned safe and sound from their difficult and dangerous task, for it cannot be denied that any disaster to such an expedition would have inflicted a well-nigh irreparable loss to the cause of zoological science.' " (Great applause, in which Professor Challenger was observed to join.)

"Professor Summerlee's rising was the signal for another extraordinary outbreak of enthusiasm, which broke out again at intervals throughout his address. That address will not be given *in extenso* in these columns, for the reason that a full account of the whole adventures of the expedition is being published as a supplement from the pen of our own special correspondent. Some general indications will therefore suffice. Having described the genesis of their journey, and paid a handsome tribute to his friend Professor Challenger, coupled with an apology for the incredulity with which his assertions, now fully vindicated, had been received, he gave the actual course of their journey, carefully withholding such information as would aid the public in any attempt to locate this remarkable plateau. Having described, in general terms, their course from the main river up to the time that they actually reached the base of the cliffs, he enthralled his hearers by his account of the difficulties encountered by the expedition in their repeated attempts to mount them, and finally described how they succeeded in their desperate endeavors, which cost the lives of their two devoted half-breed servants." (This amazing reading of the affair was the result of Summerlee's endeavors to avoid raising any questionable matter at the meeting.)

"Having conducted his audience in fancy to the summit, and marooned them there by reason of the fall of their bridge, the Professor proceeded to describe both the horrors and the attractions of that remarkable land. Of personal adventures he said little, but laid stress upon the rich harvest reaped by Science in the observations of the wonderful beast, bird, insect and plant life of the plateau. Peculiarly rich in the coleoptera and in the lepidoptera, forty-six new species of the one and ninety-four of the other had been secured in the course of a few weeks. It was, however, in the larger animals, and especially in the larger animals supposed to have been long extinct, that the interest of the public was naturally centered. Of these he was able to give a goodly list, but had little doubt that it would be largely extended when the place had been more thoroughly investigated. He and his companions had seen at least a dozen creatures, most of them at a distance, which corresponded with nothing at present known to Science. These would in time be duly classified and examined. He instanced a snake, the cast skin of which, deep purple in color, was fifty-one feet in length, and mentioned a white creature, supposed to be mammalian, which gave forth well-marked phosphorescence in the darkness; also a large black moth, the bite of which was supposed by the Indians to be highly poisonous. Setting aside these entirely new forms of life, the plateau was very rich in known prehistoric forms, dating back in some cases to Early Jurassic times. Among these he mentioned the gigantic and grotesque stegosaurus, seen once by Mr. Malone at a drinking-place by the lake, and drawn in the sketchbook of that adventurous American who had first penetrated this unknown world. He described also the iguanodon and the pterodactyl—two of the first of the wonders which they had encountered. He then thrilled the assembly by some account of the terrible carnivorous dinosaurs, which had on more than one occasion pursued members of the party, and which were the most formidable of all the creatures which they had encountered. Thence he passed to the huge and ferocious bird, the phororachus, and to the great elk which still roams upon this upland. It was not, however, until he sketched the mysteries of the central lake that the full interest and enthusiasm of the audience were aroused. One had to pinch oneself to be sure that one was awake as one heard this sane and practical Professor in cold, measured tones describing the monstrous three-eyed fish-lizards and the huge water-snakes which inhabit this enchanted sheet of water. Next he touched upon the Indians, and upon the extraordinary colony of anthropoid apes, which might be looked upon as an advance upon the pithecanthropus of Java, and as coming therefore nearer than any form to that hypothetical creation, the missing link. Finally he described, amongst some merriment, the ingenious but highly dangerous aeronautic invention of Professor Challenger, and wound up a most memorable address by an account of the methods by which the committee did at last find their way back to civilization.

"It had been hoped that the proceedings would end there, and that a vote of thanks and congratulation, moved by Professor Sergius, of Upsala University, would be duly seconded and carried; but it was soon evident that the course of events was not destined to flow so smoothly. Symptoms of opposition had been evident from time to time during the evening, and now Dr. James Illingworth, of Edinburgh, rose in the center of the hall. Dr. Illingworth asked whether an amendment should not be taken before a resolution.

"The Chairman: 'Yes, sir, if there must be an amendment.'

"Dr. Illingworth: 'Your Grace, there must be an amendment.'

"The Chairman: 'Then let us take it at once.'

"Professor Summerlee (springing to his feet): 'Might I explain, your Grace, that this man is my personal enemy ever since our controversy in the "Quarterly Journal of Science" as to the true nature of Bathybius?'

"The Chairman: 'I fear I cannot go into personal matters. Proceed.'

"Dr. Illingworth was imperfectly heard in part of his remarks on account of the strenuous opposition of the friends of the explorers. Some attempts were also made to pull him down. Being a man of enormous physique, however, and possessed of a very powerful voice, he dominated the tumult and succeeded in finishing his speech. It was clear, from the moment of his rising, that he had a number of friends and sympathizers in the hall, though they formed a minority in the audience. The attitude of the greater part of the public might be described as one of attentive neutrality.

"Dr. Illingworth began his remarks by expressing his high appreciation of the scientific work both of Professor Challenger and of Professor Summerlee. He much regretted that any personal bias should have been read into his remarks, which were entirely dictated by his desire for scientific truth. His position, in fact, was substantially the same as that taken up by Professor Summerlee at the last meeting. At that last meeting Professor Challenger had made certain assertions which had been queried by his colleague. Now this colleague came forward himself with the same assertions and expected them to remain unquestioned. Was this reasonable? ('Yes,' 'No,' and prolonged interruption, during which Professor Challenger was heard from the Press box to ask leave from the Chairman to put Dr. Illingworth into the street.) A year ago one man said certain things. Now four men said other and more startling ones. Was this to constitute a final proof where the matters in question were of the most revolutionary and incredible character? There had been recent examples of travelers arriving from the unknown with certain tales which had been too readily accepted. Was the London Zoological Institute to place itself in this position? He admitted that the members of the committee were men of character. But human nature was very complex. Even Professors might be misled by desire for notoriety. Like moths, we all love best to flutter in the light. Heavy-game shots liked to be in a position to cap the tales of their rivals, and journalists were not averse from sensational *coups*, even when imagination had to aid fact in the process. Each member of the committee had his own motive for making the most of his results. ('Shame! shame!') He had no desire to be offensive. ('You are!' and interruption.) The corroboration of these wondrous tales was really of the most slender description. What did it amount to? Some photographs. Was it possible that in this age of ingenious manipulation photographs could be accepted as evidence? What more? We have a story of a flight and a descent by ropes which precluded the production of larger specimens. It was ingenious, but not convincing. It was understood that Lord John Roxton claimed to have the skull to a phororachus. He could only say that he would like to see that skull.

"Lord John Roxton: 'Is this fellow calling me a liar?'" (Uproar.)

"The Chairman: 'Order! order! Dr. Illingworth, I must direct you to bring your remarks to a conclusion and to move your amendment.'

"Dr. Illingworth: 'Your Grace, I have more to say, but I bow to your ruling. I move, then, that, while Professor Summerlee be thanked for his interesting address, the whole matter shall be regarded as "*non-proven*," and shall be referred back to a larger, and possibly more reliable Committee of Investigation.'

"It is difficult to describe the confusion caused by this amendment. A large section of the audience expressed their indignation at such a slur upon the travelers by noisy shouts of dissent and cries of 'Don't put it!' 'Withdraw!' 'Turn him out!' On the other hand, the malcontents—and it cannot be denied that they were fairly numerous— cheered for the amendment, with cries of 'Order!' 'Chair!' and 'Fair Play!' A scuffle broke out in the back benches, and blows were freely exchanged among the medical students who crowded that part of the hall. It was only the moderating influence of the presence of large numbers of ladies which prevented an absolute riot. Suddenly, however, there was a pause, a hush, and then complete silence. Professor Challenger was on his feet. His appearance and manner are peculiarly arresting, and as he raised his hand for order the whole audience settled down expectantly to give him a hearing.

" 'It will be within the recollection of many present,' said Professor Challenger, 'that similar foolish and unmannerly scenes marked the last meeting at which I have been able to address them. On that occasion Professor Summerlee was the chief offender, and though he is now chastened and contrite, the matter could not be entirely forgotten. I have heard tonight similar, but even more offensive, sentiments from the person who has just sat down, and though it is a conscious effort of self-effacement to come down to that person's mental level, I will endeavor to do so, in order to allay any reasonable doubt which could possibly exist in the minds of anyone.' (Laughter and interruption.) 'I need not remind this audience that though Professor Summerlee, as head of the Committee of Investigation, has been put up to speak tonight, still it is I who am the real prime mover in this business, and that it is mainly to me that any successful result must be ascribed. I have safely conducted these three gentlemen to the spot mentioned, and I have, as you have heard, convinced them of the accuracy of my previous account. We had hoped that we should find upon our return that no one was so dense as to dispute our joint conclusions. Warned, however, by my previous experience, I have not come without such proofs as may convince a reasonable man. As explained by Professor Summerlee, our cameras have been tampered with by the ape-men when they ransacked our camp, and most of our negatives ruined.' (Jeers, laughter, and 'Tell us another!' from the back.) 'I have mentioned the ape-men, and I cannot forbear from saying that some of the sounds which now meet my ears bring back most vividly to my recollection my experiences with those interesting creatures.' (Laughter.) 'In spite of the destruction of so many invaluable negatives, there still remains in our collection a certain number of corroborative photographs showing the conditions of life upon the plateau. Did they accuse them of having forged these photographs?' (A voice, 'Yes,' and considerable interruption which ended in several men being put out of the hall.) 'The negatives were open to the inspection of experts. But what other evidence had they? Under the conditions of their escape it was naturally impossible to bring a large amount of baggage, but they had rescued Professor Summerlee's collections of butterflies and beetles, containing many new species. Was this not evidence?' (Several voices, 'No.') 'Who said no?'

"Dr. Illingworth (rising): 'Our point is that such a collection might have been made in other places than a prehistoric plateau.' (Applause.)

"Professor Challenger: 'No doubt, sir, we have to bow to your scientific authority, although I must admit that the name is unfamiliar. Passing, then, both the photographs and the entomological collection, I come to the varied and accurate information which we bring with us upon points which have never before been elucidated. For example, upon the domestic habits of the pterodactyl—(a voice: 'Bosh,' and uproar)—I say, that upon the domestic habits of the pterodactyl we can throw a flood of light. I can exhibit to you from my portfolio a picture of that creature taken from life which would convince you——'

"Dr. Illingworth: 'No picture could convince us of anything.'

"Professor Challenger: 'You would require to see the thing itself?'

"Dr. Illingworth: 'Undoubtedly.'

"Professor Challenger: 'And you would accept that?'

"Dr. Illingworth (laughing): 'Beyond a doubt.'

"It was at this point that the sensation of the evening arose—a sensation so dramatic that it can never have been paralleled in the history of scientific gatherings. Professor Challenger raised his hand in the air as a signal, and at once our colleague, Mr. E. D. Malone, was observed to raise and to make his way to the back of the platform. An instant later he re-appeared in company of a gigantic negro, the two of them bearing between them, a large square packing-case. It was evidently of great weight, and was slowly carried forward and placed in front of the Professor's chair. All sound had hushed in the audience and everyone was absorbed in the spectacle before them. Professor Challenger drew off the top of the case, which formed a sliding lid. Peering down into the box he snapped his fingers several times and was heard from the Press seat to say, 'Come, then, pretty, pretty!' in a coaxing voice. An instant later, with a scratching, rattling sound, a most horrible and loathsome creature appeared from below and perched itself upon the side of the case. Even the unexpected fall of the Duke of Durham into the orchestra, which occurred at this moment, could not distract the petrified attention of the vast audience. The face of the creature was like the wildest gargoyle that the imagination of a mad mediaeval builder could have conceived. It was malicious, horrible, with two small red eyes as bright as points of burning coal. Its long, savage mouth, which was held half-open, was full of a double row of shark-like teeth. Its shoulders were humped, and round them were draped what appeared to be a faded grey shawl. It was the devil of our childhood in person. There was a turmoil in the audience—someone screamed, two ladies in the front row fell senseless from their chairs, and there was a general movement upon the platform to follow their chairman into the orchestra. For moment there was danger of a general panic. Professor Challenger threw up his hands to still the commotion, but the movement alarmed the creature beside him. Its strange shawl suddenly unfurled, spread, and fluttered as a pair of leathery wings. Its owner grabbed at its legs, but too late to hold it. It had sprung from the perch and was circling slowly round the Queen's Hall with a dry, leathery flapping of its ten-foot wings, while a putrid and insidious odor pervaded the room. The cries of the people in the galleries, who were alarmed at the near approach of those glowing eyes and that murderous beak, excited the creature to a frenzy. Faster and faster it flew, beating against the walls and chandeliers in a blind frenzy of alarm. 'The window! For heaven's sake shut that window!' roared the Professor from the platform, dancing, and wringing his hands in an agony of apprehension. Alas, his warning was too late! In a moment the creature, beating and bumping along the wall like a huge moth within a gas shade, came upon the opening, squeezed its hideous bulk through it, and was gone. Professor Challenger fell back into his chair with his long face buried in his hands, while the audience gave one long, deep sigh of relief as they realized that the incident was over.

"Then—oh! how shall one describe what took place then—when the full exuberance of the majority and the full reaction of the minority united to make one great wave of enthusiasm, which rolled from the back of the hall, gathering volume as it came, swept over the orchestra, submerged the platform, and carried the four heroes away upon its crest?" (Good for you, Mac.) "If the audience had done less than justice, surely it made ample amends. Everyone was on his feet. Everyone was moving, shouting, gesticulating. A dense crowd of cheering men were round the four travelers. 'Up with them! up with them!' cried a hundred voices. In a moment four figures shot up above the crowd. In vain they strove to break loose. They were held in their lofty places of honor. It would have been hard to let them down if it had been wished, so dense was the crowd around them. 'Regent Street! Regent Street!' sounded the voices. There was a swirl in the packed multitude, and a slow current, bearing the four upon their shoulders, made for the door. Out in the street the scene was extraordinary. An assemblage of not less than a hundred thousand people was waiting. The close-packed throng extended from the other side of the Langham Hotel to Oxford Circus. A roar of acclamation greeted the four adventurers as they appeared, high above the heads of the people, under the vivid electric lamps outside the hall. 'A procession! A procession!' was the cry. In a dense phalanx, blocking the streets from side to side, the crowd set forth, taking the route of Regent Street, Pall Mall, St. James's Street, and Piccadilly. The whole central traffic of London was held up, and many collisions were reported between the demonstrators upon the one side and the police and taxi-cabmen upon the other. Finally, it was not until after midnight that the four travellers were released at the entrance to Lord John Roxton's chambers in the Albany, and that the exuberant crowd, having sung 'They are Jolly Good Fellows' in chorus, concluded their program with 'God Save the King.' So ended one of the most remarkable evenings that London has seen for a considerable time."

So far my friend Macdona; and it may be taken as a fairly accurate, if florid, account of the proceedings. As to the main incident, it was a bewildering surprise to the audience, but not, I need hardly say, to us. The reader will remember how I met Lord John Roxton upon the very occasion when, in his protective crinoline, he had gone to bring the "Devil's chick" as he called it, for Professor Challenger. I have hinted also at the trouble which the Professor's baggage gave us when we left the plateau, and had I described our voyage I might have said a good deal of the worry we had to coax with putrid fish the appetite of our filthy companion. If I have not said much about it before, it was, of course, that the Professor's earnest desire was that no possible rumor of the unanswerable argument which we carried should be allowed to leak out until the moment came when his enemies were to be confuted.

One word as to the fate of the London pterodactyl. Nothing can be said to be certain upon this point. There is evidence of two frightened women that it perched upon the roof of the Queen's Hall and remained there like a diabolical statue for some hours. The next day it came out in the evening papers that Private Miles, of the Coldstream Guards, on duty outside Marlborough House, had deserted his post without leave, and was therefore court-martialled. Private Miles' account, that he dropped his rifle and took to his heels down the Mall because on looking up he had suddenly seen the devil between him and the moon, was not accepted by the Court, and yet it may have a direct bearing upon the point at issue. The only other evidence which I can adduce is from the log of the S. S. *Friesland*, a Dutch-American liner, which asserts that at nine next morning, Start Point being at the time ten miles upon their starboard quarter, they were passed by something between a flying goat and a monstrous bat, which was heading at a prodigious place south and west. If its homing instinct led it upon the right line, there can be no doubt that somewhere out in the wastes of the Atlantic the last European pterodactyl found its end.

And Gladys—oh, my Gladys!—Gladys of the mystic lake, now to be renamed the Central, for never shall she have immortality through me. Did I not always see some hard fiber in her nature? Did I not, even at the time when I was proud to obey her behest, feel that it was surely a poor love which could drive a lover to his death or the danger of it? Did I not, in my truest thoughts, always recurring and always dismissed, see past the beauty of the face, and, peering into the soul, discern the twin shadows of selfishness and fickleness glooming at the back of it? Did she love the heroic and the spectacular for its own noble sake, or was it for the glory which might, without effort of sacrifice, be reflected upon herself? Or are these thoughts the vain wisdom which comes after the event? It was the shock of my life. For a moment it had turned me to a cynic. But already, as I write, a week has passed, and we have had our momentous interview with Lord John Roxton and—well, perhaps things might be worse.

Let me tell it in a few words. No letter or telegram had come to me at Southampton, and I reached the little villa at Streatham about ten o'clock that night in a fever of alarm. Was she dead or alive? Where were all my nightly dreams of the open arms, the smiling face, the words of praise for her man who had risked his life to humor her whim? Already I was down from the high peaks and standing flat-footed upon earth. Yet some good reasons given might still lift me to the clouds once more. I rushed down the garden path, hammered at the door, heard the voice of Gladys within, pushed past the staring maid, and strode into the sitting-room. She was seated in a low settee under the shaded standard lamp by the piano. In three steps I was across the room and had both her hands in mine.

"Gladys!" I cried, "Gladys!"

She looked up with amazement in her face. She was altered in some subtle way. The expression of her eyes, the hard upward stare, the set of the lips, was new to me. She drew back her hands.

"What do you mean?" she said.

"Gladys!" I cried. "What is the matter? You are my Gladys, are you not—little Gladys Hungerton?"

"No," said she, "I am Gladys Potts. Let me introduce you to my husband."

How absurd life is! I found myself mechanically bowing and shaking hands with a little ginger-haired man who was coiled up in the deep armchair which had once been sacred to my own use. We bobbed and grinned in front of each other.

"Father lets us stay here. We are getting our house ready," said Gladys.

"Oh, yes," said I.

"You didn't get my letter at Para, then?"

"No, I got no letter."

"Oh, what a pity! It would have made all clear."

"It *is* quite clear," said I.

"I've told William all about you," said she. "We have no secrets. I am so sorry about it. But it couldn't have been so very deep, could it, if you could go off to the other end of the world and leave me here alone. You're not crabby, are you?"

"No, no, not at all I think I'll go."

"Have some refreshment," said the little man, and he added, in a confidential way, "It's always like this ain't it? And must be unless you had polygamy, only the other way round; you understand." He laughed like an idiot, while I made for the door.

I was through it, when a sudden fantastic impulse came

upon me, and I went back to my successful rival, who looked nervously at the electric push.

"Will you answer a question?" I asked.

"Well, within reason," said he.

"How did you do it? Have you searched for hidden treasure, or discovered a pole, or done time on a pirate, or flown the channel, or what? Where is the glamor of romance? How did you get it?"

He stared at me with a hopeless expression upon his vacuous, good-natured, scrubby little face.

"Don't you think all this is a little too personal?" he said.

"Well, just one question," I cried. "What are you? What is your profession?"

"I am a solicitor's clerk," said he. "Second man at Johnson and Merivale's, 41, Chancery Lane."

"Good-night!" said I, and vanished, like all disconsolate and broken-hearted heroes, into the darkness, with grief and rage and laughter all simmering within me like a boiling pot.

One more little scene, and I have done. Last night we all supped at Lord John Roxton's rooms, and sitting together afterwards we smoked in good comradeship and talked our adventures over. It was strange under these altered surroundings to see the old, well-known faces and figures. There was Challenger, with his smile of condescension, his drooping eyelids, his intolerant eyes, his aggressive beard, his huge chest, swelling and puffing as he laid down the law to Summerlee. And Summerlee, too, there he was with his short briar between his thin moustache and his grey goat's-beard, his worn face protruded in eager debate as he queried all Challenger's propositions. Finally, there was our host with his rugged, eagle face, and his cold, blue, glacier eyes with always a shimmer of devilment and of humor down in the depths of them. Such is the last picture of them that I have carried away. It was after supper, in his own sanctum—the room of the pink radiance and the innumerable trophies—that Lord John Roxton had something to say to us. From a cupboard he had brought an old cigar box, and this he laid before him on the table.

"There's one thing," said he, "that maybe I should have spoken about before this, but I wanted to know a little more clearly where I was. No use to raise hopes and let them down again. But it's facts, not hopes, with us now. You may remember that day we found the pterodactyl rookery in the swamp—what? Well, somethin' in the lie of the land took my notice. Perhaps it has escaped you, so I will tell you. It was a volcanic vent full of blue clay."

The Professors nodded.

"Well, now, in the whole world I've only had to do with one place that was a volcanic vent of blue clay. That was the great De Beers Diamond Mine of Kimberley—what? So you see I got diamonds into my head. I rigged up a contraption to hold off those stinking beasts, and I spent a happy day there with a spud. This is what I got."

He opened his cigar-box, and tilting it over he poured about twenty or thirty rough stones, varying from the size of beans to that of chestnuts, on the table.

"Perhaps you think I should have told you then. Well, so I should, only I know there are a lot of traps for the unwary, and that stones may be of any size and yet of little value where color and consistency are clean off. Therefore, I brought them back, and on the first day at home I took one round to Spink's and asked him to have it roughly cut and valued."

He took a pill-box from his pocket, and spilled out of it

a beautiful glittering diamond, one of the finest stones that I have ever seen.

"There's the result," said he. "He prices the lot at a minimum of two hundred thousand pounds. Of course it is fair shares between us. I won't hear of anythin' else. Well, Challenger, what will you do with your fifty thousand?"

"If you really persist in your generous view," said the Professor, "I should found a private museum, which has long been one of my dreams."

"And you, Summerlee?"

"I would retire from teaching, and so find time for my final classification of the chalk fossils."

"I'll use my own," said Lord John Roxton, "in fitting a well-formed expedition and having another look at the dear old plateau. As to you, young fellah, you, of course, will spend yours in gettin' married."

"Not just yet," said I, with a rueful smile. "I think, if you will have me, that I would rather go with you."

Lord Roxton said nothing, but a brown hand was stretched out to me across the table.

THE END